I0778999

FAIR CITY BLUES

Jack Dillon Dublin Tale 5

Second Edition

FAIR CITY BLUES

Jack Dillon Dublin Tale 5
Second Edition

Mike Faricy

Library of Congress Control Number: 2023920325
paperback ISBN: 978-1-962080-69-9
e-Book ISBN: 978-1-962080-70-5

MJF Publishing books may be purchased for education, Business, or promotional use. For information on bulk purchases, please contact the author directly at mikefaricyauthor@gmail.com

Published by

MJF Publishing
https://www.mikefaricybooks.com

Acknowledgments

I would like to thank the following people for their help & support: Special thanks to Nick, Roy, Julie, Mittie, and Toui for their hard work, cheerful patience and positive feedback. I would like to thank family and friends for their encouragement and unqualified support. Special thanks to Maggie, Jed, Schatz, Pat, Av, Emily and Pat, for not rolling their eyes, at least when I was there. Most of all, to my wife, Teresa, whose belief, support and inspiration has, from day one, never waned.

"Well, maybe just a small tipple…"

PROLOGUE

rkady Sokolov was down on his knees next to the body. He pulled and tugged on the gold ring with the blue stone, but it remained on the finger. The finger was swollen, and he was unable to turn the ring, let alone pull it off. In frustration, he picked up the red-handled saw, shoved the battery into the base of the handle, set the blade against the finger, and cut it off in less than a second.

"I'm not going to tell you again, stop wasting my time, and get that taken care of, we've got a long night ahead of us," Yakov Gulin said. As he spoke in Russian, he kicked Arkady on the back of his shoulder lurching him forward.

Yakov had a low brow on his shaved head, made to appear even lower due to his one thick, bushy eyebrow. He towered over Arkady, who had been driving him crazy for the better part of the night. *Once this was over*, Yakov thought, *Arkady Sokolov just might be put to rest, too.*

"Just a little souvenir, it isn't every night—"

"I'll give you a souvenir, something to remember me by if you don't get that taken care of in the next five minutes. Now, I'm going to get the car. I'll expect the hands in that bag by the time I get back."

"Yes, sir," Arkady said, smiled his idiot grin then waved the saw in a sort of mock salute. Blood from the blade flew in all directions, and he reflexively put his hand up to shield from the spray, in the process running the palm of his hand across the saw blade and slicing it open.

"You fool. We put the plastic on the floor for a damn good reason. Now either you start paying attention to what in the hell you're doing, or as God is my witness, you're going to find yourself the next one stretched out on the floor. Tie a rag around that to stop the bleeding. I'll be back in four and a half minutes, and God help you if you keep me waiting," Yakov shouted, then stormed out of the room.

Arkady watched him head out the door, then gave him the finger once the door was closed and he wouldn't see. He pulled a rag stained with paint and grease off the workbench and wrapped it around his hand, then got down to business. He cut the right hand off at the wrist, then the left, and tossed them both into the plastic bag. He picked up the finger and easily pried the ring off at the base, dropped the finger into the white plastic shopping bag, and pocketed the gold ring. Blood from his hand began to seep through the rag, and he held it over the open plastic bag. Blood dripped into the bag as he folded the soiled rag over four or five times and tied it using just his right hand, grabbing one end of the rag with thumb and forefinger, the other end with his teeth, and pulling the knot tight. He shook his head to regain his bearings, the vodka from earlier in the night, apparently still having an effect.

He placed the saw blade against the neck, turned his head, so he didn't have to look, then pulled the trigger on the saw and dragged his way across. The blade paused for a moment, held up on bone, which caused Arkady to look. He took hold of the saw with both hands, forcing it through the upper spine until the head rolled off to the side.

That had always been the most difficult part, the victim's spine, and he took a deep breath, swallowed down whatever was in the process of rising up from his stomach, and set the saw off to the side.

The blonde hair was close-cropped, forcing Arkady to place both hands on either side of the head and lift it into the plastic bag. Although it certainly wasn't his first time, he was always more than a little surprised at the weight. The head landed in the bag with a soggy-sounding plop. Arkady quickly twisted the bag closed, letting the air out as he did so, then tied the end in a loose knot.

He grabbed the saw, stepped over to the industrial sink, rinsed off the blade, then took a sponge and wiped off the saw. He placed his hands beneath the armpits and lifted the headless corpse from under the arms, essentially folding it in half, then placed his knee against the back to hold it place while he cautiously rolled the plastic around the body. He worked carefully, making sure the blood didn't flow onto the floor before he taped the plastic closed. He'd just set the roll of tape down when the door opened.

"Are you ready?" Yakov growled as he stepped back into the room.

Arkady nodded, lifted the plastic bag containing the head and hands. "It's all in here."

Yakov gave an exasperated sigh and shook his head. "Do you ever listen? Idiot, do I have to do everything? Not in the same bag. Put the bastard's skull in a separate bag, and crush it, takes up less room that way. I'll be back in a moment."

Arkady watched him as he left the room. Once out the door, he gave him the finger again. His injured hand throbbed as he thrust his middle finger into the air, and he cursed and hoped Yakov's mother was raped by a dog, a large dog. He took a green trash bag from the roll on the workbench, opened it, and set it on the floor. He untied the loose knot in the bag with the hands and finger, took hold of the skull by the tops of the ears, and pulled it out. He laid the skull in the green trash bag, then placed a canvas drop cloth over the bag, turned the hammer sideways, and began to pummel the skull, gradually breaking it down into smaller and smaller sections. He lifted the canvas drop cloth a half-dozen times to check his progress, before continuing to pummel, until eventually, the trash bag contained nothing more than a bony sort of stew.

ONE

oira Sweeney was the focus of Dillon's comment, not that Detective Chief Inspector McCabe seemed the least bit interested. "Well then, Marshal Dillon, my first thought is that it might behoove you to stop wasting your time and mine as well. Would it not be wise to simply get behind the wheel of your vehicle and depart, with all due haste, to the office of the state pathologist and view the body?"

"I'm just thinking, unidentified, apparently floating in the Royal Canal for some time, resting peacefully on a refrigerated shelf. I'm wondering if it couldn't wait until morning? Clearly, it's not going anywhere, and as I mentioned, I have an early dinner reservation this evening at six."

It was more than just a dinner reservation. This was to be the all important third date. He'd met Moira at a party after a rugby match a few weeks back, Ireland playing England in the Six Nations tournament. A great tournament, Ireland, England, Scotland, Wales, France and Italy, with any team on any day capable of winning. Unfortunately, the match that day had gone to England, winning nine to six. But he'd met Moira at the after party, so all had not been lost. They'd hooked up in a pub the following Friday with friends, the two of them just getting to know one another a little better. They'd gone to O'Donaghue's pub the following Sunday night to listen to session music, where she gave him the perfunctory 'Have a nice week,' then headed home, alone, just to prove she wasn't a slut. Tonight was to be the all important date number three, where, since proving she wasn't that type of girl last week, she could freely hop in the sack with Dillon after dinner tonight.

"Your dinner reservation can be put back by an hour, in fact, less than that if you'd make yourself scarce and get out of my office. Now, I want you there this evening, so you'll be able to provide a full report first thing in the morning. I've got a meeting at nine, and I want you standing tall." McCabe pointed to the floor in front of his desk where Dillon was now standing. "I want you in here tomorrow morning, no later than one minute past eight. Questions?"

"No, sir. On my way," Dillon said, trying to sound positive and failing miserably.

He fled McCabe's office, hurried out to his car, and raced out of the parking lot.

He needn't have hurried. It was close to five in the evening and the Dublin rush hour was in full swing. Fifteen minutes later he was in bumper to bumper traffic that wasn't going anywhere along Drumcondra Road. People on foot had been passing him for the last ten minutes. Now they were all blocks ahead of him, and he was still moving by inches, three lanes of rush hour traffic with buses merging down to just one outside the Cat and Cage pub. Add to that the poorly timed stoplights along the way and he was late, late, late. He tried to call Moira a half dozen times but kept getting dumped into her voicemail.

He finally made it up to the Office of the State Pathologist, turned onto Griffith Avenue, pulled up onto the boulevard in front of someone's house and parked. Traffic remained heavy and he had to cross with the light, which took another three or four minutes. It was ten minutes before six, no way was he going to meet Moira on time. He called her again as a car without its blinker flashing leaned on the horn as Dillon ran across the street. He was in too much of a hurry to stop and kick out the man's headlights. Besides, he was dumped into her voicemail again, so it really didn't matter.

He entered the grounds through the wrought-iron gate. A rectangular grey granite stone just next to the sidewalk read "Marbhlann Chathair Bhaile Atha Cliath & Oifig an Phaiteolai Stáit," and below that, in slightly smaller letters the English translation, "Dublin City Mortuary & Office of the State Pathologist." Dillon rang the after-hours bell, explained who he was to the voice that came across on the speaker, then waited.

"Working late, are we?" the man clad in blue hospital scrubs, Brian McFadden, asked when he opened the door a few minutes later.

"No rest for the wicked, Brian," Dillon replied, then stepped in and followed Brian down the long hallway to the rear of the building. Framed watercolor street images of Dublin hung on both sides of the off-white hallway. He could see into most of the offices through windows next to the office doors. With one exception, all the offices were empty. They walked past the labs and the examination rooms. At this hour, it was quiet, deathly quiet, as he followed Brian into the rear storage area.

Brian walked along the wall of steel drawers, stacked five high and twenty long, large enough to hold a hundred bodies. Each drawer was numbered.

"Ahhh, here we are," Brian said, then placed a key into the lock next to the handle and pulled the drawer open. "Bit of a rough one, this is. Been in the water for at least two weeks," he said, pulling the drawer open. "We've him frozen, to slow down the decomposition."

The naked form in front of Dillon had apparently been a blonde man. The corpse was headless, and it took Dillon a moment to run his eyes back and forth over the body before he realized the hands were missing, too.

"Not much to go on," Brian said casually as if he were describing a used car. "The hands and head appear to have been removed by some powered instrument. An educated guess, I'd say a saw. Here's the reason McCabe probably decided to spice up the end of your day. Come on over to this side," he said, slipping on a pair of green latex gloves as Dillon walked around the open drawer.

When he came around and stepped beside him, Brian gave a nod, then placed his hands beneath the shoulder of the corpse and lifted. The entire body rose like a large wooden plank, exposing a tattoo covering the left shoulder blade. It was large, maybe eight inches high, an eagle, globe, and anchor, the official emblem of the United States Marine Corp. Draped across the globe was a banner that read, "Fallujah 2004."

"That mean anything to you?" Brian asked.

"Whoever he is, it's a pretty good guess he was a Marine, and he fought in Iraq. Fallujah was a hell of an ongoing battle. If he was there, he saw more than his fair share of action."

"Interesting," Brian said, sounding anything but interested. "Let me show you the other side."

They walked back around to the other side of the open drawer. Brian gave a grunt as he lifted the body again, exposing a wound from roughly the hip all the way up to the shoulder.

Dillon bent down for a closer look, then said, "What do you make of it?"

"It happened in the water, after death. I'm thinking it may be the reason he was discovered. Something, probably a large vessel, scrapped against him, just conjecture here, but probably loosening him from whatever was holding him beneath the surface. Maybe chains or rope, although there really aren't any telltale signs of that on the body. Interestingly we did recover some synthetic threads along this abrasion. Possibly a windbreaker or a jacket that was covering him.”

“Did he have clothing?”

“Yes. It’s still here, although I don’t know that there’s anything to be learned. I’ve been waiting for the Garda to pick them up. Probably good they didn’t make it today, and you can still examine them. There was nothing related to the synthetic threads we recovered from the abrasion. Come on, we can take a look,” Brian said as he lowered the body back onto the shelf and shoved the drawer closed.

TWO

T he clothing was contained in clear plastic bags labeled "evidence." A separate bag for each item of clothing. The name "Doe, John" and a reference number were written on both bags sitting on the top shelf of a metal, four-wheeled cart parked in the corner of the lab.

"Help yourself," Brian said. "My estimate is a minimum of a couple of weeks, at least in the Royal Canal. Feel free to handle them. There's a box of gloves on the second shelf of that cart. While you're looking, I'll just send an email, McCabe wanted to be kept in the loop when you arrived. Sounds like he's got you on a short leash."

"I think he lives in fear of those Russian bastards making another attempt on me. Not that he really cares, I think it's more a matter of he doesn't want to face the paperwork."

Brian laughed, then headed into his office. Dillon pulled two latex gloves from the box, slipped them on then opened the evidence bag. A sort of musty scent immediately met him as he pulled a pair of black jeans from the bag. The pockets were empty, and he held the jeans out at arm's length in front of him, turning them from front to back. He examined the pockets, the fly, and the waistband, looking for any defining label, but didn't see one. Four bits of thread were on the back, along the right side of the waist, where a label might traditionally be on a pair of jeans. Most likely, the label had been pulled off. He folded the jeans and placed them back in the bag, then opened the second bag, a pair of boxers, black cotton socks, and a black t-shirt. Again no tags on the shirt, although the frayed remnants of a tag remained on the back of the t-shirt. The back of the t-shirt along one side had a series of holes running from the bottom up to the shoulder that appeared to correspond with the long abrasion on the body. Had the tags been removed by the owner? Simply worn off? Or was someone being careful to remove all identifiable evidence? The shoes were a pair of black Nikes, but other than the Nike Swoosh, there were no identifiable marks, although they were clearly worn and not new.

"What do you think?" Brian asked, stepping out of his office. He held a mug of tea, took a sip, and grimaced. "Oh, God, but this tea is desperate."

"I think these could have been purchased just about anywhere, either in the EU or in the States. Nothing resembling a tag remains on anything, although the t-shirt and the jeans appear to have been tagged initially."

"We did find a euro in the small front pocket? You know, that little one, for coins or maybe a pocket watch."

"A euro?"

"Yeah. Irish, dated 2012, not that the year means anything or the fact it was Irish."

"Go back to those tags for a minute. Think they were just worn off?"

"Possibly, but I think it's more likely someone removed them. The next question is was it our friend in there on the shelf or whoever deposited him in the canal?"

"You send McCabe the email so he can rest easy tonight?" Dillon said.

"Just did. I'm not sure he'll rest easy, but at least he knows you're here."

"Do you know where that body was found?" Dillon said.

"Yeah, the Royal Canal. That's the plastic the body was wrapped in, that bag on the bottom shelf." Brian indicated the cart, and for the first time, Dillon noticed the clear plastic neatly folded into another evidence bag. "The plastic is heavy-duty, something maybe a contractor would use, the sort of thing you'd find on a construction site. Blood remnants would seem to indicate they laid the plastic on a floor, placed the body on the plastic, decapitated and removed the hands on your man, then rolled him up in the plastic and sent the entire package to the bottom of the canal."

"Anything from the plastic?"

"Not so much, other than confirmation it had been around the body." Brian shook his head. "There's damage along a portion of the plastic consistent with the damage along the victim's back, something apparently tearing against the corpse. It's one of but not the only reason, I'm estimating time in the water at a minimum of two weeks. There was something weighing down the body, stones, chains, something, but over time as decomposition started and the body filled with gas it rose to the surface. It would have risen sooner if the head had been left in place. The gas from decomposition…."

"I get it," Dillon said. "So you've not found the chains or stones or whatever had weighed the body down?"

"Right. Eventually, the body rose, floated some distance away, maybe quite some distance, before it was spotted."

"Who spotted it?"

"A couple, husband and wife, they were out for a stroll, pushing a granddaughter in a stroller along the canal. Have you walked along there, the Royal Canal?"

"No. Been past it uncountable times, but, no, I've never actually walked there. You got some kind of a map to show me where the body was found?"

"Amazingly, I do," Brian said, then stepped over to a stainless steel sink and dumped the remainder of his tea down the drain. "Step into my lair," he said and went back to his office. He opened an upholstered panel attached to a shelf mounted on the wall, fingered his way through a number of documents, then pulled out a tourist map of central Dublin and spread it open on his desk.

"This area," he said, circling an upper portion of the map with his finger, "is known as Cross Guns. This is Phibsborough Road, here. Do you know it?"

"I'm past there almost every day. The Brian Boru pub is just about here?" Dillon said and pointed.

"Yeah, exactly. About a hundred paces from the pub heading down Phibsborough Road toward the city center is a business called Des Kelly's. They sell beds, carpet, floor laminate."

"Yeah, I've seen the place."

"You take a turn into Des Kelly's, and the entrance to the canal is right there. There's a paved path wide enough for a car, and you can drive almost to where the body was found. Lock number seven was where it was spotted, literally up against the gate. You can't quite drive there without the Waterway Assistance. They'd have to unlock the iron barriers set across the path. They allow pedestrian and bicycle traffic only, no cars from that point forward. It's somewhat isolated, although it's fairly well traveled with local foot traffic and cyclists."

Dillon knew exactly where he was talking about. "I can be there tomorrow and check it out."

"Fancy a pint? I've time for just the one," Brian said.

"Yeah, I can fit that…Oh, Christ."

"Problem?"

"I was supposed to meet a friend for dinner." He glanced at the large clock on the wall, mounted up by the ceiling. "Supposed to meet her over a half-hour ago. God."

"I guess you're about to see if she's the patient sort," Brian laughed as Dillon hurried out of the lab.

He hurried to the lobby, then stepped outside and phoned Moira, only to get dumped into her voicemail again. He swore, then dashed across the street and over to his car.

THREE

Traffic had thinned substantially. That and racing a good twenty miles per hour above the speed limit had Dillon in front of Restaurant Patrick Guilbaud, at just a little after seven, over an hour late for their date. The restaurant was located in a red-brick Georgian building on Upper Merrion St. There was no parking in front, so Dillon drove up onto the sidewalk, set the hazard lights flashing on his car, and hurried up the front steps to the large white door.

He hurried inside, glancing left and right as he approached a smiling woman standing behind a small counter. An open book lay in front of her. A stack of menus, actually long sheets on an elegant grey paper, rested on a table behind her.

"Good evening, sir, and welcome to—" She had a French accent.

"Yes, sorry, but I'm horribly late. I had a reservation for two at six o'clock, and I don't know if my—"

"Oh, so you must be the infamous, Mr. Dillon."

"Yeah. Is she still here?"

"Yes, sir, she's been waiting for you. This way," she said, sounding like she was all too aware of the situation.

He followed the hostess into a long narrow dining room. The room had a high, curved ceiling, which gave it an almost tunnel effect. White linen tablecloths, linen napkins, elegant silver place settings, and the quiet hum of conversation filled the room. As they headed toward the back of the room, Dillon had the feeling a number of people were staring, probably whispering, "Oh look, he's finally here."

He spotted Moira at a table in the far back corner. She was dressed in a silky black sparkly number with spaghetti straps that crossed just below her neck then crossed again on her back. The cups on the dress were absolutely overflowing and made her look all the more sexy. She sipped from her glass of wine, watching as he approached. The look on her face gave nothing away.

"Hi, Moira. Sorry, I'm late. I can explain. I—"

"Sir," the hostess said, pulling a chair out for him.

"What? Oh yeah, thanks, but I think I'll sit over there," he said, taking the seat that happened to be farthest away from Moira, but feeling more comfortable that no one would be seated behind him. He glanced around. "Look, I'm really sorry. Something came up and…."

"Would Monsieur care for something to drink?" the hostess asked.

Dillon glanced over at the wine bottle sitting in the silver bucket next to Moira.

"Yeah, I think maybe I could use a glass of wine."

"Oh, please, allow me," Moira said, then pulled the wine bottle from the bucket, topped off her glass until it was almost filled to the rim, and only a drop remained in the bottle. She half slammed the empty back into the silver bucket and said, "Gee, too bad, I drank it all by myself."

"Oh, umm, that's, that's okay. I think we'll just have another bottle of that wine," Dillon said.

"Yes, of course. Coming right away, sir," the hostess said, then seemed to hurry off just as fast as she could.

Moira took two hearty gulps from her glass while she glared over the rim at Dillon. She took another gulp, then set the glass down.

"Look, sorry I'm late. You're right to be mad. It's just that I tried to call you over a half dozen times, but I kept getting dumped into your voicemail."

"Oh, really?" she said, sounding like she didn't believe him.

"Yes, really. You have your cell here? Is it on?"

She reached over, pulled her purse off the chair next to her, and placed it on the table. Dillon noticed her movements were a little clumsy. She took her cell phone out, fumbled with it and dropped it on the table, then picked it up, pressed a button, and swiped a finger across the screen. She tapped the screen two more times.

"Gee, funny," she said, then held the screen out so he could see it. "This says I didn't get so much as one fecking call from the likes of you."

"What? But that's impossible. Honest, Moira, I was calling. Here, let me try again, maybe something's wrong with your phone." He pulled his cell out, pushed the speed dial number he used to call her, and waited. He could hear the ringing on his phone, but nothing was happening on Moira's phone. He put his phone on speaker so they could both listen.

"So?"

"Can't you hear it ringing? It seems obvious your phone isn't—"

"Hello? Jack, is that you?" a woman's voice said. She didn't sound happy.

"Oh, umm, sorry. I think I really got the wrong number."

"No, you didn't. You've been calling my number almost nonstop for the past two hours. I told you never, ever to call me again. I don't want to hear from you. I do not want to see you, ever. Do you understand? Do not ever—"

He disconnected.

"Sorry about that. Well, crazy me. I, I guess I was calling the wrong number the entire time."

"Gee, amazing, there's another woman who's had just about all she can stand from you? What restaurant did you abandon her in?"

"Look, Moira, something came up at work at the last minute. I was so worried that I'd be late that I made it even worse and then made myself even more late. I'm really, really sorry."

"This is kind of the way it's going to be, isn't it? You're going to always have that one more thing you have to do, and I can just cool my heels while you're doing it, and then when we do go somewhere, you're always looking around to see if someone is going to be behind you."

"It sort of comes with the job. I have to be careful where I—"

"Yeah, maybe. Except it's not like that here, Jack. This is Ireland. We go to a pub, and we may end up talking to people we don't know. We've never seen them before, and we'll never see them again, but they're our best friend for the entire night. You just don't seem to get that."

"I get it. It's just that I'm in a business that's time sensitive, and sometimes—"

"And so apparently that means I can just sit here and drink a bottle of wine all by myself."

"Well, yeah, sometimes. I mean, no, it doesn't mean that, but well, sometimes shit happens."

"Yeah, you're right about the shit," she said and glared. "Right now, what's happening is, I have to go to the loo, so if you'll excuse me," she said and stood up.

Her short dress formed a perfect 'V' in the front, exposing her gorgeous upper thighs, then wrapped around to her fantastic rear. Dillon stared appraisingly as she walked toward the ladies' room, hoping he would be able to get things back on track for the rest of the evening.

"Monsieur," a gentleman said, interrupting Dillon's concentration. He bent over slightly, smiling and holding a bottle of wine in both hands like one might hold a newborn.

"What?"

"The wine, it is what you ordered. No?" he said in a heavy French accent.

"Oh yeah, yeah, sure, that's fine, just fine."

"Very good," he said, then made a production of removing the foil from the top of the bottle and around the neck. He slowly inserted the corkscrew, pulled the cork up, and then, with a second effort, let it pop loudly from the bottle. He twisted the cork off the corkscrew, then placed it upside down next to Dillon to examine.

"Monsieur?" he said, holding the bottle over Dillon's empty glass.

Dillon nodded, then glanced back toward the ladies' room for a moment. No Moira. He turned and looked at his wine glass. Just a small swallow sat in the glass, waiting for Dillon's approval.

"Oh, yeah, I'm sure it's just great. Go ahead, fill me up."

The waiter nodded, filled Dillon's glass, removed the empty bottle from the silver bucket, replaced it with the fresh bottle, and left just as Moira stepped out of the ladies' room.

She looked delicious in her short, sexy dress, and Dillon wondered if he shouldn't just suggest they head back to his place, then quickly decided it might be better to get some food in her and let her calm down.

As she stepped alongside him, he raised his glass of wine and said, "Here's to you, Moira. Thanks for putting up with me."

She stood next to her chair, smiled, raised her glass, and said, "I'll drink to that first part." She took a healthy sip, made two audible gulps, then set her glass back down on the table, threw a cloth object into Dillon's face, and said, "Enjoy yourself tonight," and stormed out of the dining room.

Dillon watched her leave, aware half the people in the restaurant were watching him while the other half watched Moira as she blazed a trail out of the dining room.

He looked down at the silky black cloth she'd thrown in his face. It had a small triangular section with sparkly sequins and was perfumed. He held it up between his thumbs and forefingers for a brief moment before he realized it was her thong.

The woman at the table next to him half-shouted, "Oh, sweet Jaysus."

Dillon took a sip from his wine glass, pretended to remain calm, then signaled the waiter for his check.

"Sir?"

"I think just the check, please."

"But the wine? It is just opened for you."

"Yeah, you can keep it. Just the check, please."

The waiter gave a look suggesting "crazy American's," then hurried away. Dillon stuffed the thong in his pocket, hurriedly emptied his wine glass, and paid the bill.

FOUR

Dillon gave a verbal report to McCabe at exactly eight the following morning. His report lasted less than five minutes and could be summed up in four short words, "He didn't know much."

"The corpse is headless?"

"Yes, sir."

"What about fingerprints?"

"Not much of an option, the hands were missing, sir. Both head and hands seemed to have been removed by an electric saw or knife of some sort."

McCabe shook his head. "Dreadful. God, but that's a wretched business, absolutely dreadful. Thoughts?"

"Well, the tattoo on the shoulder suggests the body is that of an American Marine, quite possibly a former Marine. I've got a call into the American Embassy to see if their staff is accounted for. I expect they are. The tattoo could theoretically reduce the pool of individuals to perhaps three or four thousand Marine veterans who were in Fallujah in 2004. Our man was blonde, that's a further subset. That said, I doubt there's anything like a record of various tattoo's, or who had a tattoo."

"Get on it, see what your sources stateside can come up with."

"Will do. I'd like to head over to the Royal Canal, take a look around the area where the body was found."

"Hoping to find something?"

"I doubt I will, but it would be nice to see what we're dealing with. Brian at the morgue said it's somewhat isolated, and like I said, the body had been in the canal for at least two weeks."

"Mmm-mmm," McCabe groaned, sounding like he thought that was a bit of a wild goose chase, but then he nodded and said, "All right, keep me informed. I want you to take Suel with you."

"That won't be necessary. I can…."

"I'm really not interested in your opinion. Take Suel with you. That's an order, Marshal."

* * *

As Dillon drove to the Royal Canal, he updated Paddy Suel sitting in the passenger seat. "So that's about it, not much to go on."

"And based on this tattoo, you're sure he's American?"

"About ninety-nine percent sure. I suppose any idiot could get the Marine Corp emblem tattooed on their shoulder, but then to have Fallujah 2004 added, that seems like a little too much, particularly for someone not American."

"Yeah. My first thought? The head and hands bit, drug-related. He's a dealer or maybe a user."

"If he was a user, there were no physical signs, the guy looked to be in pretty good shape. Nothing like marks from injections. They'll probably have blood and organ analysis back in a few days' time. We can get confirmation then. God, would you look at this idiot," Dillon said.

They were in the process of making a left turn onto Phibsborough Road. Dillon could see up ahead a block or two to the Des Kelly store Brian at the morgue had mentioned last night, where the entrance to the Royal Canal was. Unfortunately, someone had crossed the intersection, turned, then stopped just beyond the red light, so the fifteen cars turning left behind him had to wait. Horns started honking. The car remained where it was, only encouraging more honking. The driver's window on the stopped car rolled down, and a hand came out, giving everyone behind him the finger. More horns honked.

"Where do the people in this town get their driver's license from? Will you look at this idiot."

"Part of the charm of the big city," Paddy said just as the light changed and the car finally moved. A chorus of horns honked, then Dillon and the other cars sat where they were until the light changed again.

They eventually pulled into the Des Kelly parking lot. Dillon began to veer to the left to get onto the pathway along the Royal Canal.

"You mind if we walk? Should only take about fifteen minutes," Suel said.

"No, I don't mind. In fact, I'd prefer that."

"Let me out here, and I'll run in and let them know we're in the parking lot. No sense in coming back only to find you've been clamped or towed," Suel said, then climbed out of the passenger seat and hurried inside.

Dillon drove around behind the building to a small lot and pulled into a parking space. He met Suel just as he was coming out of the building.

"Everything okay?"

"Not a bother," Suel said, and they headed up along the canal. It was a sunny day, not hot, but warm, once you got moving. On the far side of the canal, a three-story building, maybe twenty years old, looked out on the canal, and next to that, a large six-story stone structure that could easily have been two hundred years old overlooked the canal. Both buildings appeared to be condos.

"You know much about it, the Royal Canal?" Suel said, then nodded a hello at the two women jogging past.

"Only that's it here, and we're walking along it, but I suspect you're about to tell me."

"Well, just one or two facts. It was built between 1790 and 1817, so over the course of twenty-seven years. It was originally built to haul freight." They were just passing a lock, a set of giant doors that held the water back. The water level on the backside of the gates looked to be fifteen feet higher than the area they had just walked past. "You can walk from here all the way to Longford along the canal, total of a hundred and forty-four kilometers."

"You ever do it?"

"Yes, I have. Once you get out of Dublin, leave behind all the litter and the graffiti on the walls, it's very nice. Will you look at this shite, for Christ's sake? The bunch of knackers," Suel said, then kicked a beer can off to the side and into the weeds.

The path was maybe ten feet wide and paved. Certainly wide enough for a car, but if you actually met someone coming head-on, one of the vehicles was going to have to back up a fairly good distance.

"I think they began to restore the canal in 1974, a volunteer group. The rest, as they say, is history."

"Do any boats actually use it?" Dillon said. They were walking past two white swans just across the canal, one of which was sitting on a nest.

"It's the rare occasion, but yeah, they do. You've got to get assistance from Waterways Ireland. They have a team of people who'll open the locks for you, follow you through. As you can tell, it's fairly tight quarters. I'd guess the locks might only be about ten feet wide. Barges used it a bit during the Second World War. I forget the exact number, but something like fourteen hundred people were more or less evicted from their homes back during the famine, walked along the canal from Mullingar all the way to Dublin. They were put on boats to Liverpool and from there to Canada. Over half died on the coffin ships on the way over to North America."

"Jesus."

"Yeah. Maybe not surprisingly, the landlord who evicted them was shot and killed that November, a bastard by the name of Major Mahon. They still do an annual walk every year in Mullingar to commemorate the event. You should go, Dillon. Didn't you tell me once your family were famine people?"

Dillon smiled and nodded at a guy pushing a stroller with twins. Both children appeared to be taking their mid-morning nap. "Yeah. To be honest, I'm pretty sure Ireland was glad to see the backside of my family. They actually landed or tried to land in Boston. Story is they couldn't because they already had enough Irish in Boston. So, the ship just sailed up the coast, around the bend and let everyone off. Technically, my family came into the States illegally. That was in 1847. They homesteaded out in Minnesota in 1853, one hundred and sixty acres of prime Minnesota farmland. Probably felt wealthier than their wildest dreams."

"You forgot the part where the US government sent you back here to punish the likes of us. All right now, just beyond this little bridge is lock number seven. The body was first spotted washed up against the lock. I'm guessing it drifted down from somewhere up the canal, but only God knows from where."

The path took them beneath a railway bridge through a small sort of tunnel that couldn't have been more than twenty feet long. Once past the bridge, the path rose slightly, and suddenly there was lock number seven.

FIVE

Bits of blue and white plastic tape that had been wound around one of the two heavy timbers serving as a lever to open the lock were all that remained to indicate anything had happened at lock number seven just three or four days ago. The tape had black letters, all capitals, that read 'POLICE LINE DO NOT CROSS.'

The path, although still paved, was decidedly more narrow, maybe just five or six feet wide. The backs of industrial buildings lined either side of the canal. Metal picket fences, maybe ten feet tall with the tip of each picket pointing out and looking sharp enough to shave with, prevented access to the industrial sites. As if that wasn't enough, coils of razor wire were wrapped along the top of the fence, adding another two feet to the barrier.

"Not exactly what I'd call romantic," Dillon said, looking around.

"Yeah. The other thing, you can't drive to this spot. Not meaning to joke, but whoever is dumping the body had to carry a lot of dead weight," Suel said.

"If I recall, I think the body was around a hundred and ninety pounds."

"Even with two people, that's quite a lot, plus they seemed to think it was originally weighed down, right?"

"Yeah, underwater for at least two weeks, maybe more."

"I'm thinking I might know the perfect spot," Suel said. "Not too far up the canal, you can almost see it from here, Broom Bridge. Come on."

It couldn't have been more than a five-minute walk, Broom Bridge. The area leading up to it seemed even more isolated. The new Luas green line station in Cabra sat behind a fairly high stone wall on the far side of the canal. The stone wall was covered in bright red and blue graffiti. The path they were on was no more than fifteen feet from the back of a number of industrial buildings, not a one with so much as a window in the brick walls facing out toward the canal. The ten-foot steel picket fence with the sharp tips turned outward, and razor wire adding another two feet ran all along the entire path, and yet amazingly, the back of every building still managed to somehow get covered with spray-painted graffiti.

Broom Bridge itself was made of stone, looked to be about two hundred years old, and was just barely wide enough to accommodate a horse and cart. A dressed stone walkway led beneath the bridge with more graffiti accented by a collection of empty beer bottles and cans.

"Is this called Broom Bridge because they used to sweep it clean?" Dillon joked.

"No, it's named after one of the directors of the Royal Canal company who lived nearby. The reason it's sort of famous is some mathematician came up with a formula as he was walking by, and he carved it in stone somewhere on the bridge back in the 1840s. I guess eggheads from universities still come here to see the stone."

"And now, some idiot is hiding a body here."

"Times change," Suel said and shook his head.

They followed the path beneath the bridge. A pair of ducks had been sitting in the sunshine at the base of the bridge and gave them a look suggesting, "You're not really going to make us move, are you?" The ducks hopped into the water when it became obvious that was indeed the intent.

Suel stopped and looked around on the far side of the bridge. The road over the bridge had the occasional car driving across, but vision from the road to the path along the canal was more or less obscured.

"You know, late at night, say after the pubs closed, it wouldn't take much for a car to pull over and in just seconds someone could drag a body from the boot of a car and have it down here where no one would see you. Foot traffic at that hour would be virtually nonexistent, or if there was somebody around, they'd probably be the sort that would lend a hand and never tell anyone," Suel said.

"Weighing it down?"

"Chains or maybe a building block or two. Where better to sink it than under the bridge? No one sits down here among all these bottles and cans marveling at the canal, and it's probably just slightly deeper beneath the bridge from whatever current is forced between the stone foundations. Maybe that same current is just strong enough after a few weeks to set the corpse free. Maybe it drifts down to lock number seven and gets spotted the next morning. Did you examine the clothing?"

"Yeah. The labels were all torn off, nothing identifiable, all of it black, Nike shoes, black jeans, t-shirt. The body had originally been wrapped in a plastic sheet that was recovered. It was a heavy plastic, industrial-strength, you might say."

"That plastic might have been there just to protect from stains on a floor, wherever it was they cut off the hands and head. That could suggest if not the murder itself, maybe the removal of those bits was done somewhere that was commercial, a trade shop, a factory, or maybe a construction site."

"Maybe somewhere near here?" Dillon said, looking around at the small factories and industrial sites on either side of the canal.

"Possibly."

Suel looked around for a moment, then walked over toward the bushes in front of the metal picket fence, grabbed a stick about three feet long, broke it over his knee, and walked back toward Dillon.

"For the sake of discussion, let's just see how long this takes," Suel said and tossed the stick into the canal. It drifted ever so slowly toward the bridge, picked up a slight bit of speed beneath the bridge as the current increased, then drifted up against some reeds and stopped just on the other side of the bridge.

"Something close to two hundred pounds, drifting into the weeds here or on the far side, it might well be delayed, held up."

"Dressed all in black, if it was on the far side, there's a pretty good chance it might not even get noticed, or even if it did, it might not be recognized for what it was," Dillon said.

A woman pushing a stroller entered onto the path through the gate off the sidewalk.

Suel called to her as she approached, identified himself as a Garda officer. "Ma'am, sorry to bother, wondering if you walk along here often."

"Is there a problem?" she said, then pulled the stroller up to face Suel as she glanced up and down the canal.

"No, not a problem. We're investigating an incident from a few days back, lock number seven."

"Oh yes, I heard about it. Saw the gardaí here the other day, and that plastic tape. It was a car, wasn't it?"

"A car?"

"Right. Heard some knackers were going to try and ram the lock open, stole a car, and drove it into the canal. Is it still down there? Anyone stupid enough to still be in it?"

"Oh, not sure, just wondered if you knew anything about the incident."

"Hmm-mmm," she said, shaking her head. "You'd think you lot would want to check down there, now wouldn't you?"

"We'll be sure to mention it to the superintendent," Suel said.

"God, you can't make it up," she said, turning the stroller around and heading on her way. "Our taxes at work."

Dillon was standing along the edge of the canal, watching the stick. It had come to rest against some reeds and looked like it was capable of remaining there through the summer. "That went well," he said to Suel.

"In a way, maybe it's a good thing she didn't know a body had been recovered, and she thinks it was just an idiot prank."

"I'm thinking that stick could be there for months before it moves. When was the last time it rained?"

"Amazingly, not for two whole days," Suel said.

"Rain could certainly increase the current, but if the body drifted to the far side, with no path along there, it could be missed for a very long time."

"Nothing on missing persons?"

"I did a quick check. Nothing that seemed to fit, the usual American things, college girls, woman from a tour group. Some kid missed his flight back to the States from four days back, nothing that seemed to jive with this incident. Think it might be worth sending someone into the canal and checking under the bridge?" Dillon asked.

"Might be. The section before the bridge is a little more well-traveled, less of a chance to miss the body for an extended period of time. On the other hand, it's just a guess on my part, and not even an educated guess at that."

"Wouldn't hurt to ask to send someone into the water," Dillon said.

"No, I suppose not. Just don't get your hopes up. The thought is awfully lean on any basis of fact, and well, there's always the ever-present budget cuts."

"Still can't hurt to ask," Dillon said.

SIX

McCabe shook his head. "Bollocks. Oh, please tell me you're not serious. Does the term *Budget Cut* have any connotation? We're lucky we aren't forced to take Dublin bus to get to a crime scene. A diver? On some wild, half-baked guess that you and Suel came up with? Was there any indication the body was dumped into the canal from the Broom Bridge?"

"It would seem…."

"Please, before you speak, Dillon, let me answer for you. No. As in 'N-O'. However, fear not, I've just the solution. Since you've time to pontificate on these sorts of grand notions, you can busy yourself in your spare time finding this young American lady, one Stephanie Johnson, late of DCU. Last seen at some raucous college party almost a week ago. I'm sure the sort of event where one drinks to the point of not remembering their name, let alone where they live. A warning, I'm under the impression family has not been informed yet, school policy." McCabe put his hand up to stop whatever comment Dillon was about to make. "A policy the staff at DCU will be only too happy to explain. Thank you," McCabe said, then handed Dillon the folder on the missing Johnson girl and sent him on his way with a dismissive wave of his hand.

"Any luck?" Suel asked, looking up from his computer as Dillon approached his desk.

"Not in so many words," Dillon said, waving the file in his hand. "Since I've time to waste on silly ideas, I can find a girl named Stephanie Johnson, apparently a missing American college student."

"Trinity?"

"No, DCU. I guess that's the good news, it's close to home."

"He didn't go for the diver idea?"

"Not exactly, although he spelled it out very clearly."

"Oh?"

"Let me quote him, 'N-O'."

Suel laughed.

Dillon wandered back to his desk, looked up a phone number on his cell, then dialed it on his desk phone, so the call would ring through as coming from An Garda Síochána, Ireland's National Police Service.

"US Embassy, how may I direct your call?" a pleasant voice answered.

"Eric Bergman in your security service," Dillon said.

"Who shall I say is calling?" the voice replied, this time still polite, but maybe not quite as pleasant.

"US Marshal Jack Dillon."

"One moment, please, Marshal."

It was a bit more than a moment, but eventually, the phone rang.

Bergman picked up on the third ring. "Eric Bergman."

"Eric, Jack Dillon here."

"Dillon, great to hear from you. How very nice of you to call and offer to take me to lunch."

"Incredible, you can read my mind, even over the phone. Your powers are nothing short of amazing. Shall we say Fallon and Byrne at one?"

"I can do that," Bergman said.

Dillon next phoned DCU to speak with someone about the missing person report on Stephanie Johnson, but he ended up leaving his name and a callback number on a recording. He phoned a contact in the Marshal's Service back in the States, but since it was just a little after six in the morning on the East coast, he left a message.

"Yeah, Gino, Jack Dillon. I'm in Dublin at the moment, calling to see if you can help me out with an apparent American body, a John Doe over here. You got my cell number, just text me when you're available, I'll call you. Thanks in advance."

SEVEN

He headed out to meet Eric Bergman from the US Embassy Security Service. The Fallon and Byrne store was located in Dublin's city center, on Exchequer Street. Dillon had always considered it a fancy grocery store until someone corrected him. Actually, come to think of it, it had been Moira Sweeney who'd set him straight, the same woman who threw her thong at him the other night in the restaurant.

"Jack," she'd said. "It's not just a grocery store, technically it's a food hall. A restaurant with a French menu on the upper floor, deli, coffee, and specialty grocery items on the main floor and a wine cellar in the basement."

Much as he hated to admit it, she'd been right. He was sitting in the wine cellar at the moment, fantasizing about Moira Sweeney and what he'd probably missed out on the other night. At this time of day, not quite half-past twelve, the place was relatively quiet, with just three other tables occupied. A number of the tables were round and sitting on top of wooden wine barrels with high wooden stools arranged around them. Racks of wine bottles covered two of the grey stone walls.

Eric Bergman bounded down the dozen stairs, taking them two at a time into the wine cellar a few minutes later. He gave a wave and hurried over to Dillon's table. His hair was close cut on the sides and neatly trimmed on top. His bangs, maybe an inch long, were gelled and standing straight up. "Jack," he said, then attacked Dillon with an outstretched hand and a death-defying grip.

"Eric, good to see you again. Get you a tea or a coffee?" Dillon asked since Bergman rarely drank alcohol.

"Coffee would be just fine."

"Two coffee's," Dillon said to the waitress, then looked at Bergman. "You got time for lunch?"

"As long as you're buying, I'll make time."

"Couple of menus when you bring the coffee," Dillon said. "So, Eric, I hope things are boring on your end."

"Oh, you know, the usual, lost or stolen passports, tourists getting in trouble after being over-served. Mercifully nothing too drastic, at least for the moment. What's on your plate that you called?"

That was Bergman, not a lot of time for small talk.

"A couple of things. Just got handed a file on a college girl apparently missing from DCU."

"Dublin City University?"

"Right. Actually not too far from my place, just a couple of blocks."

"What's up?"

"Not much at this stage. I've got a call into the school, left a message. Wondered if you had heard anything?"

"What's the name?" Bergman asked, pulling a leather-bound notebook from an inside pocket of his suit coat.

"Johnson, Stephanie Johnson, twenty-two, from Indianapolis, Indiana. Over here for a year, studying online marketing."

Bergman continued writing while he spoke. "Mmmmmm, college kid. My limited experience tells me fifty percent of the time they've taken off with a boyfriend or girlfriend, maybe left the country— nothing nefarious, just self-absorbed enough to not bother to tell anyone. Maybe they're trying to keep the relationship secret. You may find she's taken off for a week with someone else's boyfriend. They're probably somewhere in Ireland, or if they're adventurous, on the continent, maybe Paris or possibly Rome. Did the parents file the report?"

"I don't know who filed the report. I don't believe the parents are aware she's missing."

"If the parent's filed the report, the possibility of what I just described increases. They think their little angel is visiting churches, and she's really sunning naked on a beach somewhere, drinking mojitos."

"Hopefully, that's what it will turn out to be. But you're not aware of anything?"

"No, not yet. I'll check when I get back. Last name is spelled with an S-O-N?"

"Yeah."

"Okay. That's all?"

"No, unfortunately. I've got another one, not quite so nice."

"Tell me."

"About three or four days ago, a corpse was found floating in the Royal Canal, and it turns out—"

"I read something about it. Found here in Dublin, right?"

"Yeah, at lock number seven, not far from the Broom Bridge."

"I don't know where that is."

The waitress was back with their coffee and menus. "Milk?" she asked.

"Black for me," Dillon said.

"Same," Bergman said.

"Lock number seven sits between Finglas and Cabra, little more than a mile from Phibsborough Road. They're putting in a new Luas station right about there." Bergman nodded. "Here's the deal," Dillon said. "I was up yesterday at the city morgue viewing the body. Head and hands had been sawn off."

"Shit." Bergman grimaced, then took a healthy gulp of coffee.

"Yeah, male, we're guessing relatively young, late twenties, maybe mid-thirty, blonde. There was a tattoo on the back, covering the left shoulder blade, 'bout eight inches high." He indicated with his hands. "A Marine

Corp emblem, then across it a banner that said, 'Fallujah 2004.'"

"Well, that's a start, the tattoo. I can tell you I've not heard anything about anyone missing. That said, the tattoo seems to make it about ninety percent certain he would have been American. Figure 2004, that's thirteen years ago. Young jarhead private, maybe a junior officer. Yeah, aged somewhere between maybe thirty to thirty-seven."

"I was gonna say ninety-nine percent certain he was American, but okay, I'll go with your ninety."

"You're probably right on the percentage," Bergman laughed. "The other thing, the head and the hands. Two thoughts, someone doesn't want him identified and therefore, didn't want him to be found. Or, they did want him to be found, and the head and the hands were severed to serve as a warning to anyone else thinking of making whatever transgression caused that result."

"You thinking drugs?" Dillon asked.

"Yeah, certainly."

"No sign of drug use on the body. I haven't gotten toxicology reports back yet and probably won't for a couple of weeks. I'm going to gamble and say he wasn't a druggie."

"That still could mean some sort of drug tie-in. You hear horror stories of this sort of thing coming out of Mexico all the time, the decapitation, and then the bodies are hung from a lamp post or a bridge or something. That said, I'm not aware of any Mexican drug influence here.

If it's drug-related, it would seem more logical to maybe suspect a Russian influence."

"I was afraid of that," Dillon said.

"Gentlemen, are you ready to order?" the waitress asked.

EIGHT

They left Fallon and Byrne together, chatted for a minute or two out on the street, then Dillon headed back to his office. He was just pulling into the parking area behind the office building when his cell phone indicated a text message coming through. He parked, turned the car off, then pulled out his cell. The text was from Gino Andretta, the US Marshal back in the States Dillon had left a voice message for before his lunch with Eric Bergman.

Dildo, great to hear your voice. Call me at the same number anytime. Gino.

Dillon pushed a button, then sat back and listened to the phone ring.

Andretta answered on the fourth ring. "This is Gino."

"Hey, Gino, Jack Dillon. Thanks for the quick response to my message."

"Great to hear your voice, Dildo," Andretta said, using the familiar nickname. "So how's the extended vacation going over there in Dublin?"

"Exhausting, I can't keep the women away."

"Yeah, right, they probably all want to kill you. What's shaking?"

Dillon went on to explain the headless corpse lying in the Dublin City Morgue. "Any chance you can do a search and see what you come up with?"

"Hundred percent chance I'll do the search, I can start it as soon as I get off the phone, here. But chances of getting any information of value are about zero. I think about all we're going to get is a listing of Marine's who were in Fallujah. I'll try and narrow it down to ones with blonde hair, but no telling how accurate that might be, and it won't cover reddish blonde, brown, light brown. As for the tattoo, I'll try it, but it sounds pretty lean right from the start, just so you understand. What I will do then is take whatever results I get, cross-reference them with a trip outside the US in the past twenty-four months, and see what we have. That'll certainly cut the list of potentials down, but no real guarantee your boy is going to be in there."

"It's better than what I'm looking at right now," Dillon said.

"All right, let me get started. It's barely nine over here, so there's a pretty good chance I'll have something for you by the end of the day."

"You able to keep this below the radar, so Dahlquist doesn't get involved? I don't need him stirring things up." Dahlquist was Dillon's former boss back in the States. Not a fan of Dillon, nor anyone else who reported to him for that matter.

"Not to worry, I keep a very low profile around that bastard. I'm only twelve years away from retirement."

"Thanks, Gino."

"I tell you what, just to err on the side of caution, I'll send you a text message if and when I have anything. No point in getting the powers that be all excited."

"Thanks. I owe you, again, Gino."

"You can thank me if what I find does any good. Always great to chat, Dildo."

Dillon climbed out of his car and hurried over to the rear door of the building. He input his security code on the keypad, then pulled the door open once the lock clicked and hurried over to the rickety elevator.

He waited for what seemed like an eternity before the brushed chrome doors opened and he stepped inside. The elevator could maybe hold four people comfortably, but that much weight would probably pose a risk. Dillon pushed the button for the third floor and waited for the elevator door to close. The faint odor of sweat stung his nostrils, or was it just fear? The elevator remained stationary for a few seconds, then made a precipitous drop of two or three inches before it groaned its way up toward the third floor.

The doors opened on the second floor, although no one was there waiting to step on. It made another precipitous drop of two or three inches after the doors closed before groaning its way to the third floor. Once Dillon stepped off, the elevator seemed to lift an inch or two, and not for the first time he vowed to never, ever take it again.

He had to input his security code on the pad mounted next to the door labeled "Special Investigations Unit." Prior to his signing on to the unit, the desk Dillon now occupied had been vacant and therefore a repository for various tea and coffee cups, candy wrappers, dirty plates, and sundry other bits of trash. It seemed not much had changed since Dillon took up residence at the desk, and once inside the room, he focused on the debris scattered across his desk.

He stacked the tea mugs, there were four, on top of the three plates, crumbled up the candy bar wrappers and stuffed them in one of the mugs, tossed three forks and a spoon into another mug, then carried the lot to the break room, where he deposited the china and silverware in the sink and the wrappers in the trash. When he returned to his desk, another candy bar wrapper was already crumpled up next to his phone. No one at the surrounding desks looked at him, but a number of people sat red-faced and snickering.

The phone on Dillon's desk rang.

"Marshal Dillon."

"Eric Bergman, Jack. Hey, thanks again for lunch. Listen, did a quick run-through for the last twenty-one days. I've got an Emma and Stanley Johnson heading back to the states on the twenty-fifth of last month. They flew to Atlanta, ages sixty-two and sixty-four, respectively. And a Mary Jo Johnson Montrose, age forty-three, flying to the States on the second of the month. She was headed to Chicago. All three were traveling on American passports. I can send you passport information if you want it."

"Sounds like a dead end. Why don't you go ahead and send me the information anyway, the question is bound to come up, and I can show due diligence. That will shut down at least one line of inquiry. Thanks for the speedy reply, Eric. Say, I've got a pal checking data on a list of potential names on the other deal."

"The headless Marine?"

"Yeah. It'll be a needle in the haystack search, but it might tighten the list down from a couple thousand names to maybe a few hundred. He didn't sound all that promising regarding the tattoo."

"No surprise there. You want to send me that info when it arrives, I'll run it through our entry database, see if anything pops up."

"Will do. I'm guessing the earliest I might see it will be tomorrow. Then again, it could be another week, or two."

"Just let me know," Bergman said, then disconnected.

Paddy Suel came into the office, set a stack of files on his desk, and ran his hand through his hair. He looked over at Dillon and shook his head disgustedly.

"Anything I did?" Dillon asked.

"No, surprisingly. Same shite, just a different day. Anything on your friend in the canal?"

"Starting to wade through some subsets, but the chances of anything clicking are lean at best. Buy you a tea?"

"You really think that's going to help?"

"Can it hurt?" Dillon said.

"I suppose not. Yeah, come on. I'll let you buy," Suel said and headed for the break room.

Over tea, and leaning against one of the counters, Suel explained a rash of small convenience stores where the cash machines were being stolen.

"Wait a minute. The entire machine?" Dillon asked.

"Yeah, small towns and villages on the outskirts of Dublin. Bastards back a stolen vehicle into the shop, smash right through the glass, wrap a chain around the machine, pull it loose from the floor, toss it into the back of the vehicle, and they're off and running. There's been four of the damn things stolen, and they're getting it down to a split second science. Last one didn't take more than a minute and a half."

"How many people?" Dillon asked.

Suel took a sip of tea, grimaced, shook his head and said, "God, but that's awful. How many? Appears to be a crew of three, near as we can figure. Course, two of the locations hadn't bothered to turn on the CCTV. Cost savings, they told me. Anyway, a driver, plus two others who jump out and wrap a chain around the thing, then yank it loose, load it up, and they're gone."

"You got any footage on them?"

"A little. They're wearing gloves and balaclavas. Vehicles used are always found, but only because they've been set on fire. Do you believe it? Cost savings, so two of the shops didn't have the CCTV up and going. Saved about a half-euro, and now they're out anywhere from two to ten thousand euros because not running the CCTV negates their insurance coverage. Well done, you stupid bastards."

"I was going to ask if you wanted to trade investigations, but I think on second thought, I'll stick with my own headaches."

Dillon was back at his desk and put in another call to DCU, inquiring about the missing student, Stephanie Johnson. This time a live voice answered.

"Grainne Finn," the voice answered.

"Ms Finn, my name is Jack Dillon. I'm with An Garda Síochána, following up on a missing persons report regarding an American student, Stephanie Johnson."

"Oh, yes. I received your message in my voicemail."

Dillon waited a long moment for the explanation of why she hadn't called back, but it never came. "I wonder if I might stop in to your office, say in the next half hour?"

"The next half hour?"

"Yes. Time is of the essence. The faster we move on this, the better our chances of success. Are you located on campus?"

"Yes."

"If you'll let me know what building you're in, I could head right over."

She seemed to pause for a moment, then said, "Well, umm, yes I suppose that might work. We really don't see anyone without an appointment after three-thirty."

Dillon checked his watch. Not quite a quarter after three. "Could I see you a little before four?"

"An hour and fifteen minutes would be better," she said, reconfirming Dillon's long-held prejudice of academics and academic institutions in general.

"I can do that. Where are you located?"

"My office is in the Henry Grattan Building. We're just across from the bank," she said, not bothering to offer any other direction, apparently presuming he'd be familiar with the campus.

"Thank you. See you in an hour," Dillon said, but she'd already hung up.

NINE

The house An Garda Síochána had rented for Dillon was only a couple of blocks from DCU, so he headed home and parked in his driveway. He turned the car off, a grey, 2007 Dodge Avenger, then sat there while it sputtered and coughed for another fifteen seconds before the engine died altogether, and he climbed out.

"You should really get that looked at, the damage you're doing to the environment is simply ridiculous," his neighbor standing on the far side of the garden wall called to him. Her car, the exact same vehicle and grey color, was parked just behind her.

Her name was Deitora. Dillon had forgotten her last name. She was dressed in baggy jeans, a long-sleeved shirt, and a straw hat with netting covering her face and neck. She wore brown, cotton gloves and was artfully pruning a rose bush one small stem at a time. She continued working while Dillon walked through the blue cloud of exhaust to swing the wrought iron gate closed behind his car.

She was thin, pale, perhaps sixty years of age, and as far as Dillon was concerned, a major pain in the ass. Not so amazingly, she lived alone, and at least as far as he could tell had never had a visitor knocking on her door. The very few conversations he'd had with her in the past had been anything but pleasant, and this afternoon's appeared to be headed in the same direction.

"Enjoy your day," Dillon said, hopefully ending any thoughts of a conversation. As he headed for the front door, a slight breeze came across, carrying the remnants of the exhaust cloud into her front garden.

"Oh, oh, oh," Deitora half screamed, then hurried into her house coughing, and slammed the door.

Dillon unlocked his front door and called "Lucifer." His small black dog appeared at the base of the staircase and hurried toward the front door. Dillon held the door for him and watched as Lucifer wandered out into the front yard, lifted his leg against the garden wall where Deitora had been complaining just a moment ago, and relieved himself. Dillon found himself wishing she was still standing there.

He picked up the day's mail from the entry floor, a flyer from the take-away up at the shops, and another one from an insurance company. He wandered into the kitchen, tossed the fliers into the recycling bag, stood the overturned wastebasket up, stuffed the frozen meal packaging Lucifer had shredded back into the wastebasket, then pulled a bowl of chili from the refrigerator and placed it in the microwave.

He ate the chili in just over three minutes while leaning against the counter with his back to the kitchen. He
followed the chili up with a half-dozen chocolate-covered tea biscuits, then opened the front door and called,
"Lucifer, treat."

The dog was down at the far end of the front yard,
rolling on the grass. He poked his head up at the sound
of the word "treat" and hurried to the front door.

The permanently unhappy Deitora suddenly reap-
peared, this time on her knees behind the three-foot garden wall. "He certainly lives up to that dreadful name. I
hope you intend to clean that up," she said, nodding toward Lucifer's deposit just in front of Dillon's car.

Dillon glanced in the direction of the dog dropping,
shook his head, and said, "No, it doesn't really bother
me."

Her eyes grew wide, and a shocked look spread
across her face, but before she could respond, he closed
the front door.

He puttered around inside the house for another fifteen minutes before he set the alarm and headed over to
DCU. Thankfully Deitora was nowhere to be seen. He
walked a half block up to St. Pappin's Road then headed
toward the retail shops just a block away. The retail corner was made up of a dry cleaners, a Macari's take away,
a Centra store, PaddyPower betting, a EuroSpar, a Boots
Pharmacy, and last but not least, the Slipper pub.

He crossed at the light, then walked another half-
block along the Albert College Park until he came to

DCU. There was a map posted on a sign with most of the college buildings identified. According to the map, the Henry Grattan building wasn't too far away.

The campus seemed to consist of a lot of closely built structures with red brick walking paths and courtyards. He made his way to the Henry Grattan building. The automatic door opened as he approached. He stepped into a wide courtyard with a red brick floor and a glass roof three stories up. Four oak picnic tables with half of each tabletop painted blue were lined up along one side of the courtyard. To the right was the Bank of Ireland, and to the left, just after the picnic tables, was the door to the registry office with the posted hours "9:30-3:30" and below that "STAFF ONLY" painted in white.

A grey telephone that looked like it had been installed in about 1970 was mounted on the wall next to the door. The receiver was attached to the phone by a curly cord with two knots in it. A sheet of paper was taped to the wall above the phone, listing staff names followed by a four-digit extension. The list was alphabetical by last name, and Dillon found 'Finn, G' about a quarter of the way down.

He checked his watch. He was a few minutes early but dialed anyway. Grainne Finn answered on the third ring. "Yes?"

"Hi, Grainne, it's Jack Dillon with An Garda Síochána."

"You're early," she said, not sounding too impressed.

TEN

Dillon checked his watch again and wondered if she'd maybe forgotten. He'd been seated at the picnic table closest to the registry office door for the past twenty minutes. Just now, he was watching the foot traffic wander past, mostly students, and what he guessed was the occasional academic. About every third student seemed to be focused on their cell phone as they walked past. He'd lost count of the number of times people had walked head-on into one another. No one appeared to apologize. It seemed to be expected. No doubt they'd been reading that all-important text message or a breaking news story just coming through.

It was a typical college campus, young people knowing for a fact they were on the cutting edge of everything current, probably telling stories to one another about how out of touch their parents were. Individuals with life experience that could be counted in days, if not hours, playing it safe in the cushioned cocoon of academia.

Dillon was chuckling to himself about his own naivety at about the same age when the door opened, and a heavyset blonde woman wearing a grey jacket, a tweed skirt that hung just below her knees and sensible black shoes stepped out of the office and called, "Mr. Dillon?"

He raised his hand in a brief wave, stood from the picnic table, and approached the woman with a smile. "Ms. Finn?" he said, holding out his hand. He tried not to focus on the corner of her mouth, where a mole the size of a penny with hairs growing out of it had taken up residence.

"Please come in," she said, ignoring the hand and turning back to her office. The office room was large, with maybe twenty closely-cramped-together cubicles. The far wall was made up of uniformly small offices, all glass-fronted from floor to ceiling with heavy drapes pulled across the windows. She walked toward a distant corner, then maybe ten feet from the last office she turned ninety degrees in the opposite direction and stepped into a small cubicle with grey plastic walls just barely waist-high. There was a grey plastic desktop built into the cubicle and shelves hanging on two of the walls. Both shelves were lined with blue, white, and black three-ring binders. The shelves were bowed in the middle, apparently from the weight of the binders. Everything on the desktop appeared to be arranged perfectly parallel with the grey cubical wall, the phone, the rack holding a number of manila files, and a desk pad with a pen and pencil along the top edge of the pad. No personal items like a framed photo of herself or maybe her cats were apparent.

"Take a seat," she said, pointing to an uncomfortable-looking black plastic chair. She sat down in a worn, grey desk chair, pushed a couple of buttons on her phone, and then spun round to face Dillon just as he sat.

"You're with An Garda Síochána?"

"Yes, I am."

"But you sound American?"

"That's because I'm American," he said and smiled.

"May I see some identification, please."

Dillon held her eyes for a brief moment, then nodded as he felt his gaze grow colder. He reached into his pocket, took out his Marshal's badge, and opened it for her. Once she gazed at the badge, he handed her his An Garda Síochána ID card.

She shook her head and whispered, "Americans," in a dismissive tone just loud enough so he would hear.

Dillon said, "We've a report of an American student named Stephanie Johnson, who is missing."

"At this juncture that is partially correct," Grainne Finn said, pulling a thin manila file folder from a holding rack on her desktop. She opened the file and cleared her throat. "Miss Johnson arrived at the end of June for summer orientation and classes. She is enrolled in our communications and marketing program for the term of one year, at which point she was scheduled to graduate. That said, she has missed the past two weeks of classes, and well, as of now—" She lifted a sheet of paper in the file and paused before reading the sheet below. "Yes, it would appear her graduation will be all but impossible."

"You said the report of her missing was partially correct. Has she been seen somewhere?"

"At just about the same time her absence from class was brought to our attention, her roommates contacted us. She resides in a rental unit not far from here, just over on Collins Avenue actually. They were due to pay their monthly rent, and then suddenly, Miss Johnson was nowhere to be found. The girls rent from a private party. She's responsible for her portion of the rent payment, so at this point, she is in arrears."

"What did her family say?"

"We haven't contacted them."

"Why not?"

"For starters, she is still enrolled. We'll be letting another seventeen days pass before we send an official notification to her family. Our experience with students, particularly *American* students, is they seem to feel a compunction to run off to the continent in search of adventure for a week or two. It's why we usually have a thirty-day waiting period before we contact the authorities, in this case, you, apparently."

"Then what am I doing here?"

"I believe one of her housemates actually contacted An Garda Síochána, once their rent came due. I can assure you. It certainly wasn't anyone from this office."

"Could you give me some contact information on the housemates? I'd like to start there and see—"

"I'm sorry, but that's privileged information, and we simply don't pass that on without a written—"

Dillon felt something snap inside. "Let me explain something. I've two cases I'm dealing with at the moment. One is the headless corpse found in the Royal Canal a few days ago. The other is this young woman. If she is found headless or stuffed in the trunk of a car or raped and being held against her will, that's going to come back and haunt you, and by extension, the university. Now, while I understand the concern and applaud your efforts to keep this information private, I would suggest you might wish to reconsider and cooperate, at least in this particular instance."

She seemed to think about that for a moment, then picked up her perfectly positioned pen and wrote a note on a perfectly positioned pad of paper. She tore the note from the pad, repositioned the pad of paper to line up perpendicular to the wall of the cubicle, then set the pen back in the exact same position.

"Here is the address of the house the girls are renting. You can talk to them."

"Do you have their names?"

"I do, and I can provide those to you in seventeen days. I'm sure if they're truly concerned, they'd be more than happy to talk with you and tell you their names, Detective Dillon."

"It's Marshal Dillon," he said, getting to his feet. "It's been…interesting, Ms. Finn. Enjoy the rest of your day." He extended his hand and received a cold stare in return.

ELEVEN

The main entrance to DCU was on Collins Avenue. Dillon fled the company of the not-so-charming Grainne Finn and walked out to Collins Avenue. He crossed the street, walked down past a block of identical two-story attached homes until he came to the address he was looking for.

Much like the place he was living in, a three-foot wall ran along the front sidewalk. The small front lawn had been replaced by an asphalt parking area, although no vehicles were parked there at the moment. Two bicycles were chained to a bike rack up against the front of the house. The front of the unit was a type of stucco referred to locally as pebble and dash. It had been painted white.

As Dillon approached the front door, he could hear classical music from inside, not a radio or a CD, but what sounded like an instrument being played, in this case, a violin.

He rang the doorbell, and the music stopped. A moment later the door opened, and a girl he guessed was in her early twenties opened the door.

"Yes?" she said.

"Hi, my name is Jack Dillon. I'm looking for the housemates of Stephanie Johnson. I'm with An Garda Síochána," he said, then handed her his business card.

She was dark-haired, with dark brown eyes magnified behind her glasses. She looked at the card, then at Dillon. "Kristy," she called. "Kristy, you better come out here right now."

A door at the end of the hall opened, and a girl stepped out. She was blonde, in stocking feet, wearing blue jeans plus a DCU sweatshirt that looked fairly new. She was eating what looked like a salad from a large wooden bowl. She set the bowl on a small table next to the staircase, chewed once or twice, then swallowed and smiled at Dillon. "What, exactly, is this about?"

"He's with the police," the first girl said, handing Dillon's card over to her. "It's about Stephanie."

"Is she okay?"

Both girls had American accents, probably from the Midwest, Dillon thought, but with a bit of a twang, suggesting maybe southern Ohio or Indiana.

"We received a missing person report. I believe someone here filed the report?"

"Oh, yeah," the dark-haired girl said. "We informed the school, and they said something about waiting a couple more weeks, and we didn't want to do that, so that's when we filed a police report. It's really not like her, like Steph. She just all of a sudden disappeared. We all split the rent. There's three of us living here, and all of a sudden, when it came time to pay, she suddenly wasn't around."

"Do you want to come in?" Kristy said.

"Oh, yeah, sorry 'bout that. We can go into the living room. Umm, I'm Barb Kruger," the dark-haired girl said and stuck out her hand.

"Jack Dillon," he said, shaking her hand. He followed the two girls into the living room.

There was a flatscreen sitting on a coffee table next to the fireplace. The fireplace had a sign that read "Out Of Order DO NOT USE" taped to it. Two formerly white couches were lined up alongside one another. One of the couches had a large pink stain running down the arm and across the seat cushion, probably red wine, a lot of red wine. A black leather couch was positioned against the back wall of the house, perpendicular to the white couches. None of the couches matched, and all of them looked the worse for wear. Pillows and blankets were scattered on each couch, suggesting a good deal of time spent lying in front of the flatscreen. Four mismatched wooden chairs were lined up in front of the window that looked out onto the street. An empty wine bottle sat in the far corner on the floor. A metal stand with an open music book resting on it stood in front of the picture window, and a violin and bow rested on one of the wooden chairs.

Dillon grabbed a seat on the leather couch against the back wall. The girls sat next to one another on the couch closest to Dillon with their hands folded in their lap. They sat up straight, looking like they were waiting to be called into the principal's office.

"So, what can you tell me?" Dillon said.

"Well, she just sort of all of a sudden wasn't here," Barb said.

"Yeah, and the landlord is hassling us for the rest of the rent."

"He said he'd give us one more week, then we have to pay it," Barb said, sounding like it was going to be tough coming up with Stephanie's portion of the rent.

"Do you think she might have run off, maybe went back to the States? Or could she just be on the continent in Paris or Rome or somewhere, soaking up the sun on a nice beach?"

"Pretty sure she didn't go back to the States," Kristy said as the two girls looked at one another.

"Yeah, she hates her mom," Barb said.

"Actually, we think she's probably with Pauly," Kristy said.

"Pauly?"

"This guy she met, his real name is Seamus, but he kind of looks like Paul McCartney."

"Paul McCartney, the Beatle?" Dillon asked.

"Yeah, that's one of the bands he was in, well, and Wings along with a ton of solo stuff. Not that Pauly, I mean Seamus, can play any instrument. God, he can't even carry a tune."

"Yeah, but he's really nice."

"Umm-hmm, and cute." Barb nodded.

"Is he a student at DCU?"

"No, he's a Dub. Works construction or something. He and Stephanie have been going out for a couple of months."

"Have you checked with him?"

The girls looked at one another for a moment. "We don't know how," Kristy said.

"We don't know where he lives, don't have a phone number for him," Barb said.

"Don't even know his last name."

"And we haven't seen him since Steph disappeared. He used to be here almost every evening, and suddenly, he's nowhere to be found."

"You think they may have gone somewhere together, maybe over to—"

"Well," Kristy said. "If they were going to be traveling, she wouldn't have left her passport here, so they can't be going too far."

"And from what we can tell, she didn't pack any of her clothes. The dresser in her room is still full. All her shoes are here. It's just not like her."

"Do you have pictures of her?"

"Just a couple from a party," Kristy said, pulling out her phone.

Dillon pulled his wallet out, took out a business card, and handed it to her. "Could you email me those photos, please. You said she left her passport here, can I see it?"

"I'll go get it," Barb said and hurried out of the room.

Kristy punched a number of keys on her phone, glancing back and forth between Dillon's business card and her phone. "There, that should be coming across in just a few—" Dillon's phone suddenly pinged, alerting him to an incoming text message. "Oh, wow, that was really quick."

He pulled out his phone, glanced at the screen. "You're KF101094?"

"Yup," she said.

Barb suddenly hurried back in the room, handed a passport to Dillon along with a framed 4x5 photo. He glanced at the passport, a dark-haired young woman who looked like she could be twenty, maybe. She wore bright red lipstick and had dark, severe eyebrows that Dillon figured were more penciled than natural. As he paged through the passport, he said, "Does she have any identifying marks? Maybe a tattoo?"

The girls looked at one another for a moment. "She has a scar on her tummy, had her appendix removed, I think her senior year in high school," Barb said.

"Yeah, and then, well, a shamrock tattooed on her butt, on the right cheek. We kinda all got one like that after a party one night."

"Yeah, after that party," Barb said and nodded toward the framed 4x5. "It was a costume party. That's Pauly with her."

Dillon flipped through the last few pages in the passport. There was only the one stamp, from when she'd entered Ireland on the twenty-eighth of May. He picked up the framed photo, just an average-looking young couple, dressed for a costume party. Stephanie wore what looked like a flapper's dress from the 1920s, with row after row of fringe. Her hair was curled as opposed to straight, like on her passport photo. Pauly, or rather Seamus, had on jeans and a t-shirt advertising the Gravediggers pub, and what looked like a silk tie around his forehead. He appeared to be carrying an orange squirt gun.

Dillon must have made some sort of face because Kristy said, "He was supposed to be a gangster."

"Yeah, the party theme was the Godfather, and all of us had pizza and way too much wine," Barb said.

Dillon swiped his finger across the screen on his phone. Then clicked on the images that had just come through in Kristy's email. "Can you send me this one from the costume party? I'd like to get one of her boyfriend, Seamus."

"I don't have one of him. I've just got the ones of Steph by herself at the party."

"Was he trying to avoid having his picture taken?"

"Umm, no, not really. More a case of me not wanting to be caught taking pictures of a friend's boyfriend, if you get what I mean."

Dillon nodded, then said, "Mind if I hang onto this photo?"

"No, go ahead, if you think it would help."

"And you don't have any idea where he lives or what his last name is?"

The girls shook their heads.

"And he wasn't a student at DCU?"

"No."

"Used to always give us a hard time about having an easy life, sleeping in and not having to go to work," Kristy said.

"He worked construction or something like that," Barb said.

"Construction?"

"Yeah, he told us they were doing a kitchen once," Barb said.

"And that bathroom where there wasn't room for the shower, but the lady wanted it put in any way, so they had to remove the bathroom door, remember?" Kristy said, and they both laughed.

"Yeah, now everyone could watch her shower, and she was a big fatty."

"So he was doing work on homes as opposed to tall buildings?"

"Yeah. Besides, I don't think there are any tall buildings in Dublin," Barb said.

"Or in the rest of Ireland," Kristy added. "He did fix a couple of things here, some drawers in the kitchen that wouldn't close."

"And he put some insulation around the front door so the wind couldn't blow through."

Dillon thought for a long moment, then said, "I'm going to check out some things. If you hear anything from Stephanie or Seamus for that matter, you call me right away. What's the name of your landlord?"

They both gave a worried look.

"I'll just call him, tell him we're looking into the matter, and I'll expect him to allow the two of you to remain here until further notice. Hopefully, that will take some of the pressure off. Okay?"

"That would be great," Barb said. "Thanks for helping, Marshal."

"Don't thank me until we get this sorted," Dillon said. "Just remember to give me a yell if you hear anything. Promise?"

Both girls nodded.

"And email me the name and phone number of your landlord. I'll give him a call. Anything else?"

The girls looked at one another, then shook their heads.

"Okay, I'll be in touch," Dillon said and headed for the front door.

TWELVE

illon hadn't made it the three blocks back to his place before his phone rang.

"Where the hell are you?" Paddy Suel said as soon as Dillon answered.

"Just leaving DCU. Missing American student, only no one seems to think she's really missing. Her room-mates just want the rent paid. What's up?"

"A call from out on the Dollyer. Someone's kids found a bag."

"A bag?"

"Yeah, a plastic bag on the beach. Don't know if it washed up on shore or what. I thought of you as soon as I heard about it."

"Oh?"

"A pair of hands in the thing. The kids, couple of young lads, ages five and six. Apparently, they were chasing one another around with the bag when their mother copped on. She sounded a bit over the top when she called it in. You're at DCU?"

"Just heading toward my car," Dillon said, crossing Ballymun Road and heading down St. Pappin's toward his place.

"Perfect. You can meet me over there, Dollymount Strand, in Clontarf. You go onto Bull Island just off of Clontarf Road. There's a mess of posts sunk into the beach to stop fools from driving their cars any farther. I'll meet you there. Shouldn't be more than a few minutes behind you."

"I'll be waiting," Dillon said. He walked another block along St. Pappin's, then down Dean Swift to his place.

Ten minutes later, he drove out on the wooden bridge to Bull Island. He pulled a short distance onto the beach and parked next to a long line of 6x6 timbers embedded in the sand just as Suel had described. He parked next to three Garda cars, then looked down the beach toward a woman talking to two gardaí. The gardaí were wearing high visibility fluorescent green vests. Both looked to be taking notes, and even from this distance, Dillon could tell the woman was upset. Two little boys were chasing one another around in circles, not far from the adults, and Dillon headed off in their direction. As he approached, he could hear the boys laughing. When he was maybe fifteen feet away and obviously heading toward the group, the boys quickly ran to their mother.

One of the officers glanced at Dillon, frowned, then took a step toward him and held his hand up to stop Dillon from coming any closer. "If you'll just hold on a minute, sir, we'll finish up with the lady, and then we'll attend to whatever *your* problem is."

"Name's Marshal Jack Dillon, I'm assigned to An Garda Síochána. Meeting Detective Sergeant Paddy Suel out here. He should be along any moment."

"Dillon? That American?"

"Yeah."

"Sorry, sir, sort of focused on the lady here." He motioned Dillon to join them. "Seems the little lads found a not so pleasant surprise on the beach."

"Jack Dillon," Dillon said, and nodded at the other officer and then the woman. "Please don't let me interrupt."

"I was just after saying I tell the boys to never, ever pick anything up on the beach," the woman said as her lower lip started to quiver. She was wearing jeans and tennis shoes with pink socks that came up just to the top of the shoe, leaving her ankles exposed. It was windy on the beach, and she wore a dark blue jacket. Her dark hair was pulled back in a ponytail and hung down to just above her shoulders. She didn't appear to be wearing makeup, not that she really needed any. Dillon pegged her age at maybe thirty-five.

The boys had gone back to chasing one another and calling each other names. They were wearing short sleeve shirts and had windbreakers tied around their waists. One of them seemed to shriek about every fifteen seconds.

Farther down the beach toward the water, two more officers were crouched examining something on the ground. They were dressed in uniforms and wearing the same high visibility vests along with what looked like cotton masks over their nose and mouth. One of them was taking pictures, presumably of the bag with the hands, while a third officer stood about ten feet away from them, ready to move any casual observers on their way.

"We've your initial details, Mrs. Talbot. If you could stop into the Garda station later today or sometime tomorrow just to make a formal statement, that would be grand."

"Will the boys need to be there? At this stage, I'd really like to minimize their involvement," she said, then glanced at the two children, still chasing one another back and forth.

"No." One of the Guards smiled. "I don't think that will be necessary. Just yourself will be fine."

"Can we leave then? I need to get them home. I want to give the two of them a long, hot bath."

"Of course. By all means, and thank you for your time."

"So dreadful," she said, shaking her head. "Okay, Michael, Patrick, come on, time to go," she called and headed off in the direction of the cars. The boys chased one another around for a few seconds longer than hurried to catch up with her.

One of the gardaí turned toward Dillon. "That's it, down where your man is photographing close to the water's edge. From here, they'll be bringing the bag and contents to the morgue over on Griffith Ave for examination."

"Where'd those kids find them, the hands?"

"Apparently in the plastic bag. Not sure if it washed up on shore or was buried on the beach or just left there. The older lad started to chase his younger brother with one of the hands until their mother confiscated it and returned it to the bag. She called 999." He glanced at his watch. "That was just a little over an hour ago. Care to walk down and take a look?"

"Let's go," Dillon said, and the three of them headed toward the group at the water's edge.

The two officers with Dillon nodded at the one keeping people at a distance, although, in fairness, there were only a handful of people walking past.

"How's it going, Timmy," one of them called.

"Boring up till now, but I'm sure there'll be a crowd once word gets out that you're here."

"More gorgeous women just waiting in line," he said, which brought a chuckle from everyone.

As they drew closer to the two cops examining the hands, one of them looked up, said something to his partner, then headed toward Dillon and the other two gardaí. "Just going to grab the cooler from the van to place the bag in, and we're finished," he said.

"Mind if I have a look?" Dillon asked.

"Suit yourself," he said, then headed back across the beach toward the vehicles. Dillon watched him for a brief moment, then saw a car pull up and park next to his. Paddy Suel climbed out and looked around. Dillon waved his arm for a few seconds before Suel spotted him, waved back, and stepped off in their direction.

Dillon approached the gardaí staring down the beach at two people flying a very large kite. Both had their feet planted firmly on the beach, legs braced, and still, the kite was dragging them along as they attempted to reel it in.

"Looks like a lot of work," Dillon said, and the officer turned with a surprised look on his face.

"I'm Jack Dillon. I'm with the Special Investigations Unit. I report to DCI McCabe," he said.

"McCabe? Well then, you're used to being told to get the thumb out," the gardaí said and laughed.

"Yeah. I hear that on a very regular occasion. You're going to take these to the morgue?"

"Soon as he's back with the cooler. I'm Tom White, by the way," he said and held out his hand.

Dillon shook it and said, "Can I take a look?"

"Feel free."

"You got any thoughts?"

"Thoughts? Yeah, a couple. Maybe more questions than answers."

"Such as?" Dillon asked. He took out a pair of blue latex gloves from his coat pocket, slipped them on, then knelt down and carefully opened the white plastic bag.

The bag had handles and large red letters that said, "Smart & Final." It consisted of a heavier duty plastic than say a sandwich bag or something a butcher might place a cut of meat in. As Dillon cautiously opened the bag, the smell of meat gone bad, really bad, wafted out of the bag, and he reflexively jerked his head back.

"Yeah, a bit manky smelling," the gardaí said. "What I don't get is why here? It doesn't make sense on the beach, well, unless you wanted it to be found."

"Maybe someone tossed it into the ocean thinking it would be carried out, and instead, it just washed up on shore," Dillon said.

There were two hands inside the bag, along with a lot of maggots. One of the hands, the left one he quickly determined, was missing the ring finger. Based on the size, he thought there was a pretty good chance they belonged to a male. Both had what looked to be a wound on the back of the hand like a nail had been driven through them. Crucified?

"I don't think it washed up. According to the mother of the little ones, they found the bag up there on the dunes. This is just where she got hold of it and left it. Initial examination doesn't seem to suggest it was in the water for any length of time. Not that large an item, the two hands. If you wanted to hide them, why not just bury the things in a farm field somewhere? Take all of five minutes, and they'd never be found. Amazing, the things were still here for two little boys to find, or someone's dog hadn't run off with them."

"What do you make of the ring finger missing on the left hand?" Dillon asked.

"It was cut off," the officer said with a deadpan look on his face.

"Gee, really?"

The gardaí smiled, said, "Can't be absolutely positive, but if I had to hazard a guess, I'd say it was done at the same time the hands were removed. It looks to be the same sort of equipment, an electric or power device. Maybe a saw or possibly a knife, although my money's on a saw. Not a power saw, you know, the sort with a round blade like what you'd cut lumber with, but a smaller type. The sort used for cutting pipe and the like. It appears to have cut in a back and forth motion, and I'm guessing a blade with fine teeth as opposed to a knife blade."

"And those wounds on the back, the guy was crucified?"

"That was our first thought too. Actually, they're bullet holes. You look closely you can see stippling around the wound, shot close up. Whoever it was, I'd guess the final minutes, maybe hours, couldn't have been all that pleasant. Probably tortured. Hell of a deal."

"Poor bastard. You're dropping this off at the morgue?" Dillon said, folding the plastic bag closed and standing. He pulled off the gloves, placing one inside the other, then tied a knot to contain the smell or anything else they may have picked up. He stepped away from the bag, gave it a final glance, and took in a deep breath of fresh air.

"Yeah, bit on the ripe side, aren't they? Here comes my man with the cooler. Who's your one with him? Suel's his last name, what's his first name?"

"Paddy. Paddy Suel," Dillon said, then called to Suel. "You can forget it. I've got the case all wrapped up and solved."

"Well, isn't that just grand. Think of the time it will save me because now I can get right to fixing all the mistakes you've no doubt made."

"When you get to the morgue, check in with Brian," Dillon said to the gardaí. "We were going over a body, John Doe, just yesterday. Pulled from the Royal Canal a few days ago. There's a good chance this might just tie in, no hands or head on the body," Dillon said.

Both gardaí looked out over the Irish Sea, and the one holding the blue plastic cooler said, "A head could be anywhere out there, just bobbing around."

"Or even anywhere around here," his partner said. "You've damn near five kilometers of beach and dunes."

"You want to take a look?" Dillon said to Suel.

"Tonight? No thanks, I'll take a pass. I've a steak dinner coming my way tonight."

THIRTEEN

Dillon and Suel waved goodbye to the two officers as they backed their van up, then headed back onto the wooden bridge and off Bull Island.

"You think it's related to your headless body?" Suel asked.

"I'd say there's an awfully good chance. Be great if they could lift the prints from those hands."

"What kind of shape were the hands in?"

"I'll tell you tomorrow after your steak dinner."

"Speaking of which, if you've nothing else, I just might head home and get cleaned up."

"I'll see you in the morning."

Dillon gave Suel a wave as he drove off, then stared down the beach. The couple with the large kite had the thing reeled in and were carrying it along the beach. The kite still caught in the wind, and from time to time, the guy adjusted his hold, so it didn't blow away.

Five miles of beach and sand dunes, Dillon thought. *The head could be anywhere out there.*

He called McCabe but ended up leaving a message. He told him about the hands and suggested they have a search done of the area, looking for the head.

He drove back the way he'd come and parked in front of the girls' house on Collins Avenue. The door opened just a second after he rang the doorbell. This time it was blonde Kristy who answered the door. "Oh, hi. Forget something?" she said.

"No, not really. I was just thinking you mentioned Seamus worked construction. Do you know if he had a specialty? Maybe he was an electrician or a plumber or something."

She seemed to think for a moment, then shook her head. "God, sorry, but I never even thought to ask."

"How'd they meet, Seamus and Stephanie?"

"Oh, one night over at the Slipper, up on the second floor. They had a big DCU event, live band and all. That was back in June."

"But he didn't go to DCU, right?"

"Yeah, that's right, but there were signs for it up all around campus, and at the Slipper too, so there were some local people there. He wouldn't have been the only one there who wasn't a student. I guess he just asked her to dance, and then, well, things clicked. Kind of romantic, in a way, you know."

"Yeah, romantic," Dillon said, and then climbed in his car and drove across the street and onto the campus. He walked into the Henry Grattan building. The offices where Grainne Finn's desk sat were closed and dark. He picked up the antique phone next to the door and dialed her extension, hoping to leave a message, but the phone just continued to ring, and eventually, he hung up.

On his way out, he stopped to peruse a bulletin board hanging alongside the door into the campus bank. There were notices for a debate club, a Fianna Fáil student group, yoga lessons, the French club, and a play that apparently had ended two weeks ago. Then, thumbtacked to the far, upper right corner was a flyer for the DCU Sub-Aqua Club, complete with pictures of people in wet suits standing in front of a large body of water.

Divers. He immediately thought of the Royal Canal and Broom Bridge and copied down the phone number, then walked back to his car and drove home.

FOURTEEN

Dillon had a quiet dinner at home, potatoes, broccoli, and a pork chop while Lucifer rested at his feet ready to pounce on any crumbs. A pen and paper rested next to Dillon's plate, and he occasionally wrote down a building trade that would be associated with home construction. The list just kept growing. He finished dinner, placed the dishes in the sink, tossed a treat to Lucifer, then turned his computer on and Googled building trades.

The building trade list immediately tripled in size to over sixty different occupations. He'd have to find another way to look for Stephanie Johnson and Seamus. He scrolled through over a hundred cable channels on his flatscreen, couldn't find anything that caught his interest, and went to bed a little after ten.

He was in the office just before eight the following morning. There was a note waiting on his desk from McCabe that said a team would be searching the immediate area of the dunes at Dollyer that morning. He left a voicemail message on the DCU Sub-Aqua line, grabbed a fresh coffee, and called Brian at the Dublin morgue.

"Hi, Brian. It's Jack Dillon," he said once Brian answered.

"Now, I wonder why you're calling. Amazing, I've been in the office for all of about four minutes, and here you are on the other end of the line before I even have a tea in my hand."

"You want to grab one and call me back?"

"No. Listen, I'll be examining that pair of hands from the beach later this morning. Feel free to join me if you'd like. I took a quick look and think there's a fairly good chance we'll be able to lift some prints and run them through our database, see if we can get some identification."

"Any initial thoughts?" Dillon asked.

"Not really, other than I think there may be a fairly good chance they belong to our unidentified headless man. Bit of luck, the two children finding them, as awful as that sounds."

"Yeah. I was talking to the gardaí on the scene yesterday. We all had the same thought. If they belong to our friend from the Royal Canal, that's wonderful. The mother was pretty upset. Hopefully, the incident won't affect those two little kids. Of course, it raises a number of questions."

"Such as?"

"Why put them in a plastic bag and toss them in the dunes? If you were going to just toss them, why not up in the mountains or out on some farm? One of the gardaí said you could bury them in just about any field, and no one would ever know. Take all of about five minutes to do it."

"Bit reminiscent of the situations down in Mexico."

"Yeah, we talked about that briefly. Down in Mexico, they seem to be sending an unmistakable message. You don't do as we say, and here's your end result. If those hands match up with the body, I'd say his last moments weren't all that pleasant," Dillon said.

"You're referring to the bullet holes?"

"Yeah, well, along with cutting off the hands and the head. A pretty good indication of torture, don't you think?"

"Possibly. Although I couldn't determine any indication whatsoever on the torso or legs that torture was involved, I don't know. I guess that will be for you to find out. I should be finished with my examination around mid-morning. Stop by, oh, say eleven, and I can give you an initial summary."

"I'll see you then, Brian, and thanks in advance."

Dillon hung up, took about four steps from his desk before the phone rang.

"Jack Dillon," he answered.

"Hi. I'm returning a call that was left for the DCU Sub-Aqua club," the voice replied.

FIFTEEN

Dillon explained to Dennis Conlin what he hoped to accomplish on the Royal Canal. "We're guessing the body may have been hidden beneath the Broom Bridge, maybe weighed down somehow. Eventually, it came loose and drifted down to lock number seven."

"Not that far a distance. If that happened at night, it could have floated down to the lock before daylight."

"You're familiar with the canal?"

"Pretty much, I'm a Dub, grew up in Cross Guns. So what exactly are you looking for?"

"Well, to be honest, I'm not really sure. Just trying to prove our suspicions. If we could get someone in the water, look for something like a heavy chain, maybe building blocks or even a suitcase weighed down with rocks, it might answer some questions and probably raise others."

"When do you need this done?"

"No hard and fast deadline, obviously the sooner, the better, and I have to add, about all I could afford to pay you would be a pint of Guinness afterward."

"Let me make some calls around and see if I can dig some folks up. I'd be up for it myself."

"Really? That would be great if you could."

"Thanks, but it's strictly for selfish reasons, could be some great press and publicity potential for the club," Conlin said.

"I'd be happy to attest to just about anything you want."

"Let me get back to you," Conlin said and hung up.

Dillon headed into the break room and grabbed a coffee. Paddy Suel was just coming into the office with a stack of files when Dillon returned to his desk.

"Late night reading?" Dillon asked and indicated the files.

"Bloody ATM's. Bastards snagged another one out in Rush last night."

"How many does that make?"

"Five and counting. No further along than we were at the beginning. What's the latest on your headless man?"

"I'm at the morgue later this morning for a summary of the hands. Brian seemed to think they're from the body. We can get fingerprints and…."

"Fantastic."

"Yeah. And I've got a guy with a diving group at DCU willing to go into the water at Broom Bridge and see what he can find."

"You get fingerprints and then an ID on that corpse, it might go a long way to wrapping that up."

Dillon's phone rang later that morning. "Jack Dillon."

"Brian McFadden, Jack." The voice echoed, and Dillon figured he was on a speakerphone, maybe still working on the pair of hands in the lab or maybe performing an autopsy on someone else. "I've been examining those hands. Almost positive they're from our John Doe. We're taking prints now. We'll make a tissue comparison, and I'm putting a rush on the results. If you want to join me in, oh, say an hour or so, I should have some definitive results for you by then."

"I'll be there," Dillon said and disconnected. He went to give McCabe a short update, but he wasn't in his office. Dillon made a few more phone calls, ended up leaving messages, then sent Gino Andretta, the US Marshal in New York, a brief email telling him he'd call toward the end of the morning, New York time.

He parked alongside the Dublin morgue on Griffith Avenue an hour later and hurried inside. Brian McFadden was leading him back to his office a couple of minutes later, talking over his shoulder as he hurried down the hall.

"Yeah, despite deterioration, the wrists still more or less line up. We'll have more conclusive results sometime tomorrow, but I expect them to match. One other item, well, actually two," McFadden said, opening the door to his office. He picked up a white mug from his desk emblazoned with the Dublin Coat of Arms, a castle with three towers on fire.

"Interest you in a tea and some biscuits?"

"You talked me into it," Dillon said.

"I'll be back in a minute. Grab a seat."

Dillon sat down in the only other chair and waited. McFadden returned a couple of minutes later. He carried a metal teapot. Steam was drifting out of the spout, and he set the teapot on a thick file on his desk. He pulled a desk drawer open, took out a box of chocolate-covered tea biscuits and another mug. This mug was blue with "I love Dublin" in white letters over a large red heart. He blew into the mug as if he was getting rid of dust, then placed the mug in front of Dillon. He helped himself to a couple of biscuits, then handed the box to Dillon and said, "Here. No doubt you need some sweetening."

Dillon took a couple of biscuits and set them on the edge of the desk next to his mug. "You mentioned two items?"

"Hmmm-mmm. Oh, yeah. The bullet holes in the hands, small caliber, fired from a distance of not more than three inches. Stippling on both hands, fired through the back of the hand. It would appear the hands were forced down on a wooden surface." As McFadden spoke, he wrapped his hands around his tea mug as if he were forcing it onto the desktop. "Wood residue on both palms, possibly from a chair or a table, or maybe just a board."

"While the victim was alive?" Dillon asked, then nodded, and McFadden filled his mug with tea.

"It would appear he was alive, based on wood residue suggesting the hand was forced, pushed up against the wood surface and some bruising on the hands. Purely conjecture, but there would be no obvious reason to add pressure to the hand if the individual wasn't offering some resistance. Which brings us to the next bit of information, the missing finger."

"From the left hand, the ring finger."

"Yes, digitus medicinalis," McFadden said, then followed up with a loud slurp of tea and a smile. "Did you get a look at it in the bag?"

"In the bag? No, to tell you the truth, I didn't even know it was in there. In all honesty, the smell was so bad I just closed the bag. I guess I completely missed it."

"Not to worry, it was in the bag. Removed from the hand by the same tool used to sever the wrists. If I might hypothesize a possible reason."

Dillon nodded as he stuffed one of the chocolate biscuits into his mouth.

"Physical evidence points to a ring on the finger, apparently a large ring, heavy, possibly gold. Whoever the basement surgeon was, he, or she, wanted that ring. Perhaps it was a diamond or some sort of precious stone, probably gold, and that may have appealed. Anyway, I'd say the finger was removed to get at the ring as opposed to cutting the finger off as some sort of torture. Most likely done after death."

"Interesting."

"Maybe. That's for you to find out. I'll forward summations to you once we get results back from the lab. Have you searched the area for your man's head?"

"We're in the process. I don't expect much. To be honest, I'm surprised we even found the hands. If I had to make a guess, I'd say someone made a mistake in not disposing of them more aggressively."

"The best laid plans," McFadden said.

"Thanks for the update, Brian," Dillon said. He took another sip of tea, then stood. "Anything else pops up, let me know."

"As always," McFadden said. He took another slurpy sip of tea, grimaced, and set his mug on the far side of the desk. "Oh, dreadful."

Dillon drove back out to Dollyer to see how the search for the head was progressing, but once there, he couldn't spot anything resembling a search team, and so he headed back to the office. He was almost there when his cell phone rang. He pulled over and answered the call.

"Jack Dillon."

"Dennis Conlin, with the DCU Sub-Aqua club."

"Yeah, Dennis, what'd you find out?"

"I've got three, well, four guys, counting me, eager to please. We'd love to get into the Royal. When did you want this done?"

"The sooner, the better, I'll adjust to your schedule," Dillon said, hoping sometime in the next week.

"Perfect. We can be there this afternoon, a little after two if that works for you?"

"Really, that's fantastic. I'll make it work," Dillon said.

"We'll meet you at Broom Bridge. Will you be in a Garda vehicle?"

"I suppose I could be. Is that important?"

"It'll eliminate some curious people. That portion of the canal, there's a number of folks with a lot of time on their hands. With an official vehicle parked there, they'll head in the opposite direction."

"I'll be there, with lights flashing," Dillon said.

SIXTEEN

Dillon pulled off the road and onto the entrance of the Royal Canal walking path at Broom Bridge. Just as promised, he had the lights flashing on a sedan he'd drawn from the motor pool. The vehicle was white with a fluorescent green and blue checkered pattern all around the base of the vehicle. The word "GARDA" was painted in large blue letters on the sides, front and rear of the vehicle. As he pulled over to park, he noticed two men walking toward him along the canal. They glanced in his direction then suddenly made an immediate about-face and quickly headed off in the opposite direction.

Dennis Conlin and four friends showed up in a van that looked like a product of the 60s about ten minutes later. The van had large flowers, and the semblance of a beach scene painted on the sides. The words, "Going to a dive" were spray-painted in red letters across the side of the van.

"Jack?" Conlin called, hurrying out from behind the steering wheel.

Dillon had been leaning against the Garda vehicle, looking at the canal and trying to ignore the flashing lights. He gave a small wave and walked over to the van.

Conlin opened the double rear doors and began unloading air tanks. He was dressed in a black wet suit and some sort of wet suit boots. He looked to be maybe late twenties, with neatly trimmed dark hair, a trimmed beard that looked to be about a four-day growth, and a flashing smile. *A chick magnet,* Dillon thought.

Three of the guys with him sort of stood off to the side. They all appeared to be a little younger, maybe in their early twenties, and were wearing wet suits. Conlin introduced them while he continued to unload items from the back of the van. Each one stepped forward, shook Dillon's hand. Dillon nodded as he shook hands, repeated their individual names, then immediately forgot all the names except Conlin's. He shook Conlin's hand once he stepped back, and the other three stepped forward to grab their individual equipment.

A fourth man was dressed in jeans, a green fleece jacket and a faded blue baseball cap with the Dublin logo. He had a square black bag slung over his shoulder and a camera hanging around his neck.

"That knacker with the camera is Jerry. He's gonna be taking pictures if it's all right with you. He's with The College View, the school paper. We're always looking for new members, and this will be good press."

Dillon nodded, shook hands, and then Jerry stepped back and started taking pictures as they grabbed their equipment. "Can I help carry something?" Dillon asked.

"Thanks, but no. We're each responsible for our own equipment."

They walked together down the slight hill to the canal, setting their equipment along the edge of the path and sitting down on the stone wall lining the canal around the bridge. Their legs from the knees down were dangling in the water. Although the water was murky, you could see the bottom along the edge and bits of debris, most of which looked like tin cans.

"How deep is it under the bridge?" Dillon asked.

"Five to six feet along most of the canal, maybe seven or eight feet beneath the bridge."

"That's where most of the large items tossed into the canal end up. A shopping trolley, bottles, bicycles, that sort of shite. Knackers like to watch them splash, I guess," one of the guys said, then slipped into the water. He left his air tank standing on the walking path and waded out toward the middle of the canal. The water rose to his shoulders before he reached the middle. He turned around and waded back to where the others were sitting. He grabbed a weight belt with a knife attached and wrapped it around his waist.

One of the guys half laughed and said, "Why would it be easy?"

As the others slipped into the water, three ducks maybe twenty feet away took off quacking before they flew maybe another hundred feet farther up the canal landed back on the water.

As Conlin slipped into the water and strapped on his air tank, Jerry began taking pictures, clicking away with his camera. "And you said you're looking for a heavy chain or building blocks? That sort of thing?" Conlin said.

"Based on our examinations, the body was in the water for a period of time. It washed up at the lock just down there, lock number seven. Right now we're thinking it was weighed down beneath the surface. Maybe a heavy chain, possibly building blocks, something like that. It somehow came loose and floated down to the lock. At least, that's what we're thinking at this point."

"Okay, let's see if we can come up with anything," Conlin said, and then waded out toward the middle of the canal.

About the point where the water grew to chest high, he pulled a diving mask down over his face and inserted the mouthpiece on the breathing apparatus. The other three lined up on either side, pulled their masks down, put the breathing apparatus in, and then floated on the surface as they slowly headed toward the bridge.

They swam, not quite abreast, but stretched out across the canal, faces immersed in the water, each apparently searching a designated section approximately five feet across. They slowly traveled beneath the bridge and continued on for maybe another hundred feet, then turned around and retraced their route, swimming past

Dillon for maybe another fifty feet before they stopped and seemed to gather for a brief chat.

All the while, Jerry traveled along the walking path, taking pictures, racing ahead another ten or fifteen feet, and taking more pictures. More than once, Dillon thought he was about to fall in.

When they stopped to talk, Dillon was tempted to ask if they'd seen anything but kept his mouth shut.

They turned and slowly headed back toward the bridge, this time occasionally stopping while someone pulled something out of the water and placed it on the edge of the walking path. At one point, Dillon thought one of them had come up with a head, but it turned out to be nothing more than a deflated soccer ball with one side completely crushed in and weeds and algae on the side.

Over the next hour, they hauled up an orange traffic cone, what looked like a length of flexible plumbing pipe, a large athletic bag, a wrought iron gate, some sort of metal rack on wheels, a bicycle, the apparent scorched remains of a motorized scooter, another bicycle, a small outboard motor, the barrels from a double-barreled shot-gun, a wheelchair and a spring frame for a bed.

They made another pass back up the canal past Dil-lon, then Conlin led them back to the wall where they'd first climbed in. He rested his elbows up on the walking path, pulled his mask onto his forehead, and said, "I'd say that pretty much does it. We could go on down to-ward the lock, but from the way you described it this would seem to be the logical place to drop a body, it's more or less hidden from view, and you could drive to the bridge, park just where you're parked and not have to carry the body too far. I'm trying to think like they would, and it seems to me that even in the middle of the night, they'd want to get this done as fast as possible and then just get the feck out of here."

"Let's take a look at what you guys dredged up," Dillon said. "You had me going for a minute there with the soccer ball."

They all laughed, and one of the guys said, "You should have seen it in the muck. Had a big stone next to it, and I thought for sure it was your man's head."

They all climbed out of the water, set their tanks and weight belts along the edge of the canal, then walked along, looking at the various items they'd brought to the surface.

"Maybe this," one of them said, touching the rusted wrought iron gate with his foot. It looked like something from the Victorian era. Heavy ornamental branches and vines with leaves and flowers that comprised the sides, top and bottom of the gate. Just a hint of flakes from silver paint appeared here and there. "They could have tied your man to it, a couple of big guys would swing it back and forth, toss him into the middle of the canal."

Dillon nodded, said, "Yeah," trying to envision the act. He placed a hand on the gate and lifted it just a few inches. It was heavy. "All that rust, I'm guessing it's been down there for more than just a couple of weeks, but best not to discount it entirely."

They looked at the metal rack on wheels, the spring frame for a bed, and the wheelchair, but all seemed to have the same problem. Based on rust, algae and weed growth they'd been down beneath the water far longer than a few weeks, maybe more like years.

"What about this?" one of them said, then kicked the large athletic bag. At one time it had been red with blue trim, and white letters. The letters appeared to be some sort of white tape, and only three of them remained, characters that seemed to suggest the Cyrillic alphabet. The bag was large enough to hold a body if maybe it had been bent over. The zipper across the top was still zipped closed, but a large rip extended just below the zipper along the entire length of the bag. "Damn thing's got bricks in it. No wonder it was so heavy."

Dillon looked at the bag. The handles were worn, but not from being in the water. There was a plastic luggage tag hanging from one of the worn leather handles and attached with a cheap chrome chain. Dillon looked at the tag but didn't touch it. On closer examination, the bag looked to be nylon or some other synthetic, and the handles he'd initially thought to be leather now appeared to be some sort of plastic. He could make out some of what was written on the tag, although he couldn't translate it, definitely a Cyrillic alphabet. There were a half dozen bricks in the bottom of the thing, buff-colored bricks. Two of them had remnants of mortar on them like they'd come from a construction site or maybe a derelict building.

"Who pulled this out?" Dillon asked.

One of the guys raised his hand. "Guilty, officer," he half laughed.

"You remember where you got it?"

"Yeah, I think so. Just over there on the far side," he said, then turned and pointed toward the corner of the bridge.

"Can you check and see if there are any more of those bricks in the canal? I think—" But the kid had already jumped back in the water and was hurrying to the far side of the canal.

When he finished, and the other two had done a thorough search of the area, they'd come up with six more bricks, all buff-colored. Three of the bricks were broken in half and looked to have a fresh gash across them.

"What do you think?" Conlin asked.

"I'm thinking this looks like a very good possibility. I'm going to run it to the labs, but can I buy you guys a late lunch, first?"

"You don't have to do—" One of the guys started to say, but the one closest to him elbowed him in the arm, and he shut up.

Dillon slipped on the latex gloves from his coat pocket and carried the bag up to the car. Water seeped out from the bottom of the bag, and he carried it with his arms extended away from his body in a failed attempt to avoid the water dripping onto his shoes. He leaned the bag at an angle against the rear tire of the car, letting more water drip out while he walked back down for two trips to retrieve the loose bricks.

Conlin and the divers hauled their equipment up to the van. Then while Conlin loaded it into the back of the van, the other three hauled the remaining items they'd recovered from the canal up toward the street, piling them against the stone wall.

"How about I meet you guys over at Hedigan's Brian Boru pub?" Dillon asked. "I'm buying."

"It would be bad form to refuse," Conlin laughed as they all climbed into the van.

SEVENTEEN

Suel thought for a half-second and said, "Contact Irish Waterways."

Dillon was back in the office and had just finished telling Paddy Suel about the athletic equipment bag with the tear and the bricks. After the late lunch and pints of Guinness with Dennis Conlin and friends, he'd taken the athletic bag to the Forensic Science Laboratory based at Garda Headquarters in Dublin's Phoenix Park.

"Red and blue with a Cyrillic alphabet, the thing sounds Russian. That's their colors, anyway. And it's how big?" Suel said.

Dillon stretched his arms out and said, "A good four feet. I'm thinking you fold the body at the waist, the head's removed, the body's wrapped in a plastic sheet, and yeah, it could fit in there, maybe. The gash along the back and the shoulder might be consistent with something causing the rip along the length of the bag. The bricks in there were meant to weigh it down, keep it on the bottom. Unfortunately, something tore the thing open, some of the bricks fall out, and the body rises to the surface."

"Like I said, contact Irish Waterways. It's not as if you've got people swimming around in there, and someone unzipped the bag. Waterways will have a log of any boats going through the canal. I know they've been moving a few boats over the last couple of months or so, and you need a crew from Irish Waterways to open and close the locks, so they'll have a log of who and what has gone through the lock. Might just give you a better idea of when and how that body rose to the surface and floated up to the lock."

Dillon went back to his desk and phoned Irish Waterways. The number he called turned out to be for the headquarters, which was located in Enniskillen, Northern Ireland. He had to concentrate to translate the hard northern accent on the other end of the line before they mercifully transferred his call to the Dublin office, which he should have called in the first place.

After explaining what he needed to four different people, he ended up speaking with a woman named Jennifer Cassidy.

"And you're with An Garda Síochána?"

"Yes, here in Dublin."

"Mmm-mmm," she said, not sounding all that sure. "It's just that you sound American."

"That's probably because I am American. I've been detailed to—"

"Could you give me your number and I'll call you right back?"

"Sure thing," Dillon said. He gave her his number and then rang off.

It wasn't the first time someone heard his accent and had a hard time believing he was with Dublin's police force. He expected his phone to ring in the next five minutes. It actually rang in about 60 seconds.

"Marshal Jack Dillon," he answered, smiling to himself.

"Oh, umm, Marshal, Jennifer Cassidy. I'm so sorry, but we just can't be too careful nowadays, you never know what some—"

"Don't worry about it, Jennifer. Happens all the time."

"It's just that your accent, you sound…."

"My accent? Are you kidding? I'm the only one in this town without an accent."

She paused for a long moment, then laughed, "Oh yeah, brilliant, I get it. Yeah, yeah. All right, so how can I help you, American Marshal?"

Without going into too much detail, Dillon explained the situation finishing up with, "So, if I could get a log, say for the past three months of boats that have passed through lock number seven on the Royal Canal and maybe contact information for owners of the boats, that could prove helpful to our ongoing investigation."

She seemed to think about that, then said, "What I would need is a request on letterhead listing the specifics you just gave me, along with your contact details. If you could email that to me, I can print a copy off on our end for records and email you the information yet this afternoon."

"I can do that," Dillon said, thanked her for her time then disconnected. Twenty minutes later, he sent the email on its way, then hurried into the break room for a coffee.

There was just barely a cup of coffee left in the pot, and one swallow from what he poured into his mug explained why no one had taken it. It had probably been on the burner since eight yesterday morning, and he feared it was strong enough to remove the glaze on the inside of his mug. He debated pouring it down the sink for a moment lest it eat through the plumbing, then did so anyway and hurried back to his desk. Jennifer Cassidy's email arrived a half-hour later with an attachment.

There had been a total of five boats through lock number seven over the past three months. One of the five had been just four days earlier, bringing the list of possibles down to four vessels. There were two vessels that had gone through the lock five weeks ago, both passing through on the same day, and Dillon focused on them. Both were listed as belonging to a Dublin company, Lundy Transfer.

He called the number listed and left a message. His call was returned maybe twenty minutes later.

"This is Dermot Lundy. I received your message. Now what's the problem?" He sounded under pressure.

"Actually, not really a problem, Mr. Lundy, and thanks for returning my call." Dillon went on to give a basic explanation of what he was looking for, then said, "So what I was hoping to do was to talk to whoever was piloting the boats on that particular day, see if they had any recollection of striking something beneath the waterline."

"So, there's no problem, no questions about how much fuel we used and whether it was rebated diesel?"

"Rebated diesel?"

"It's marked gas oil, and it's green. We've to pay a tax, at the end of the year I might add, not right now."

"I've no idea what you're talking about."

"You're sure?"

"Absolutely. I just have a question about striking something. I'm working on dates relating to an ongoing investigation. Your vessels are two of five that went through the lock within a certain time frame. I'm not at all interested in what type or how much fuel you used."

There was a long pause before Lundy finally said, "Hold on, I'm searching for the phone number now. Ah, here it is. You got a pencil ready?"

"Fire away," Dillon said.

Lundy gave him the phone number, then said, "PJ Connolly. You'll not find a grumpier bastard, nor a better man on the canal. Good luck," he said and hung up.

Dillon phoned the number he'd been given, and a moment later, a voice growled, "Hello," after the second ring.

"PJ Connolly, please."

"Who's calling?"

"My name is Jack Dillon. I'm with An Garda Síochána. I had a couple of questions about—"

"I don't believe it. The bastard actually filed a complaint? I didn't even hit him that hard. In fact, come to think of it, I didn't even hit him. Stupid eejit had the piss on and, umm, he just fell down in the pub. All I did was help the plonker up off the floor. And this is the thanks I get? You're telling me the bastard—"

"No, no, Mr. Connolly, if you'd let me speak for a moment. I've no idea what you're talking about. I have a question on a vessel, actually two vessels, that you took down the Royal Canal some weeks back. I'm wondering if you might have a memory of anything that happened near the Broom Bridge that day." Dillon glanced at the notes in front of him and mentioned the date, then waited for a long moment before Connolly said anything.

"Broom Bridge. You're referring to the two Lundy boats? Both fifty-footers and not in the best of condition."

"Yes, the Lundy boats. As a matter of fact, it was Dermot Lundy who suggested you'd be the man to talk to."

"Derm Lundy, he sure as hell would have no idea. Not half the man his father was, God bless him."

Dillon ignored that last comment and pressed on. "I'm involved in an ongoing investigation, and there's a question—"

"An ongoing investigation? About the canal and Broom Bridge? This have anything to do with the body they recovered at lock number seven? If you're asking did I see anything, the answer is no. As God is my witness, I would have contacted the authorities the moment I'd seen anything like that. That the reason you're calling?"

"No, sir, at least not exactly."

"Well, like I just said, if you'd bother to listen. I didn't see a damn thing if that's what you're asking. Seems to me there's enough foot traffic along there that someone would have spotted the thing. My opinion, it was dumped at night after we passed through and then spotted the very next day. When did they see it? It was the couple with the wee one no later than ten in the morning. Right? And the gardaí were there immediately."

"Actually, that is right," Dillon said, hoping he'd hidden the surprise in his voice, Connolly remembering that a couple with a baby stroller had initially made the call to the gardaí. "Do you recall running against anything below the surface?"

"Running against anything? No, can't say that I do. Course, the problem with that is the Lundy vessels we had were being salvaged. They'd both been submerged for quite some time. The engines on them were inoperable, so we'd attached engines the day before, noisy damn things, with a vibration all to themselves that would have drowned out any other sound. We had to yell just to communicate."

"Nothing rose to the surface?"

"No, we weren't traveling at any particular speed. Anyone walking along the pathway would have passed us by. Speed, it took the better part of the day to make it from Broom Bridge to the other side of Phibsborough Road, where we tied up for the night. A person could walk it in under an hour without an effort."

"I see. Mr. Connolly, thank you for your time," Dillon said, but Connolly had already hung up.

"How'd it go?" Suel called across from his desk.

"About what I expected, no way to confirm that the two boats I think may have ripped the sport bag actually did so. That doesn't disprove it, it just doesn't confirm anything, although the dates would seem to match up with what Brian McFadden was thinking."

"What's next?"

"That ID tag on the bag. If it had an address, that would be great."

"Don't hold your breath," Suel said.

EIGHTEEN

Actually, "don't hold your breath" turned out to be sage advice. Dillon received a call from the Forensic Science Laboratory the following morning. He'd been in the process of spinning his wheels and getting absolutely nowhere for the better part of the morning attempting to locate Seamus, the construction worker and Stephanie Johnson, the student from DCU when his phone rang.

"Marshal Jack Dillon."

"Marshal, Teresa Muldoon, with the Forensic Science Lab. We spoke yesterday. You dropped this athletic bag off for examination."

"Oh, wow, that was fast. I didn't expect to hear from you for days."

"Well, sorry to say that's not too far from the truth. Your item is in the queue, and we'll get to it when we get to it. That'll be at least a week if not longer, budget cuts, short staff, and a ban on overtime."

Shit. "Unfortunately, I'm familiar with the drill. But thanks, Teresa. I do appreciate the call, and if anything—"

"Actually, the reason I'm calling is I was able to get that address label translated."

"Really?"

"Yes. I've got a friend, she's Russian, and she came in this morning to take a look. By the way, we both commented, a cheap bag, and she said they were sold back in 2014 as a tourist item at the Olympics that were held in Sochi, Russia. Do you remember?"

"Yes, I mean sort of. So it's Russian?"

"Oh yes, most definitely. There's a tag inside, manufactured in Russia. She said they made millions of the things. Once the winter Olympics were over, they flooded virtually every store with the things. It became a bit of a disaster. All the stores were forced to purchase the bags and then try to sell them. Of course, no one was interested in buying. I guess places were giving the things away just to get rid of them. She said although the bag was initially associated with the Sochi Olympics, you shouldn't assume there was some sort of connection to the actual event like someone participating or even going there."

"Mmm-mmm."

"She was able to translate a portion of the address tag."

"Really?"

"Yes. I'm sending all this information in an email to you, but the address tag is for the name, Alyona Sokolov, that's a woman's name, by the way. The street address is impossible to read other than the number six. The town is Samara, a city of about three million, in the southeastern part of European Russia."

"Three million people?"

"Yeah, and that surname, Sokolov, I guess it's one of the most common names in Russia. Sorry."

"Well, actually, this is more information than I had before your phone call, Teresa, so I appreciate you making the time, and thanks for the info."

"Yeah, good luck. Oh, a couple more things, there was a two-euro coin in the bag, dated 2014, Spain, not that that makes any difference. And the bricks in the bag, we'll be doing a further analysis, but just at a glance they appear to be wire cut bricks, popular throughout the nineteenth century virtually everywhere, not only in Dublin but every town and village throughout the country."

"So nothing unique?"

"No, unfortunately, in fact, just the opposite. They're everywhere. Sorry," she said, and Dillon envisioned her giving a shrug of her shoulders and half-smiling as she said that last word.

"This is still more than I had. Thanks, Teresa. I really appreciate the call."

"My pleasure. Sorry, it's not better, but maybe the name will help."

"I'll be checking it out. Thanks again."

"Okay," she said and hung up.

Dillon drummed his fingers on the desk. A city of three million, one of the most common surnames in a nation of a hundred and forty-six million, and no idea if Alyona Sokolov had ever been in Ireland let alone still here. Would it make sense to leave her name tag on the bag for exactly that reason, because she wasn't here? Still, it was a Russian bag.

Dillon thought back to his initial arrival in Dublin and the attempts on his life, always the Russian connection, although they seemed to have settled down for the last two months. Was this an upturn? A coincidence, maybe not even related?

He accessed a Dublin database, searching for Alyona Sokolov, and not all that surprisingly came up empty-handed. He went national, going through all thirty-two counties in Ireland, north, and south, and still came up empty-handed.

"How's it going?" Paddy Suel said, walking past with a mug of tea from the break room.

"Does the term "dead end" have any connotations?"

"Your lads in the water didn't find anything?"

"Actually, yeah, they did." Dillon went on to tell Suel about the bag with the bricks and the two-euro coin. "Pretty sure that's what the body was in. Just hoping the address tag on the bag might have led somewhere. Unfortunately, it didn't."

"Well, except that it's Russian, and we've got a running game with that bunch of knackers, the Russians. We've got a fairly complete dossier on Alexei Bazanov and his contacts, at least the ones we're aware of. Might be worth it to have a look. It's in the data section online. You should be able to access it."

"Surprisingly, that's not a bad idea," Dillon said and started clicking keys on his computer.

"The other thing," Suel said, then slurped tea from his mug and made a face. "That name on the address tag, you mind if I give it to one of our eager up-and-coming lads? I've one in mind that might have a bit more luck than either you or I looking that name up."

"That would be great. Please put him on it, I'd like nothing better than to have him find something where I couldn't. Here," Dillon said, writing the name Alyona Sokolov on a note pad followed by the city, Samara. "I guess this is one of the most common surnames in Russia, and by the way, Alyona is a woman's name, and the city has a population of something like three million. Does the term "needle in a haystack" have any connotation?"

NINETEEN

Alexei Bazanov was thought to be the guy who gave the go-ahead on the shootout at the airport, where six people were killed, three more wounded, including Dillon. Of those killed, three of them were Russian, and Dillon had shot all three. So, if indeed Bazanov was involved, what was the connection between him and the frozen, headless American body in the Dublin morgue?

Dillon phoned Brian McFadden at the morgue and ended up leaving a message. McFadden returned his call maybe a half-hour later.

"Jack Dillon."

"If you've got another body, we simply don't have any more room," McFadden said.

"Brian, thanks for calling back."

"What do you need? Or were you going to invite me out for dinner with you and a couple of hot American women?"

"I don't know any American women or Irish ones for that matter, and certainly none that are hot."

"Can't blame me for trying. What can I do for you?"

"The fingerprints you took from those hands, can you send me that file?"

"I suppose I could," McFadden said, sounding like he wasn't all that sure about doing so.

"I want to send them over to a guy I know with the Marshal's Service in New York. He'll run them through their database. I was going to do it yesterday, but I got side-tracked with the guys diving in the Royal Canal."

"How'd that go?"

"Actually, I think we may have found a large athletic bag, the kind used for equipment, pretty good chance the body may have been stuffed in that. A big rip along one whole side, just below the zipper, bricks in the thing to weigh it down. I'm thinking the rip might match the damage along the back of the body. You mentioned you found some fibers on the body?"

"Yeah, nylon, sounds like they could be from that bag. What color was it?"

"Red and blue, from the Sochi Olympics in 2014. Apparently, the Russians made millions of the cheap things, then forced retailers to buy them after the Olympics. This one had an address tag on it, although the damn address was more or less unreadable."

"An address for here in Dublin?"

"No, some town in Russia, Samara," Dillon said, glancing at the notes on his desk. "City of something like three million people. Anyway, can you email me those prints? I'll shoot them over to my Marshal friend and then cross my fingers and hope he can come up with a name."

"Soon as I'm off the line, I'll send them your way."

"Oh, okay, then listen to this, Brian," Dillon said and hung up his phone.

An email from Brian McFadden came through with the fingerprint file attached five minutes later. Dillon forwarded the email to Gino Andretta in New York and Eric Bergman at the US Embassy in Dublin. Along with the fingerprints, he added the woman's name, Alyona Sokolov, from the name tag and referenced the Russian city, Samara, on the off chance that might trigger something.

TWENTY

The phone rang toward the end of the day. "Marshal Jack Dillon."

"Hi, Jack. Brian," McFadden said. "Say, I'm just checking to see what night you'll be free to buy me dinner."

"Just about any night will work, the McDonald's on O'Connell Street is open seven days a week. What do you have?"

"Just heard from the lab. They found two different blood types on samples from the hand's and that plastic bag we sent them."

"Two different blood types? How the hell does that happen? Are the hands from two different people?"

"No, nothing like that. You want an educated guess? Whatever idiot was cutting the hands off ended up cutting himself in the process and left a sample of his blood in the bag. It's almost like the stupid bastard stuck in his calling card."

"The folks from the lab are sure?"

"No question, blood type from our victim is A positive, that's the same for thirty-five point seven percent of the US population. The second sample is O positive, no question it's a different type." As he spoke, Dillon made a note of both blood types.

"Just for the record, can you tell me what percent of the Russian population would have an O positive blood type?"

"Russia? Hang on just a minute, let me check on that." Dillon could hear the keyboard clicking in the background. "Here we go. Hmmm-mmm. Yeah, I suspected as much. O positive is the most prominent blood type in Russia. Population of a hundred and forty-six million people, and forty-six percent are O positive, damn near half the country. You coming up with Russia based on the address tag on that bag they fished out of the Royal Canal?"

"Yeah. Doesn't it seem like this second blood type would reinforce that thought?"

"Possibly. Maybe. Just a minute." More keyboard clicking in the background. "Except that O positive is *the* most prominent blood type in Ireland, the UK, and the US as well."

"Oh, shit."

"Still, it tells us a little bit more about at least one of the individuals involved, the fool that cut themselves. You find them, we'll be able to link the knacker to those hands."

"Appreciate the call, Brian. Anything else develops, let me know."

"You'll be the first one on my list," McFadden said, then hung up the phone.

Dillon sent an email to Gino Andretta in New York and Eric Bergman with the US Diplomatic Security Services in Dublin, alerting them to the two blood types. His phone rang fifteen minutes later.

"Jack Dillon."

"Jack, Gino. Got your email a moment ago. I got a hit on those fingerprints you sent off."

"A name?"

"Yeah, former US Marine, First Lieutenant Matthew Schmidt, Second Battalion, First Marines. That last name is spelled S-C-H-M-I D-T. From Berlin, North Dakota."

"Berlin, North Dakota? Never heard of it."

"Small wonder. Population of thirty-four in the 2010 census. I'd say it's the kind of rural place you probably have to leave once you're out of high school. That's what Schmidt seems to have done. Graduated Northwestern University in 2001, enlisted in the Marines, graduated OCS, 2002. By 2004 he's a First Lieutenant in Fallujah. Seems to have left the Marines in 2006 for the DEA."

"DEA? The Drug Enforcement Agency?"

"That's what I'm coming up with."

"Why the hell hasn't the embassy or An Garda Síochána been alerted? He's been dead for at least a couple of weeks, maybe as long as a month from what we can determine, and there's been no report of him missing? That doesn't seem to make any sense."

Andretta seemed to scoff on the other end of the line. "You ever think just maybe they didn't want you to know?"

"Yeah, well, something ain't right, that's for damn sure. Send me what you got on him," Dillon said.

"I will. Word of advice, Jack?"

"What's that?"

"Watch yourself. Just the nature of the beast, the DEA. They deal with some rather unsavory folks. Move carefully."

"Thanks, Gino. I'll be careful. Send that stuff over, please. I'll print it off and erase the file."

"Good idea. Coming your way as I speak."

The email came across a minute after Dillon hung up the phone. He printed off two copies, then deleted the email. He took the copies out of his printer, slipped them into his inside coat pocket, then stepped out of the office, took the elevator down to the ground floor, and went out to the parking lot. He got in his car, drove a couple of blocks away, pulled over, phoned Eric Bergman at the US Embassy, and prayed he wouldn't have to leave a message.

The phone rang four times, and Dillon was just about to hang up when Bergman answered. "Eric Berg-man."

"Eric, Jack Dillon."

"Jack, héy. Sorry, I haven't gotten back to you, but I've drawn a blank on those fingerprints. Absolutely nothing to report other than that, a big fat nothing."

"You got time to meet me for a pint tonight?"

"A pint? Yeah, I suppose," Bergman sort of dragged that last part out. "Everything okay?"

Dillon didn't answer directly, instead, he just said, "How about the Palace in an hour?"

"Make it an hour and a half, and I'll see you there."

"You got it," Dillon said and hung up.

He sat behind the wheel for a very long moment, thinking, drumming his fingers on the steering wheel. Then he turned the key in the ignition and headed home.

He pulled in front of his place, parking partially on the sidewalk, leaving enough room for foot traffic on the one side and cars to pass along the narrow street on the other.

He walked through the front gate, hurrying toward his front door before he had to speak to Deitora, just now in the process of trimming back a rose bush in her front garden.

"Mr. Dillon, a moment of your time, s'il vous plaît."

"Actually, I'm afraid I've just a minute or two and—"

"That's all the time I intend to spend. Your dog was barking this morning for a good long while, continually. I suggest you do something to ensure a little more peace and quiet for the rest of us." She brushed the veil hanging from the brim of her straw hat. "My morning tea was cut short, interrupted, with all that racket."

"I'll talk to Lucifer."

"Talk to— I'd say there was something bothering the dog. Either that or it's simply disturbed. Perhaps the latter is more probable." She said that last bit under her breath. "There, I've said my piece. Do with it what you will."

Dillon was about to suggest what she could do with it, then thought better of the idea. "Thank you. I'll look into it."

"Very well," she said, then took a step back and said, "Oh, and while you're at it. The view from my front garden is not at all pleasing." She nodded at the four piles Lucifer had left scattered around Dillon's parking area and small front lawn over the past few days.

Dillon physically bit his tongue, smiled, and gave her a polite nod. He set his key in the front lock, then opened the door. The house alarm began to beep, and he input the access code, disarming the alarm, then called, "Lucifer."

A moment later, the dog hurried down the staircase with a black sock in his mouth. Dillon retrieved the sock, sent Lucifer out into the front garden to leave yet another pile and closed the door behind him.

TWENTY-ONE

Dillon gave a quick glance toward his front door just before he pulled away from the curb. Now there were five piles of Lucifer's special greeting scattered across the front, and Deitora was nowhere to be seen. He smiled as he drove around the corner and headed for the Palace.

He was seated in the backroom in one of possibly twenty-five chairs pushed up against the wall. The chairs were upholstered in red faux-leather, almost as old as Dillon and very comfortable. Small, round wooden tables and stools were scattered throughout the room. There were just a half-dozen people in the room at the moment, but that would change over the course of the next hour, and the room would remain more or less full until closing. Dillon had ordered two pints of Guinness, which sat on the table in front of him, untouched. He spotted Eric Bergman heading his way a few minutes later.

"Hi, Jack. You waiting long?" Bergman called as he approached the table.

"Here just a couple of minutes," Dillon said.

Bergman grabbed the chair next to Dillon so they'd be sitting side by side, both with their backs against the wall facing the entrance to the room.

"Is that Guinness for me, or are things so bad you're drinking double-fisted?" Bergman asked.

"That one's for you."

They both lifted their pint glass, clinked them together, gave the traditional Irish toast, "Sláinte," and took a healthy sip.

"So, I came up with a big fat nothing," Bergman said. "It was a long shot anyway, but I was hoping we might have gotten something on those fingerprints. Your Marshal pal in New York find anything?"

"Gino?" Dillon said and took another sip. He gave a quick glance left and right as he set his glass down. The ladies' room was located on the lower level, and the stairs leading down were in the corner of the room. All eyes, including Bergman's, were momentarily focused on two attractive dark-haired women just heading down the stairs. They seemed to be speaking Spanish or maybe Italian.

Dillon reached into his coat pocket and pulled out a copy of the information Gino Andretta had sent him. "Here's something you might find interesting reading," he said and handed it to Bergman.

Bergman gave a questioning look as he unfolded the sheet of paper and started reading. He glanced up at one point, looked like he was about to say something, then returned to the sheet of paper.

When he'd finished reading, he refolded the sheet in half. "Mind if I hang onto this?"

"That's your copy to keep," Dillon said.

Bergman slipped the sheet inside his coat pocket. "So let me get this straight. The DEA apparently has someone here, and we're completely unaware of it," Bergman said. As he spoke, he quickly scanned the room and reflexively placed a hand in front of his mouth.

"Looks that way," Dillon said. "Is there a way he could be here on a need-to-know basis?"

"Oh yeah, I mean, I suppose if they were working some black operation, yeah. They wouldn't necessarily check in with us. That would seem to make sense just from a security standpoint on their level. I didn't mean it like that exactly. But wouldn't you think he'd come up somewhere on the standard radar, as a tourist or someone entering the country. I'll go back to the office tonight and run this information, see if anything comes up."

"You can run it in the morning, at this stage—"

"No, I want to check it out tonight. Something ain't right. Let's say the guy gets smuggled in here on a top-secret flight or some bullshit, you'd think we'd still be alerted once he disappeared, if for no other reason than to help try and find the poor bastard. Something ain't right here. Guy's been dead for the better part of a month, his unidentified body is lying frozen in a drawer in the God damned Dublin morgue, and no one even asks a question?"

"Be my guest. You find anything, anything at all, call me. I don't care what time it is."

"Let me finish my pint first," Bergman said, then took a large sip.

They spoke in soft voices for the next fifteen minutes, Bergman studying each person who entered the backroom and took up a seat. By the time they were ready to leave, the backroom was full, and the front room along the bar was standing room only.

They finished their glasses at the same time, then stood to leave. Dillon carried the empty pint glasses up to the bar and set them next to three other empties, then headed out the door.

Outside on the street, Bergman looked around before he spoke. "The thing that bothers me is it would seem to be a given that this individual if he's on DEA business, wouldn't be here on his own. It's just not adding up."

"You know anyone in the DEA?"

"No, not really."

"Do they have anyone officially in the embassy?"

"Not that I'm aware of. The little I know, Ireland would be at best a second-tier posting. There are just a lot of other places they'd be before here, like just about all of central and South America, Africa, Afghanistan, Asia. God, Ireland? Based on my knowledge, it doesn't make any sense," Bergman said, shaking his head.

"Let me know what you find out," Dillon said, then they shook hands and went their separate ways.

TWENTY-TWO

Alexei Bazanov was furious, so mad he was spitting as he shouted. "Were you listening? No, it's not impossible. It's already too late. They know. They've recovered the bastard's body, something I told you could not be allowed to happen. Something you swore would be impossible, and yet now it is done. First spotted by grandparents pushing a child in a stroller. Fuck! Now, after you promised me I need not worry, they've recovered the hands I insisted you remove. You assured me, promised me, swore on your mother's grave they would never be found, yet two children, little boys no less, found them. They've recovered the bag you put the body in, and just in case they wouldn't be able to put two and two together, you left an address tag on the bag." Bazanov was glaring, red-faced, and shaking. As he sat down behind his desk, he could hear his heart pounding. He took a deep breath in an effort to calm himself before he had a heart attack.

He was a short man by any standard, just over five feet. His head was shaved on the sides, long on the top and combed straight back, although just now long strands of hair hung down to his ears on either side of his head.

He brushed his hair back with both hands and looked at the large figure standing on the opposite side of his desk. At six and a half feet, Yakov towered over Bazanov. His massive arms hung out from his sides, looking like he carried two invisible barrels. His bald head glistened as his eyes remained focused on the floor of Bazanov's study. Yakov had been with him for a number of years. He had never been the brightest bulb on the tree, but he was fiercely loyal to Alexei, and up until this moment, that had seemed to be enough.

"It was Arkady who—"

Alexei Bazanov held his hand up to silence Yakov. "I don't want to hear excuses. Arkady Sokolov is one of a number of problems that are going to have to be eliminated, do you understand?"

Yakov nodded, was about to speak when Alexei held his hand up again. "Please, not another word. I'm not interested in what you have to say." He filled the small crystal glass sitting on his desk with vodka, thinking, *Could it get any worse*, then realized it already had and downed the vodka.

"Where does she live, Arkady's sister? Moscow?"

"No, down south, Samara," Yakov said.

Alexei shook his head in disgust, wrote down the woman's name, Alyona Sokolov, along with the name of the city. "One more loose end that apparently I'll have to tie up. I swear to Christ you've made a complete mess of what was supposed to be a very simple task."

"If I might just explain—"

"Please," Alexei said, feeling his blood pressure beginning to rise again. "Please just do not say another word. Can you do that? Remain quiet? Just shut the hell up?"

Yakov wasn't sure if he should answer. After a second or two, he decided it might be best not to.

"The same individual has returned once again to become a large pain in my ass. This American with the Garda. This Dillon. Jack Dillon. Another loose end that now I'm forced to deal with. I should have put an end to him before." Bazanov looked up and glared at Yakov. "But, it seems I'm surrounded by incompetents."

"If I might suggest—"

"Suggest what? You haven't done enough damage already?"

"If you'd let me, I can clean up this entire mess, eliminate the American, bring an end to any further investigation."

"And you plan to do this how, exactly?"

"Someone we have used before. He can be controlled. I'll make sure of it, won't let him out of my sight and—"

"Please, I don't wish to hear any more. Just get out of my sight and deal with this problem once and for all."

"If I might just suggest an option that I think will end all your worries…."

"No, you cannot."

"I know this will work, I think."

Bazanov gave a loud sigh, seeming to surrender for a brief moment, then looked up, still red-faced, and stared at Yakov. "No. What you can do is get out of my sight while you're still able. Go on, get out. Get out. Get out. Get out," Alexei shouted, growing louder with each command until he jumped from his chair, picked up the crystal glass, and threw it at Yakov just as he hurried out of the room. The glass shattered against the oak trim along the edge of the door.

Bazanov took a couple of deep breaths in an effort to calm himself as Yakov's footsteps quickly faded down the hallway. He took a final deep breath, then sat down, slowly exhaled, and grabbed the bottle of vodka only to realize he no longer had a glass.

TWENTY-THREE

S omeone had parked their car, a white 2016 BMW, across Dillon's driveway, so he had to pull around the corner and park on the short, dead-end street. He walked back up the sidewalk, thought about leaving a note on the windshield, then decided he didn't need the hassle. He opened his gate and noticed the five piles left by Lucifer over the past few days were nowhere to be seen.

The drapes on Deitora's front window were pulled closed, although a light appeared to be on in the sitting room. Her car, a Dodge Avenger exactly the same as Dillon's, was still parked outside the front door. He debated about ringing her doorbell for a brief moment, thanking her for cleaning up after his dog, but then decided he didn't need a reaming tonight. He unlocked his front door and entered his house.

"Lucifer. Hey, Lucifer, come on, boy."

He heard what sounded like the dog jumping off the bed upstairs. A moment later, he heard Lucifer coming down the stairs and poking his head around the corner.

"There you are. Come on outside, pal," Dillon called, and held the front door open. Lucifer seemed to consider the offer for a moment before he hurried outside. He stopped on the front stoop, apparently looking for Dillon's car or maybe just the deposits he'd left scattered around the front over the better part of the week.

Dillon rummaged around in his refrigerator, pulled out a pork chop that had been sitting on a plate for three or four days, and set it on the kitchen counter. He placed the pork chop between a stale ciabatta roll he found on the back shelf, squirted some mustard on the lot, and called it dinner. He ate the sandwich in just over three minutes while standing at the kitchen sink. Once finished, he went out to the front hall, opened the door, and called for Lucifer before he realized the dog was standing right there on the stoop, waiting to be let inside.

He settled onto the couch in the sitting room, turned the TV on then lowered the volume to zero using the remote. He turned on his Kindle, clicked onto the book he was reading, and proceeded to reread the same page a half-dozen times in between thinking of Marine First Lieutenant Matthew Schmidt and the missing DCU student, Stephanie Johnson.

A little after ten Dillon's cell phone rang.

"Jack Dillon."

"Jack, Eric Bergman. Hope I'm not calling too late."

"No, just up reading, or at least trying to. What's up?"

"I've been searching online since we left the Palace, and I've come up with absolutely nothing, no record that I can find of a Matthew Schmidt entering Ireland. I'll put in an official request tomorrow morning, but we would usually have something, particularly if he was working on the DEA clock while over here. Absolutely no record of anyone by that name entering Ireland or departing Ireland for the States. At least not for the past two years."

"You went back that far?"

"Yeah. This wasn't adding up from the moment you handed me that information. The more I look at it, the more questions I have."

"You'll keep me posted," Dillon said.

"Yes, and please do the same for me. I'm worried something's going on we're not supposed to know about. Invariably, that leads to problems."

TWENTY-FOUR

Dillon pushed Lucifer to the side and mumbled something. Lucifer was back a second later, whining and nuzzling the back of Dillon's head. "For Christ's sake, don't tell me you have to go outside?" Dillon grumbled, then looked at the digital clock on the bedside table. Not even four in the morning.

"No," Dillon groaned firmly and pushed Lucifer away.

He was back nuzzling Dillon's head, only this time he barked once or twice.

"For God's sake, will you just let me sleep?" Dillon groaned, knowing it was already too late, he was awake. He lay there undisturbed for maybe ten seconds before the dog was back at it again.

"Oh, for the love of God, all right, all right, come on," Dillon growled and climbed out of bed.

Lucifer seemed to look at him, then snuggled down between the two pillows as Dillon pulled on a pair of sweat pants.

"Oh, no. Come on, you woke me. Now you're go-ing—"

It sounded like something metal bouncing off the concrete, something sort of heavy outside— a high-pitched clanging or ringing for just the briefest moment. Dillon walked over to the bedroom window, moved the curtain ever so slightly, and glanced out the window. The street appeared deserted. He listened carefully, thought he maybe heard something, but maybe not.

Lucifer seemed to groan and then whined.

"What is it, boy?" He quietly pulled the top drawer open on the bedside table, grabbed the nine-millimeter pistol from the drawer, and inserted the clip. He chambered a round, then stepped out into his hallway. Lucifer remained on the bed, hiding between the pillows.

Dillon looked out the hallway window without moving the lace curtain, but couldn't see anything. He did notice that the white BMW that had been parked in front of his driveway was now gone. He waited three or four minutes, straining his ears and searching the street, but still didn't see anything and decided it was just his imagination fueled by Lucifer being a pain in the ass.

"Idiot," he said, stepping back into the bedroom.

He was about to set the pistol back in the drawer when the explosion went off. He felt the concussion through the stucco and concrete walls of the bedroom, heard the sound of broken glass as the bedroom walls and windows vibrated, and a cloud of flame illuminated the street. The explosion was followed by the sound of a distant car quickly accelerating and disappearing into the night.

"Jesus Christ," he screamed and hurried down the stairs with the pistol in his hands. He cautiously crouched at the bottom of his staircase, holding the pistol at arm's length, scanning the hallway for anything out of place. Orange and yellow flames from in front of Deitora's home were illuminating the hallway and the sitting room. Dillon remained crouched as he made his way to the sitting room, then scanned it with his pistol, moving across the room. The room was empty, and he hurried back to the end of the staircase, quickly entered the kitchen, and went through the same process. The room, and in fact, the entire first floor was empty.

He ran back upstairs, dialed 999, and placed an emergency call to An Garda Síochána. He identified himself, described the explosion then hung up. He slipped into a t-shirt, jeans, and shoes, then stared out the upstairs hallway window, watching for any movement. Lights were on in four homes across the street, although he couldn't see anyone stepping outside. The flames from what was left of Deitora's car continued to burn, although nowhere near as large as just a few minutes ago. What looked like a tire and a rear portion of the vehicle was burning out in the middle of the street.

Not too long after that, the distant sound of a siren could be heard, and then another. Dillon stood in the dark, looking through the lace curtains, trying to discern movement, but he never did see any.

Once the first Garda vehicle pulled up, Dillon went out the back door, around the side of the house, and opened the side gate that led into the front garden.

He glanced left and right, saw the headlights of another Garda vehicle coming down the street, and behind it a fire brigade truck. He slipped the pistol into his waistband and pulled his t-shirt out to cover it. He waited a moment, then approached the two gardaí standing on the sidewalk, staring at the burning rubble.

They glanced up at him with shocked looks on their faces. The entire front window of Deitora's home was gone. Just some jagged pieces of glass around the outside edge of the window frame remained. The lace curtains and drapes in her front window appeared shredded and scorched. The right-hand portion of the drapes was hanging outside the window over the stucco exterior. All the lights were off in the house.

"I'm the guy who called this in, or maybe just one of the people who called," Dillon said as he approached. He looked up and down the street. Virtually all the homes had their lights on. Neighbors were silhouetted in the windows, looking outside, although Dillon appeared to be the only one actually out of his house.

Someone from the fire brigade truck wearing a long, high-visibility coat, a fire fighter's helmet with an air tank strapped to his back, was in the process of foaming the tire and car debris out in the street with a handheld fire extinguisher.

"You live here?" one of the officers asked.

"No, I'm next door. The woman who lives here is Deitora—"

"McGra?" the gardaí said, finishing Dillon's sentence. Both gardaí stared at one another.

"Deitora McGra?" one of the gardaí asked again.

"Yeah. I couldn't remember it before, but that's her last name, McGra."

"The old bitch— er, umm, woman who calls constantly to complain," the other said.

"She'd complain about the weather on a sunny day if we'd listen."

"I'm with An Garda Síochána," Dillon said and smiled. "Jack Dillon."

They both gave him a questioning look.

"Special Investigations Unit."

"Oh, yeah, DCI McCabe," one of them said.

"You're the Yank. And you're living next to Deitora McGra, now that's funny."

"Funny as long as it's not you or me," his partner said. "We better check, make sure she's okay," he said, then hurried over to the front door and pressed the doorbell.

Four men with large fire extinguishers had surrounded what was left of the car and began foaming down the burning wreckage, now more smoldering than actually burning.

"We might as well get out of their way," the gardaí said and began to move away.

"Jesus Christ, will you look at— Officer, you better come check this out," one of the fire crew shouted. "Hold off, lads," he said, and everyone stopped spraying their fire extinguishers.

The officer glanced at Dillon, then took a half-dozen steps over toward the fireman and half-shouted, "Fucking hell." He called to his partner at the front door, "Jerry?"

TWENTY-FIVE

There was an ambulance crew inside attending to Deitora McGra, who was apparently refusing to leave her home and get checked out at the hospital. Four more Garda vehicles were parked up and down the street. The medical examiner had wheeled a gurney up next to the wreckage, which had at least stopped smoldering, although the air still reeked of burnt fuel and melted plastic. A black body bag rested on top of the gurney, unzipped and pulled open, just waiting for the remnants of whoever had been under the car when it exploded.

"Nothing more we can do here, so we're going to take the remains over to the morgue, and they can see what they get there in the lab. You want to photograph and check the pockets, or what's left of them, be my guest," the Medical Examiner said, then stepped back and pulled the mask covering his nose and mouth down around his neck.

Dillon recognized the man, but couldn't recall his name. He was dressed in a white hazmat suit, one of two at the scene tonight.

"Marshal Jack Dillon. We've met before," Dillon said, extending his hand.

"Oh yeah, Dillon. It was over near the Stag's Head, that lad, the musician who'd been shot. American, wasn't he?"

Dillon nodded.

"Yeah, Fintan Burke," he said, taking Dillon's hand. "Good to see you again. What are you doing here?" he asked, looking up and down, taking in Dillon's t-shirt, jeans, shoes, but no socks. "Another—"

"I just live next door." Dillon nodded toward his house.

"Bit strange, this one. I don't suppose there's an outside chance your man was working on his car in the middle of the night?"

"If he was, it would have been a complete surprise to the owner. He doesn't live here. Any thoughts?"

"Yeah, he was blown to bits. We'll see what the lab results are. I don't know, smoking underneath the engine, and he cuts a fuel line? That seems a bit far-fetched, but I suppose just about anything's possible. We see a lot of stupid things."

Dillon nodded.

"If I have to hazard a guess, I'd maybe think a bomb," Burke said. "Whoever lives here, are they political?"

"Not that I'm aware of. An older woman, she can certainly be a pain in the ass, but from that to putting a bomb on her car? Seems a bit of a stretch."

"Yeah. Course, you never know. She says something to someone who's just a little off, they take offense, and suddenly you've got this sort of situation," he said nodding at the curtains softly flapping out of the shattered window. He indicated the various people collecting samples, taking photographs and notes, not to mention the fire brigade collecting equipment, and returning it to their truck. "All seems just a bit mad."

"I don't know that car certainly wasn't anything to brag about. I should know, I'm driving the exact same kind," Dillon said, then suddenly thought, *What if the bomb had been meant for me?*

The same vehicle, the same year, same color, only Dillon's car wasn't parked in front of his house because someone had parked in front of his driveway. He'd parked his car around the corner.

The front door to Deitora's house opened, and the two gardaí he'd spoken to earlier hurried outside, closing the door behind them.

"How'd it go?" Dillon asked as they passed by.

"Just as mean as ever. She'll survive," one of them said, and they hurried up the street toward their car.

TWENTY-SIX

Dillon was halfway to Deitora's front door when it opened, and she stood in the doorway in a brown, terrycloth dressing gown with what looked like some kind of flannel wrap around her hair.

He swallowed hard, then said, "Deitora, are you okay?"

"And what a foolish question. Yes, I guess I'm all right. I suppose I've you to thank for this," she said and nodded at the smoldering, burned-out wreckage, all that remained of her car. She suddenly stepped out of the house, made her way around the wreckage, then leaned over toward her garden to examine her rose bushes.

"Mmm-mmm, mmm-mmm," she said, going from one bush to the next. She suddenly stopped and said, "Oh, dear. My Kordes Robusta doesn't seem to have fared quite so well." She reached down, picked up what looked like a portion of a bumper about a foot long leaning against the rose bush, and tossed it back into the pile of wreckage. "I'd better get the clippers," she said and headed back into the house.

The sky to the east displayed a razor-thin line of grey. It wouldn't be sunrise for another hour, and Deitora was going to start pruning her roses. She was back outside a moment later, rose clippers in hand.

"Is that the red rose?" Dillon asked, not knowing what else to say.

She gave him a dismissive look, shook her head, and began trimming. "No, it's scarlet."

Dillon picked up a large portion she cut, and half tossed it into the car debris. "Ouch, damn it," he said, then reflexively shoved his thumb and forefinger into his mouth after impaling them on thorns.

"Careful of the thorns," Deitora said, giving him a quick scowl, then resumed her pruning, only now wearing a smile. She pruned the bush back to about a quarter of yesterday's size, then stepped back and said, "Well, I guess now we'll just have to wait and see."

"Can I make you a coffee?" Dillon said.

"No, thank you. But you could join me for a tea if you wish."

Dillon wanted to say no but heard himself doing just the opposite. "A tea would be nice, thank you," he said.

"I'd prefer not to leave my house unattended."

He looked around at the four men from the fire brigade, the three Garda vehicles still parked in front of the house, six or seven officers sorting through the rubble. Two more gardaí were across the street, beginning to talk to neighbors, asking if anyone saw anything. *Unattended?* he thought.

"Best to leave your shoes on," Deitora said as they entered her home.

Dillon had never been inside before. The place looked like what he would have expected, everything in its place, a crucifix on the wall opposite the front door with a small holy water container mounted on the wall below, literally the first things you'd see once you entered. With the exception of the front window being blown out by the blast, it was all very neat and tidy.

"Let me just put the kettle on," Deitora said, then dipped her fingers in the holy water and blessed herself as she headed toward the kitchen. "Please wipe your feet before you head into the sitting room." She made a beeline for the kitchen, leaving Dillon in the front entry. She closed the kitchen door once she entered, just in case he had any ideas about following her.

Dillon went into the sitting room. Both sets of curtains were now hanging out of the window. Dillon set about removing them from the heavy wooden curtain rod, carefully laying them over the brown leather couch opposite the fireplace. He noted that the floor had already been swept, and bits of glass and whatever else had resulted from the explosion had already been cleaned up.

"Here we are, Marshal," Deitora said a few minutes later. She had changed into slacks and what looked like a fleece jumper. The cloth around her head had been removed and her hair had been brushed. Dillon couldn't recall ever telling her he was a US Marshall, in fact, other than her complaints about the piles Lucifer had left behind and her suggestions he should wash his car, cut the grass, rake the leaves, close the garden gate and not accept junk mail, he really couldn't recall ever having an actual conversation with her.

"Do you take milk or sugar with your tea?" she asked as she set a tray on a buffet against the wall. The buffet, in fact, all of the furniture in the room with the exception of the leather couch, looked to be antique. The floor was covered by a thick oriental rug, royal blue, and red, and appeared to have been recently vacuumed. Outside, occasional conversational noise from the gardaí could be heard, although Dillon was unable to make out exactly what was being discussed.

"Thank you. No milk or sugar for me," Dillon said as he hurried over to the tray. There was a plate with two different tea biscuits, one chocolate covered, the other sugar-coated, which glistened in the headlights shining through the window space.

"Do you have someone you can call to seal that window?" he asked.

"I've left a message for my handyman. He should be here later this morning."

"Are you all right? This explosion was…."

"Yes, I can assure you, I'm quite all right," she said. "A word to the wise. This nonsense was meant for you. They made a mistake, but I wouldn't count on them being as careless next time, and we both know there will be a next time."

Dillon nodded and took a long sip from his tea mug.

"I was a nursing superintendent in Croatia, then Bosnia, after that with the UN in Somalia, well, until they pulled us out. It will take a lot more than some fool who can't read a proper address to frighten me off."

Dillon took another long sip of tea, then nodded. In a way, he wasn't surprised. In fact, he was glad. He set his mug back on the tray next to the plate with the tea biscuits. "Thank you for the tea, but I'd better get ready for work. It's bound to be a very long day."

"Thank you for your concern. Now mind yourself and be careful," she said, then added, "And clean up after your dog, please."

"I will," he said. "Call me if you run into any difficulties covering up that window."

She smiled, set her mug down, and said, "Let me see you to the door."

TWENTY-SEVEN

Dillon spent the better part of the morning going over the car explosion with McCabe.

"I would really like someone posted out in front of her house," Dillon said. "If only to make her feel a little more secure."

"And they're sure it was a bomb and not someone trying to steal the vehicle?" McCabe said.

"Well, I'm as sure as I can be without the final results from the crime lab. And who steals a car by crawling underneath and fooling with the engine? A 2007 Dodge Avenger no less. A ten-year-old car? I'm having a hard time believing it. Besides, her car was an exact copy of what I'm driving, year, model, color, everything."

"Did you drive your vehicle in this morning?"

"Yeah. Like I said, on a fluke, I had to park around the corner. Whoever it was who was killed, that was the first of two mistakes. They were on the wrong vehicle."

"And the second?" MacCabe asked, then smiled and said, "Oh. Yes, of course."

"Obviously not the smartest guy," Dillon said.

McCabe shook his head. "Better return your car back to the motor pool today. They'll issue you a different vehicle, but I want you to plan on changing it every twenty-four hours."

"That's going to be a real pain."

"And that's not really my concern. Plan on doing it anyway. Now, what do we know about the *victim*?" McCabe said, adding emphasis to the word that suggested anything but a victim.

"From what I saw, about all they had were a pair of legs from the knees down and two shoes, more like work boots actually."

"We'll have to see if they can come up with anything. From this moment forward, I want you with another officer at all times."

"With all due respect, sir. That's going to slow us down. I've got an ID on the body from the Royal Canal, and now I'd like…."

"I read your report first thing this morning, Dillon. The Russian aspect is interesting, but inconclusive at this stage. We need more facts."

"I can get them. It would just be better if I could proceed on my own without having to take someone off whatever they're working on just to tag team with me."

McCabe seemed to think about that for a long moment, then said, "Okay. For the time being, you're on your own. If you're out investigating anything that has to do with this morning's explosion or the body from the canal, Smith was the name?"

"Schmidt, sir, Matthew Schmidt, with the Drug Enforcement Agency in the States."

"Right. Anything to do with him, Alexei Bazanov, or anything Russian, I want you paired up with someone, Suel, Murphy, Carney, someone. It becomes a problem, you let me know. Clear?"

Dillon was about to argue the point, then decided against that course of action. "Got it," he said, trying to sound agreeable.

"Excellent. Now get back to work."

Dillon went back to his desk and phoned Grainne Finn at DCU. He ended up leaving a quick message and hung up. His phone rang no more than two minutes later.

"Marshal Dillon, I'm afraid I just missed your call. This is Grainne Finn. What can I do for you?"

"Thank you for returning my call. I was just checking in to see if you learned anything regarding Stephanie Johnson."

"Stephanie Johnson? Well, no. I thought I had made it clear when we met earlier. Under the circumstances, our policy is we still have the better part of two more weeks to wait before we react. You did speak with her roommates, did you not?"

"The other two girls in the house? Yes," Dillon said, looking at the file on his desk. "Barb Kruger and Kristy." Dillon couldn't remember Kristy's last name if indeed she ever told him.

"I can appreciate your concern, but in my experience, it is just about time for Ms. Johnson to turn up. The two-week mark seems to be when they resurface, realize they've made a big mistake in a relationship, adventure, or both, and set about making things right."

In other words, she had no new information, or, if she did, she wasn't about to share it with Dillon.

"Can't thank you enough for your time, Miss Finn," Dillon said, then hung up. He phoned the girls' house, thinking he should have done that to begin with. Someone answered after a half-dozen rings.

"Umm-mmm, hello." Then there was the sound of something crunchy being chewed.

"Barb or Kristy, please," Dillon said.

"This is Barb."

"Hi, Barb. Sorry to bother you. This is Marshal Jack Dillon with…."

"Oh, yeah, I guess you're calling about Steph. Nothing to worry about. Seamus finally stopped over here yesterday and gave us the rent money. Thank God. We barely had enough time to get it to the landlord before he was going to start eviction proceedings."

"So is she back at your place?"

"Back? Well, ummm, no, not really."

"What does "not really" mean?" Dillon said.

"Just that she's not here. Seamus said they were living together and everything and—"

"Living together and everything?" Dillon said. "Has she dropped out of school?"

"I don't really know about that."

"What did she say?"

"Oh, she wasn't here. Seamus said she was busy but sent her apologies, and then, well, he just gave us the rent money and said he had to meet up with some folks."

"Did he give you cash?"

"Yeah, three hundred and fifty euros."

"I don't suppose you were able to get an address from him?"

There was a loud crunch on the other end of the line and then what sounded like more chewing. "He gave us an address to forward her mail to."

"Did he take any of her clothes or books or anything like that?"

"No, but they or someone was apparently here later in the day because a bunch of her stuff was gone. Not to worry, we've got a girl lined up who's going to move in, so we're covered for the rent."

"I wasn't really worried about your rent. I was thinking more of Stephanie and why, apparently, no one has seen her."

"Oh."

"Can you think of any way to get in touch with her?"

"Not really," she said as another loud crunch followed up by more chewing came across the phone line.

Somehow he wasn't surprised. "What was the address he gave you?"

"Oh, umm," She paused for a moment, clearly swallowing whatever it was she'd been eating during their conversation. "Just a minute and I'll get it for you. It's just out in the kitchen. Oh, yeah, here it is," she said a moment later, and read the address off to Dillon, who wrote it down then repeated it back to her.

"Yeah, that's it. Are you going to go there?"

"I'll want to just touch base, make sure everything is okay."

"Oh, yeah, I s'pose," she said, sounding like his response was a novel suggestion that had never occurred to her before. "Well, if you see her, could you maybe not tell her where you got the address. We kinda don't want her to know about filing the police report. 'Specially since she's apparently just fine."

TWENTY-EIGHT

lexei Bazanov asked again, "Dead? You're sure?"

"Positive," the voice on the other end of the phone said.

"Have they been able to identify him?"

"Not yet. Fortunately, there wasn't much left to identify."

"But how? What happened?"

"Apparently he'd been drinking. Yakov's instructions were to make sure the American was eliminated. It would appear he built a bomb about three times as powerful as normal, and then, well, apparently it went off as he was installing it."

"At the American's home?" Bazanov asked.

"Actually, not quite."

"What do you mean, not quite?"

"Apparently he was installing it on the wrong vehicle. The car actually belonged to an elderly woman. She lives next door to the American."

"The wrong vehicle? The wrong house? And the gardaí are involved?"

"Yes, of course. The explosion was bad enough, but now a body? Well, you can just imagine."

"What in the— Is there no one capable of doing anything properly? I tell them to dispose of a body, it's found within a week and a half. 'Remove the hands,' I say, 'destroy them.' They end up gift-wrapped, and a child brings them to the police. A child. I want the American eliminated, and this fool decides it would be a good idea to get drunk before installing the bomb on the wrong vehicle. I'm becoming rather frustrated," Bazanov said, then took a couple of deep breaths to calm his heart. He could hear the pounding in his ears.

"I'm sorry to be the bearer of bad news, but I thought you would want to know immediately. I only found out just a moment ago myself and thought it best to call you right away."

"Thank you. You hear anything else, please let me know," Bazanov said and hung up. He drummed his fingers on the desk for a long moment, then, against his better judgement he summoned Yakov.

The large man entered the study a minute later. He hurried in front of Bazanov's desk, never really looking up. Now he stood with his head bowed, appearing to be in abject surrender as he murmured, "How may I be of service."

Bazanov chose his words carefully. "Was there any activity last night you wish to make me aware of?"

Yakov seemed to squirm a bit, then without looking up from the floor, said, "I had hoped to eliminate a slight problem for you, the American."

"And?"

"There seems to have been a small situation."

"A small *situation*?"

"Arkady Sokolov had a friend, Dmitry, who was supposed to place a device in the American's car. But that didn't work out so well."

"Didn't work out so well?"

"Yes, sir," Yakov said in barely a whisper.

"He apparently placed the device in the wrong car, in front of the wrong house, and blew himself up. Which saves me the time of having him slowly killed for being such a stupid idiot."

"That was the wrong car?" Yakov said.

"Yes. And the wrong house. Does anyone think anymore? And this was with the help of your friend Arkady Sokolov? The same genius who hid the American body that was never to be found, only to be located by grandparents and a small child. The same fool who was going to dispose of the hands only to have them found by children playing. Correct?"

"Yes, sir," Yakov said in barely a whisper.

Bazanov studied the giant in front of him focusing on the floor, for a long moment, then, despite his misgivings, said, "It would please me to see and hear no more of Arkady Sokolov."

Yakov looked up from the floor and smiled. "It would be my pleasure to make this so. Please, consider the task done, and I assure you that no one will find a trace of him, ever."

"That would make me very happy, Yakov. I think the sooner you take care of this problem, the better it will be for all of us. I trust you understand what it is I need."

"Yes, he will vanish without a trace, disappear never to be found, he will be erased from—"

"Yakov, simply eliminate him, and please, please, please, no mistakes, no witnesses, no one finding him. I've had enough disasters for the time being."

"On my mother's grave," Yakov said, raising his right hand.

"Or your own," Bazanov replied. "If this isn't done properly."

Yakov nodded, then hurried from the room.

TWENTY-NINE

illon pulled up across the street from the three-story stucco building on Drumcondra. At some point, the stucco had been painted white, and could definitely use a second coat. The navy-blue trim around the windows and front door was peeling in a number of places. Dillon counted nine doorbells attached just to the right of the front door. Number seven was supposedly the unit Stephanie Johnson had moved into with her boyfriend, Seamus. Logic would seem to suggest it was one of three units on the third floor.

He climbed out of his car and waited a moment for a small break in the traffic before he crossed the street. As soon as there was a break in traffic, he hurried across the street and rang the doorbell numbered seven.

He stepped back from the front door and studied the building for a few seconds, noticed that the second and third-floor units all had items of food sitting out on the window sill. Two rather large, fat pigeons were on one of the window sills on the second floor, attacking what appeared to have been a loaf of bread.

A moment later a female voice said, "Yes."

"Stephanie Johnson," Dillon said, trying to sound official.

"That's me?"

"Stephanie, my name is Jack Dillon. I'm a US Marshal attached to An Garda Síochána. We need to talk."

"The police? What's this about?"

Dillon smiled and nodded at two women who had slowed as they were walking past, obviously interested in what was going on. He nodded in a way that suggested, *Nothing to see here, just keep moving.* Eventually, they resumed their normal pace, one of them looking over her shoulder and staring as they departed.

"Hello? Hello?"

"It's about your dropping out of school, along with a missing person report that was filed on you. If you could let me in, or come down and we can talk in some public place you would feel comfortable in, but I have to make sure that you're okay."

"I'm fine, really. Everything is going—"

"I need to see you, Stephanie. Why don't you buzz the door, and I'll be up in a minute to chat."

There was a pause, and then, amazingly, the door buzzed, and Dillon heard the front door lock give an audible click. He opened the door and stepped into a narrow stairway of steep steps, covered with dark green plastic tile and edged with silver metal trim that looked like it came out of a catalog page from 1955. His footsteps echoed as he made the steep climb, then took the next flight up to the third floor.

Number seven was right next to the staircase, and he took a couple of seconds to catch his breath before he knocked on the door.

Stephanie Johnson answered the door almost immediately.

She was of medium height with shoulder-length dark hair, not quite black, and parted down the middle. She had bright blue eyes beneath severe black eyebrows, a somewhat long nose, and shapely hips. Dillon guessed she might be in her second trimester, which would seem to answer a number of his questions.

"Stephanie?"

"Yes."

Dillon showed his badge and warrant card. She gave a quick glance, then looked at him with an expressionless face.

"Can I come in for a minute or two and talk to you?"

"I suppose. Yeah, sure, come on in. Seamus is at work. He gets home around five," she said and held the door open for Dillon to step in.

The unit was small, just a one-room efficiency apartment. A double bed was in the center of the room, with a kitchen countertop and a small range and refrigerator up against the wall that looked out onto the street. There were two windows, one in either corner of the wall. Both windows were open, and traffic noise drifted up from the street outside.

A metal card table chair sat alongside the bed, and Stephanie sort of focused on the floor, looking slightly embarrassed and said, "Can I get you a tea or something?"

"No, thanks. That's nice of you to offer, but I'm fine. I just have to ask a couple of questions, and then I'll get out of your hair."

"Yeah, I can guess what you're probably thinking. Not too many people know. I haven't told my parents yet. They're going to go absolutely bird shit."

"So, that's why you left school and the place you were renting?"

"I was starting to show, and I, we, just needed some time to get things figured out."

"My only concern is that you're safe, not being held against your will, and other than that, I'm pretty much out of your hair."

She suddenly seemed relieved, and she visibly exhaled. "Oh, thank God, so my folks didn't send you?"

"Your folks, no, they didn't. The school, DCU, apparently waits a month before they contact family, but I'd guess you're coming up on that time pretty soon. You might want to talk to the school, then best to get in touch with your folks. They're going to be worried."

"They're gonna go crazy is what they're gonna do."

Dillon looked around the place for half a second. A small chest of drawers stood against the wall at the end of the bed. A shelf made from plastic milk crates and three pine boards held some folded clothes and four plates. There wasn't a table anywhere in the place.

"Yeah, I know, it's not much, but it's all we can afford. I'm looking for work, applied for a work visa, but
because I'm American, it gets complicated pretty fast."

"You're okay, Stephanie?"

She looked at Dillon and her eyes started to tear up,
then she swallowed and nodded a few times. "Me? Yeah,
yeah. We're going to make it. We'll be fine."

Dillon took out his wallet and handed her a business
card. "Hey, you guys need anything I can help with, just
give me a call."

"Oh, thanks, and thanks for not lecturing me. I
know, I know, but sometimes things just happen," she
said, then placed her hands across her growing stomach.
"Seamus is really good to me, and he's working really
hard. It's just that there's literally nothing to rent in this
town, and everything is so expensive."

"What kind of work are you looking for?"

"I'll do just about anything, but I can't get a work
visa, at least not yet."

"Well, if you'd be interested in doing some light
cleaning, I could always use it at my place. I'm on the
bus line, you could grab a number 13 just outside, and
it'll drop you two blocks from my place. I'm close to
DCU."

She looked at his card and smiled. "Thanks. That's
very kind of you. I might take you up on that."

"When are you due?"

"One hundred and twenty-two days. Just eighteen
weeks," she said, looking around the place as if to say,

Where is the baby going to go? "Like I said, if I can be of any help, you just call, okay?"

"I will," she said, then held out her hand to shake. "Thank you," she whispered. She pulled Dillon closer and gave him a peck on the cheek. Her eyes started to tear up again as Dillon stepped out into the hall, and she quickly closed the door behind him.

THIRTY

illon was in the break room about to grab a candy bar for a late lunch when a text message came across his cell phone. *Calling in 15 min. Get to a secure locale. G*

He didn't recognize the number but knew it was from Gino Andretta, back in New York. Something was up. He stuffed the candy bar in his shirt pocket and headed out to the parking lot. As he stepped outside, he remembered that he'd turned his car back into the pool and hadn't drawn a new one, so he hurried around to the sunny side of the building and waited for the call. It came through a few minutes later.

"Free to talk?" Gino asked.

"Yeah, I'm outside enjoying the sun for a change. What's up?"

"Matthew Schmidt, your DEA agent, turns out there's something dark going on, surprise, surprise. My source said it's on a need-to-know basis. Maybe only a half-dozen folks knew about the operation, well, at least until Matthew Schmidt turned up missing. They're still trying to decide what to do as far as the body is concerned. Family is beginning to bring some heat to the game, got a couple of members of congress involved. His death is liable to go public at any minute."

"Congress? When was the last time those bunch of fools accomplished anything?"

"No argument there. The only thing is this could be a win-win situation for them. They come out having gone to bat for a rural family trying to learn information on their son who's working for a federal agency, and you can suddenly see how it could pay big dividends with no real downside for them. Anyway, it looks like the DEA has been trying to keep a lid on everything and they're about to fail."

"What did you learn about the actual operation?"

"Not much. A Russian connection, but no names coming out as of yet. Rumors of heroin and Afghanistan, but again, nothing I could get confirmation on."

"Was he working alone, Schmidt?"

"Apparently. I'm trying to find out if anyone was in there with him, but it's pretty hushed up. His record, at least up to this point, has been exemplary."

"Strange, they'd make no effort to contact us. The body getting discovered in the Royal Canal made headlines here. You think they'd know about his murder. Any idea how he got in here? According to my contact at the embassy, they appear to have avoided Irish passport control and any contact with the US Embassy."

"Could be as simple as being flown in on something like a mail flight, and he just walked off the plane, got in a car, and drove away. If you're looking for a wild and crazy option, maybe someone in a boat just dropped him on the shore, and they were picked up. The country is an island, after all. It wouldn't be that hard to do. A false passport certainly isn't out of the question."

Dillon thought about that. All the options seemed to make sense.

"You ready for the weird part, now?"

"There's a weirder part?" Dillon said.

"Yeah. I think I got a possible address for you."

"An address? You're kidding?"

"Nope. 85 North Circular Road, an area in Dublin, called Phibsborough. You familiar with it?"

"Sort of. It's not too far from Phoenix Park. A great big park with—"

"With a zoo, a coffee shop, the Irish President's residence as well as the residence for the American Ambassador."

"You know it?" Dillon asked.

"Been there," Andretta replied.

"So let me get this straight, this is, or maybe was a black operation. You don't know how he snuck into the country. You can't get the name of anyone who might have been with Schmidt. But you got an address?"

"Possible address. It's owned by a company that's a front for the DEA, Sysdigi Inc, supposedly out of

Springfield, Virginia. They own property everywhere from Miami and Bogotá to Kabul."

"Hmmm-mmm, anything else?"

"That's pretty much what I've been able to dig up so far. Something else turns up. I'll let you know."

"Thanks, Gino. This is a big help. I'll check the address out today. You get anything else you let me know, okay?"

"You'll be the first person I call. Hey, Jack, be careful out there. Keep your head down."

"Thanks, Gino, I will. Make sure you do the same."

"Little different danger over here in IT."

"I owe you one."

"You owe me more than one," Andretta said and hung up.

THIRTY-ONE

Sitting at his desk, Dillon put a call into Paddy Suel, hoping they'd be able to connect but got dumped into his voicemail again. It was the second call he'd made to Suel in the past half hour. He decided no harm could come from just driving past the address on North Circular Road Gino had given him, scoping it out in the event he decided they should investigate it further.

He quietly left the office and went down to the motor pool.

"Well, if it isn't the Marshal. Word has it you're about to become a daily visitor," Sergeant Bourke said.

He was a large man, in a large uniform, and Dillon had always figured him for a former athlete maybe eighty or a hundred pounds ago. He had close-cropped hair, red at one time, now more grey along the sides and thinning on the top. Dillon had always found him pleasant and armed with uncountable hilarious, one-liners. He'd been introduced and told Bourke's first name more than once, something that always seemed to go in one ear and immediately out the other. It was something basic, the first name, Mike, Mick, Mark, Mel, though past experience had taught Dillon whatever he guessed would be wrong. So he stuck to the generic, Sergeant Bourke.

"Yeah. Bit of a surprise, the bomb meant for me ended up taking out the neighbor's car."

"Along with the little that was left of your man. Were they able to determine an ID yet?"

"Not as far as I know. At least for the time being, I've been instructed to draw a different vehicle every day. I'd say for today that shiny red Mercedes coupe out there might just be the perfect fit."

"Indeed. However, DCI McCabe seemed to have your happiness headed in a slightly different direction."

"Oh?"

"Yes, a 2008, Chrysler PT Cruiser," Bourke said and flashed a wide grin.

"A PT Cruiser?"

"A 2008 PT Cruiser."

"I don't think—"

"I'm afraid you'll have to, Marshall. Besides, it's a year newer than that litter box you've been driving."

"Does it have to be a—"

"I'm afraid it does. DCI McCabe picked it out especially, for the likes of you. You can take it up with him if you'd prefer. It's purple if that's any consolation, Marshal."

"Mmm-mmm," Dillon said, not really sounding all that sure.

"A year newer, and well, I'm afraid I've been instructed you're not to have any other choice."

"Then I guess I'll have to take it," Dillon said.

Bourke flashed a wise smile and said, "Good idea. Coming right up, Marshal."

The PT Cruiser was indeed purple, with a smell faintly reminiscent of a pub the morning after some wild event. The floor in the rear was covered with empty take-out boxes, food wrappers, and three or four plastic bottles half-full of Lucozade.

Dillon pulled out of the motor pool, then stopped on the street next to the first public trash bin he saw and shoveled out the back seat. He drove for ten minutes through Glasnevin and Phibsborough, then took a right onto Cabra Road and the next left onto North Circular Road.

The road was made up of multiple-story, attached brick houses that had all been changed into flats. What had once been elegant, two and three-story Victorian and Georgian homes had been transformed into six and eight-unit flats. Just now, Dillon was stopped at a traffic light. He glanced out the window and counted ten doorbells on the door frame of the unit on the corner. The vast majority of the structures appeared to have front doors and windows with peeling paint, small front gardens overgrown with weeds, and overflowing trash bins. The odd-numbered building addresses were on his right-hand side and the even numbers on the left. The building on the corner with the ten doorbells was number 65.

Each front garden was lined with a three-foot-high brick wall and fence of Victorian-styled wrought iron fencing, usually painted black, but occasionally green or silver, mounted on top of the brick wall. Most, but not all, featured a wrought iron gate and a hedge growing behind the wrought iron fence. Dillon thought back to the rusted gate the DCU divers had pulled out of the Royal Canal.

He made a left-hand turn at the corner and parked. He stepped out of the PT Cruiser, slipped on a pair of mirrored sunglasses, and headed back to North Circular Road, figuring he'd get a better chance to look at the place if he could leisurely stroll past.

THIRTY-TWO

He had walked halfway down the block when he noticed three men heading toward him. One of them wore a hoodie sweatshirt, grey with a crest or seal centered on the sweatshirt, and the words "Dublin" above and "Ireland" below the crest in dark blue letters. As they approached, Dillon thought they might be discussing him, but couldn't pick up what exactly was being said. As they drew closer, the man in the middle said something, then stepped aside so that Dillon could pass between them. They weren't speaking English, and Dillon's thought was the language sounded like Russian or maybe Polish.

As he came alongside, the man in the hoodie suddenly reached over and grabbed his mirrored sunglasses. The man on the other side punched him in the stomach. Dillon dropped to his knees more as a defense than from the power of the punch and rolled off to the side. The man who'd dropped back attempted to kick Dillon but missed. They all turned and took off in the direction they'd just come, not really running, but jogging down the sidewalk, looking over their shoulders, laughing, hooting, and slapping one another across the back of the head.

Dillon quickly got to his feet and headed in the opposite direction, back toward the PT Cruiser. When he reached the corner, he looked over his shoulder. The three had already slowed to a walk, and the one who'd taken his sunglasses gave a wave, shouted something Dillon couldn't make out, and laughed.

Dillon walked around the corner, then ran to the PT Cruiser. He slid behind the wheel, started the car, then raced down the street to the corner, made a sharp turn, and sped down the length of a very long block. He took the first right, heading back toward North Circular Road. Four young boys, maybe twelve or thirteen, were standing on the far corner.

The boys were dressed in sports uniforms, blue shorts, and jerseys with yellow stripes along the side of the shorts and jerseys. The shoulders on the jerseys were yellow, and the chest was emblazoned with the letters GAA: Gaelic Athletic Association. All four boys were holding hurleys, a cross between a short hockey stick and a baseball bat, made out of ash.

Dillon pulled to the curb, jumped out and hurried over to the boys. "Hey, lads, what team are you on?"

They looked at him with more than a little suspicion before one of them finally said, "Na Fianna." Two of his friends gave him a look that suggested he keep his mouth shut.

Dillon glanced over the hedge and up North Circular Road. The three guys were still walking toward the corner. The one wearing his mirrored sunglasses had just taken them off, waved them in front of his pals, then put them back on, said something, and they'd all laughed.

"Can I see that hurley?" Dillon asked the kid who'd told him the team name. "Just like to hold it for a moment. I tell you what, here," he said, taking out his wallet. "You can hang onto this if you're worried about me keeping it." He pulled a twenty-euro bill out of his pocket and handed it to the kid, who then flashed an ear-to-ear grin at his pals.

"You can hold mine, too," one of the others said and held his hurley out.

"Thanks," Dillon said, "but one should be enough." He slowly swung the hurley a couple of times like a baseball bat, adjusted his hands slightly for better balance. "Nice, very nice, good feel to it. You get this here in Dublin?" he said, looking over the hedge.

The three were maybe twenty steps away and counting.

"It was me older brother's, he gave it to me," the kid said.

"Sounds like a nice guy," Dillon said, taking two steps toward the brick pillar at the corner. A trimmed hedge ran along the sidewalk. Now he could hear their voices as they approached, caught the same laugh from one of them. He couldn't understand what they were saying, but he was pretty sure they were speaking Russian.

He turned and faced the boys, tightened his grip, spread his feet apart, and smiled.

Four more steps, three, two—

Dillon spun and swung the hurley, catching the guy wearing his sunglasses right in the teeth. He made a momentary gurgling sound before he dropped to the ground. The sunglasses sailed off his head and onto the sidewalk, maybe ten feet behind him.

His friend, the one who'd punched Dillon, gave a surprised look, took a half step forward before a vicious upward swing of the hurley caught him on his chin. His jaw slammed shut with an audible noise as his eyes rolled up into his forehead, and he dropped to the ground. The third guy was already running full speed in the opposite direction down the block. Dillon stood over the two, glaring, hoping one of them would make a move, but they were out. He turned back to the four boys standing wide-eyed with their mouths hanging open and shocked looks on their faces.

"Real nice. Good balance," he said and handed the hurley back to its owner. "You guy's keep that twenty. Appreciate you helping me out." He walked over and picked up his sunglasses from the sidewalk, wiped them off on his shirt, and walked back toward the two figures on the sidewalk.

Blood was flowing from the mouth of his first victim, dripping down onto the front of his hoodie. What looked like at least two teeth rested on his chin. He appeared to be in some fairly serious pain as he groaned something unintelligible and slid back against the brick wall in an effort to crawl away. He raised a hand as a sort of surrender and gurgled out, "Net, net." "No" in Russian. As he spoke, he sprayed more blood down the front of his grey hoodie sweatshirt.

His partner was slowly beginning to come round, eyes blinking as his head rolled from side to side. Dillon gave the bloody figure against the brick wall a polite nod, thought about saying something, but decided against it, then calmly walked back to his car and climbed behind the wheel.

When he pulled up to the corner, he nodded at the boys still standing there with their mouths hanging open and gave them a two-fingered salute. They gave a sort of absent wave as he turned right and headed back toward his office, deciding this probably wasn't the best time to slow down and examine 85 North Circular Road.

Halfway up the street, he glanced in the rearview mirror just in time to see the four young athletes laughing and skipping across the road toward a corner store. The kid holding the twenty-euro note was waving it in the air. The two recipients of Dillon's loving attention remained on the sidewalk. Their friend, who took off running, was nowhere to be seen.

Hopefully, the kids would waste the money on sweets and sodas.

THIRTY-THREE

J ust as he entered the parking lot, Dillon's phone rang.

"Where are you?" Suel said once Dillon answered.

"Just pulling into the parking lot in back. I was out running a quick errand."

"You had called earlier," Suel said, then apparently said something to someone wherever he was. "Sorry about that. You still there?"

"Yeah. I'm on a short leash after that idiot blew himself up last night. McCabe has placed me under penalty of death and a threat of having to clean both restrooms before he has me drawn and quartered if I so much as think about going anywhere on my own. Now, apparently, I need an escort just to go to the break room for a coffee. I got an address for the American found in the Royal Canal. It's over on North Circular Road, close to Phoenix Park. I wanted to go past it, maybe ring the doorbell see who answers. You interested in acting as my chaperon?"

Suel chuckled for a moment. "An address? Tell me you're joking."

"No, I'm serious. Not sure how good it is, but it's better than what I didn't have earlier."

"I've got to talk to someone on these ATM robberies. He's sort of on that end of town. You're welcome to come along. We could swing by North Circular on the way back."

"When you thinking of going?"

"Ready to head out now. Just stay in the parking lot, and I'll meet you down there."

"I'll be waiting next to the door," Dillon said as he pulled into a parking space and turned off the PT Cruiser.

It took Suel fifteen minutes to make it down to the parking lot. Not that it was a problem. Dillon leaned against the building, took in the rare bit of sun shining down on him, and replayed the hurley incident in his mind a few dozen times.

"Sorry about that," Suel said, hurrying out the back door and pulling his suit coat on. "Every time I was ready to leave, someone else had another question. Sometimes I think I should stop being the kind, gentle soul that I am."

"Yeah, that would help. Not. Who are we going to see anyway?"

"A gentleman by the name of Jasper Akintola."

"And he is?"

"He *was* the man working behind the counter in one of the ATM robberies. At this point, he's my most credible eyewitness. He's given an initial statement. This is just a followup chat."

They were standing alongside the car Suel was driving, talking over the roof of the car. He pushed a button on the car key and the locks clicked open. Dillon climbed into the passenger seat and buckled up. Suel tossed a computer bag in the back seat, slid behind the wheel, started the car, then pulled the seat belt across his chest.

"You still dealing with five ATM robberies?" Dillon asked.

"For the moment. Their success rate has been such that I don't see whoever is pulling these to be slowing down anytime soon."

"Still taking them just a couple of minutes?"

"I only wish. They were averaging ninety seconds. A damn minute and a half," Suel said as he pulled out of the parking lot. "Now, with the last one, they managed to cut twenty seconds off their time from the moment they crashed through the front window to when they jumped back into the car and drove off a mere minute and ten seconds later. Hell, it usually takes me longer than that just to get settled behind the wheel."

"A minute ten?"

"Yeah, nothing short of amazing. By the way, almost half of the shops aren't recording. Oh sure, they've got the camera's up there, mounted inside and outside the building, not that they do any good. They're either just for show, or they're old enough to need film physically installed, and these cheap bastards aren't going to take the time or spend the few cents to pay for that. They'd rather take their chances, negate any insurance coverage they have, and hope to hell they're not the next victim. Bunch of wasters, if you ask me."

"And this Jasper—"

"Jasper Akintola, a Nigerian fellow, quite nice actually. He was working when they came rolling through the front window, pulled the ATM off its steel pad, tossed it into the rear of the vehicle, and drove off almost ten thousand quid for the better. Not a bad payday for ninety seconds' worth of work."

"I don't suppose he's got film?"

"No, but he's just an employee. Plonker that owns the place has five or six locations around the city and wasn't in the mood to spend the euro or two it would have cost to have the camera operating. I've got film from an earlier robbery, the one out in Rush. Hopefully, this Jasper will give the nod it's the same lads."

"Be nice to get the bastards."

"God, I've blisters on me arse from the heat coming down. We'll get them sooner or later, but not soon enough for my taste."

THIRTY-FOUR

J asper Akintola lived in a section of Dublin called the Liberties. The Liberties was one of, if not *the* original suburb of Dublin. An area just outside the walled city, it originated back in the twelfth century. Guinness's St. James Gate was in the Liberties, and Jasper Akintola's flat was just a few blocks from the Guinness brewery on Thomas Street.

The flat was one of four located just above a small newsagent in a decrepit three-story building in the middle of the block. The building looked to be at least a hundred and fifty years old. The green paint on the small door next to the newsagent shop that hadn't peeled was faded. The address 142 was tacked to the top of the door frame in brass numbers. The top tack in the number one had been missing for quite some time, and the brass number hung upside down. Four doorbells were attached to the upper right side of the door frame. They were labeled with numbers one through four and no names. Suel pressed number three, holding the button down for a good ten seconds.

"I talked to him on the phone before we left, so he's expecting us," Suel said once he'd removed his finger.

A minute later, they could hear someone stomping down the steps inside.

The door opened, and a tall, thin black man stood and smiled at Suel. He wore jeans and a white sleeveless t-shirt. He had brown leather sandals on his feet. "Detective, nice to see you again. How are you today?"

"I'm fine, Jasper. Thank you for letting us interrupt your day off."

"It is not a problem," he said, then focused his attention on Dillon.

"Jasper, this is Marshal Dillon. He's working with me today."

"Nice to meet you," Dillon said, extending his hand.

Akintola took Dillon's hand, wrapped his long thin fingers around it, gave a vise-like grip, and shook.

"May we come in and show you the tape?" Suel said, lifting up the laptop he carried.

"Please, follow me," Akintola said, then turned and hurried back up the steep set of stairs. The stairs creaked loudly as Suel and Dillon followed him up. There was no handrail, but there were holes in the wall about every four steps where one had previously hung. The air was heavy, stale, and unpleasant smelling. It reminded Dillon of spoiled food.

Akintola turned a corner at the top of the stairs and walked up another flight to his apartment on the third floor. The second set of stairs was just as steep as the first and creaked a bit louder.

"Apartment" was a generous term. The unit, if it could be called that, consisted of two small rooms and a bathroom. Although the only window was open, the air remained stuffy, and traffic noise drifted up from the street below. Items were stacked on virtually every flat surface, and there was something cooking on the stove in a large cast-iron pot.

A woman stood at the little two-burner stove. She turned and smiled as they entered. She had a small, sleeping child strapped onto her back. She wore a cloth covering over her hair and was dressed in a long cotton sort of shift that appeared to be off-white or maybe just in need of a wash. There was no more than a foot of counter space next to the stove, and it was covered with pots piled one on top of the other along with a stack of four mismatched plates.

"This is my wife," Akintola said, not bothering to introduce her by name. She nodded shyly before she quickly walked back into the small bedroom with the child and closed the door behind her.

Akintola took two stacks of clothing from the small wobbly table positioned just below the window. He piled the stacks one on top of the other, then set them on the floor.

"Please, that is enough room for your computer?" he said.

"This will work just fine," Suel said, setting the computer on the table and opening it up. He pushed a button on the side, and the computer made a noise that sounded like a piano chord as it slowly came to life. A minute or two later, Suel had a copy of the security tape from one of the ATM robberies up on the screen.

"Here, Jasper, please sit down so you can view this tape. It's just about a minute and a half long," Suel said as he pulled a wooden chair out from the table. It appeared to be the only chair in the unit.

Akintola sat down. Suel pressed a key on the computer, and the security video began. The tape consisted of a series of slightly blurry black and white images, one taken every two or three seconds, so that as it played, it didn't appear as a smooth movement, but more like a series of jerky images. There was no sound from the tape.

The camera appeared to have been centered on the ATM, which was standing in a corner next to shelves holding paper towels, napkins, toilet paper, and disposable diapers. Suddenly the window seemed to explode as a dark vehicle crashed through the glass. Two figures were immediately alongside the vehicle, pulling what looked like a chain from out of the rear. They both wore balaclavas over their faces, hoodie sweatshirts, and what appeared to be black leather gloves. While one of them wrapped the chain around a trailer hitch of some sort, the other wrapped the chain around the ATM three separate times, then quickly stepped back and apparently shouted something. The chain tightened, and suddenly, the ATM was yanked from its foundation and lying on the floor. The figures were immediately on either side, hoisted the ATM into the back of the vehicle, and then hopped in, and they were gone.

There was a green digital readout in the lower right-hand corner of the screen running a twenty-four-hour clock. The vehicle had crashed through the window at exactly 14:17:00, seventeen minutes after two in the afternoon. They fled the scene at 14:18:37, just a minute and thirty-seven seconds later. This was just the third robbery, and they'd cut another twenty seconds off their time since then.

Akintola stared at the screen and shook his head halfway through the tape. When it had finished, he looked up at Suel.

"It looks like the same ones, but I think they were even faster in our store, and they had a different car. They seem to know what they are doing. I would guess they were in the store before, maybe many times, but there is no way to know. And as you know, our owner did not have film in our cameras."

"But from what you can see, it's the same bunch?"

Akintola nodded. "They had said something, but I didn't understand it, just a word or two."

"Was it a foreign language?"

"Maybe, maybe not. It could have been Dublin."

"They said 'Dublin'?"

"No, their voice, the accent, it might have been the Dublin talk, but it could have been a foreign language. This, I don't know. Then one, he hits the other."

"What do mean he hits the other?"

"Like this," Akintola said, holding out his right hand and moving it upward. "How do you say he smacks him?"

"Slaps him?" Dillon said.

"Yes, that is it, slaps him, on the back of his head. Almost like they had scored a goal in the football. You know?" Akintola said and looked from Dillon to Suel.

A light flashed on in Dillon's brain.

"Run that tape again," Dillon said.

"I don't think I can tell you any more," Akintola said.

"Let's just watch it again. Then I might have a question."

Akintola sort of shrugged and turned back in his chair to face the computer screen.

Suel reached down and clicked the arrow to replay the video. The vehicle suddenly crashed through the glass, and the two figures appeared. Dillon focused on the figure wrapping the chain around the ATM. His back was to the camera as he wrapped the chain, then tucked the loose end behind two coils of chain and stepped back. Once the ATM was on its side he hurried around to the far side to hoist it into the back of the vehicle.

"Stop the tape, Paddy," Dillon half-shouted.

Suel quickly reached down and pressed a key.

"Can you back it up, just a frame or two?"

Suel backed the tape up a little too far, then slowed the movement and went forward two frames.

"There, stop it. Can you enlarge that?"

Suel enlarged the frame to two hundred percent, making it just a little more blurry and taking up almost the entire screen.

"Jasper," Dillon said. "This guy in the hoodie sweatshirt. Is he the one who slapped the other on the back of the head?"

"Mmm-mmm, I don't know that I can be certain."

"Think about it. Remember what they were wearing. See that hoodie sweatshirt." Dillon pointed to the screen. "It's grey, and the letters are blue. That's a crest in the center, and it says 'Dublin' on the top and 'Ireland' on the bottom. The writing and the crest are written in—"

"In blue letters. Yes, it's the same as the one who robbed our store."

"And he was the one who slapped his partner on the back of the head?"

"Yes, yes." Akintola grinned and looked up at Dillon. "It's him, I remember now, and they laughed, both of them."

"You know how many of those hoodie sweatshirts there are? They might as well be wearing black Nike shoes," Suel said.

"What if you narrowed it down to someone in a hoodie like that speaking Russian and slapping his pal on the back of the head? I think, as of this afternoon, he might be missing a few front teeth."

THIRTY-FIVE

Alexei Bazanov half-shouted into the phone, "What do you mean they were assaulted? Assaulted where? By who?"

"We were just walking down the street, North Circular Road, and suddenly this crazy man came around the corner carrying a hurley and swinging it. We tried to get out of his way, tried to take the hurley from him, but he hit Grigory in the face, knocked a bunch of his teeth out. I grabbed him just as he hit Andrei and knocked him out. He shook me off, and then he took off running. I went after him, but he was so fast, and I didn't want to leave them lying on the sidewalk, no telling what would happen if the Garda got them."

"And this happened on the street? In broad daylight?"

"Yes, sir. North Circular Road. He seemed to come out of nowhere. I think he was hiding around the corner, just waiting for someone to come by, and unfortunately, it was us."

"How long before they're able to get back to work?"

"Probably a week, maybe more. I think—"

"A week?" Bazanov screamed into the phone.

"Well, maybe a couple of days. If the healing goes well. We got some pain medication for Grigory, but he really should see a doctor."

"Do not take him to a doctor or to any hospital. Do you hear me?"

"Yes, sir, but he really needs some attention, he…."

"Where are you now?"

"We're back in our flat."

"All right, now listen to me carefully, like your life depends on it because it does. You are not to leave your flat for anything, is that clear?"

"Yes, sir."

"I'll send someone over there shortly to look at Grigory. Is Andrei all right?"

"His chin is black and blue, and he bit his tongue when he was hit. He— just a minute. What? I'm talking with Bazanov now. Okay, all right. Sir, he says he has a terrible headache. I think maybe a concussion when he hit his head on the sidewalk."

"If I find out this happened in a bar or you three were caught with someone's wife, there won't be enough left of you to bury when I'm finished. Do you hear?"

"Yes, sir, but it happened just like I said. I can show you the corner. Grigory's blood is all over the sidewalk."

"All right, all right, I'll send someone over there. Until you hear from me, you are not to leave the flat. Is that clear? This put's the entire ATM operation on hold, which gives the police time to catch up. I'll need you back to work in forty-eight hours, no later. Goodbye."

"That might be a bit too…Hello? Hello?" Viktor said, but Alexei Bazanov had already hung up.

Bazanov stood at his desk, taking deep breaths in an effort to calm himself. *Fools*, he thought. Something wasn't adding up. He walked to the window of his study and looked out toward the sky. Surprisingly, the day appeared to be sunny, although he felt like he'd had a permanent rain cloud hanging over him for the past three or four weeks. Fools, that's what it was. Fools not taking the business seriously. Lesson learned. He'd been too kind, far too understanding. The body of the American found almost before it was cold. The bag with his hands found by children. Children! The bomb attached to the wrong vehicle at the wrong house by a drunken Dmitry. It served the fool right, although there was a good chance if they identified Dmitry's remains, Alexei's name might possibly be linked. Now this, some crazy person attacking three men in broad daylight. It didn't add up, didn't pass the smell test.

He needed vodka, lots of it, and a woman, and not in that order.

THIRTY-SIX

S uel laughed. "You told them you just wanted to hold it?" The two of them, Dillon and Suel, were standing on the corner at North Circular Road, where Dillon had retrieved his sunglasses.

"Yeah. There were four of them here in uniforms, kids, twelve, maybe thirteen years old. I gave one of 'em twenty euros if he'd let me hold his hurley, and then I just waited till those bastards were here, stepped out, and nailed two of them. The third took off up the block and just kept going. I don't think I could have caught him even if I'd been in the car. Look, here's the blood from the one I hit in the mouth. The blow knocked my sunglasses right off his head, and they landed over there," Dillon said and pointed to an area about ten feet away.

There was a large bloodstain on the sidewalk. More blood was on the brick wall, where it looked like the victim had spit a number of times. Dillon scanned the sidewalk for teeth but didn't see any.

"And you just left them here?"

Dillon shrugged. "I got my sunglasses back, and I didn't see the point in putting them under arrest for assaulting an officer. I figured they'd gotten enough for one day. Last time I saw them, they were lying here with dazed looks on their faces."

"You think they were speaking Russian?"

"I know they were."

"You're sure?"

"Yeah. I couldn't tell when they punched me at the other end of the block, but I was pretty sure when I heard them coming down the sidewalk here. Then, when he was just lying there bleeding and spitting teeth and saying 'no' in Russian, yeah, I'm sure. When Jasper Akintola mentioned one of them slapping his partner on the back of the head, it all of sudden clicked. That move, a foreign language, the hoodie sweatshirt, three of them. I know it's all circumstantial, but it's better than what you don't have. Bastards have to live somewhere around here, certainly within walking distance," Dillon said, then sort of slowly turned around to look up and down the street.

Most of the two and three-story homes had been turned into multiple flats, probably not all that much better than the hellhole Jasper Akintola and his wife were living in. The only difference here was the overflowing garbage bins stacked in front of every structure.

"As long as we're here, you want to check out number 85?"

"You got a warrant?" Suel asked.

"A search warrant? No. All I've got is a possible address, and my fingers crossed. Be a shame to come this far and not at least try." Dillon glanced at the corner unit, number 97. "Is the warrant a problem? It's just a few doors down, Paddy."

Suel gave a loud exhale, then looked around and said, "Not really a problem. I just want to make sure we're prepared. You have a pair of gloves?"

Dillon pulled out a pair of blue latex gloves from his pocket and flashed a smile.

"All right, let's give it a try," Suel said, and they headed up the block.

Number 85 was about a third of the way along the street. It was a three-story building with nine steps leading up to an industrial metal front door painted a glossy blue. Ten doorbells were mounted on the side of the door frame, identified by numbers one through ten. The building address was two numbers taped onto the front door, black numbers on a reflective silver background that had been crookedly attached to the door. What looked like a CCTV camera was mounted on the second story of the building and appeared to be focused on the front stoop.

"You wouldn't happen to know the unit number, would you?" Suel asked.

"No. All I got was the street address."

Suel shook his head, slipped a hand into one of his latex gloves, and began holding each doorbell down for a few seconds. A voice came over an intercom before he'd pushed all the doorbells.

"Yeah."

"An Garda Síochána," Suel said.

"Feck off, ya bollocks," the voice said and disconnected.

"He must have dealt with you before," Suel said, and went back to pushing doorbells. A woman's voice answered on the last one. "Yes."

"Good afternoon," Suel said. "Sorry to bother. An Garda Síochána."

"Oh, finally. Let me buzz you in," she said and disconnected. A moment later, there was a loud buzz, and they heard a lock on the door snap open.

Dillon made a surprised face, pushed the door open, and said, "What was that unit number?"

"Ten, I think."

They entered a hallway with elaborate cornice and crown plaster moldings, most likely a hundred and fifty years old from a time when the homes and the neighborhood had been exclusive. An elaborate circular design in plaster was positioned in the center of the ceiling. The door to the left was numbered 1, and the door on the right was numbered 2, both with the same stick-on black numbers with a silver background as the address on the front door. What had at one time been an elegant staircase banister leaned noticeably to the left and led up to the second floor.

More elegant plaster molding ran along the ceiling and the four doors on the second floor. Something indecipherable in black spray paint had been sprayed on the far end of the hallway wall.

As they climbed the staircase to the third floor, a woman leaned her head over the banister and called, "An Garda Síochána?"

"Yes, ma'am," Dillon said.

"Thank God, finally. I think I placed my first call almost a month ago. I've lost count of how many times I've called since then. I suppose I should see some identification before we go any further," she said.

They pulled out their badges and warrant cards as they reached the top of the stairs and let her examine them. Dillon guessed her age at maybe fifty. Her auburn hair was nicely done, and she wore black slacks with a white blouse. She appeared to have a pleasantly toned figure. Her hands appeared soft, and her nails sported a French manicure.

"Hmmm-mmm, Suel. You wouldn't happen to have family down Wexford way?"

"No, I'm just a coulchie from Sligo," he said and smiled.

"Dillon, perhaps Roscommon?"

"No, ma'am, Minnesota."

She got a look on her face and then cocked her head. "American? Well now, maybe I'll get some answers. Your young man, the American, is the one I was worried about. Haven't seen him since the night I called. I'm sorry, won't you come in. Can I offer you a tea?"

"That would be grand," Suel said. "Milk please."

"And—" She gave a questioning look toward Dillon.

"Just plain tea, no milk or sugar. Thank you."

"Please come in," she said, holding the door open.

They entered an apartment with ten-foot ceilings, more elaborate cornice, and crown plaster moldings. The wood floors had been refinished at some point. Dillon thought they were pine by the looks of the grain. The room they stepped into had a fireplace centered on one of the walls with a leather couch and four upholstered chairs. Dillon figured you could have fit all of Jasper Akintola's flat in this one room and still have space left over. It looked like a bedroom was off to one side, and a kitchen off to the other.

"Please, make yourselves comfortable while I put the kettle on. I'll just be a minute."

Suel settled into one of the upholstered chairs. He pulled a magazine from a stack on the coffee table and pointed at the address label. The magazine was addressed to Noreen O'Bannon at this address. Suel glanced at two more magazines in the stack, then nodded at Dillon as he sat in the far corner of the couch. Dillon took a small notebook and a pen from his coat pocket and set them on the coffee table.

A few minutes later, she came back into the room carrying a tray with three mugs, a tea kettle, and a plate of chocolate-covered tea biscuits. She set the tray on the coffee table, then settled into the opposite corner of the couch from Dillon, essentially sitting between the two of them.

"There now, we'll just give that tea a moment before we pour, but please feel free to help yourself to a biscuit."

Suel took a biscuit.

Dillon turned halfway to face her and said, "May I call you Noreen, ma'am?"

"Oh yes, please, that would be just fine. Your manners are very good, Mr. Dillon," she said, then shot a look at Suel as he stuffed another chocolate biscuit into his mouth.

THIRTY-SEVEN

They'd been talking for over a half-hour, or rather listening as Noreen O'Bannon told them about the incident that brought her to call the gardaí a month ago. Her night's sleep had been interrupted by late-night shouting sometime after midnight, and what sounded like something being broken against the wall in the unit next to her's.

She'd only met her neighbor twice, both times little more than a quick passing in the hallway. He was fairly young, she guessed early thirties, with close-cropped blonde hair. He'd smiled and nodded, but never really spoke to her other than a polite, "Hello."

"Never even bothered to tell me his name, although I could tell he was American," she said and had chalked him up as a bit of a recluse. Other than the night of the incident she hadn't heard any noise coming from the flat. She'd knocked on his door twice after the incident, but never received a response and had simply assumed her neighbor was either out or possibly already asleep.

"Since that night, I haven't heard so much as a peep coming from next door, and after phoning the gardaí a number of times, I've simply had to give up and move on." She gave Suel and Dillon a disapproving eye as she said that last bit.

"And could you confirm the date you called An Garda Síochána?" Dillon asked.

"Yes, I can, as a matter of fact," she said and pulled out a cell phone from the front pocket of her slacks. She swiped the screen with her finger, then rapidly moved both thumbs to arrive at some site. A moment later, she smiled and said, "Yes, here it is, that was on the eleventh of last month, at just ten minutes after midnight. And, as I already mentioned, I was most unhappy with the reply I received. 'Give us a call if it continues,' they told me. Honest to God, your man could have been murdered, and they wouldn't have been bothered. I got nowhere with the three or four calls over the next few days, no response, no call back, not so much as an acknowledgment, and I finally just gave up."

Dillon hoped he hadn't shown a reaction. "And no activity next door since then?"

"No. Thankfully things seem to be back to normal. Everything has been nice and quiet."

"And the last time you saw your neighbor, Mr. Schmidt?"

"Oh, I couldn't really say. Is that his last name, Schmidt?"

"Yes, Matthew Schmidt."

"Hmm-mmm, I never would have guessed. Well, the last time I saw him was certainly a while before the incident, a week, possibly two weeks before that dreadful night, but I wouldn't be able to give you an accurate date. As I said before, he seemed pleasant enough, but we never really had a conversation. I've actually seen his two friends more than him of late."

"Friends?" Suel asked, leaning forward in his chair.

"Well, yes. Oh, I hope I haven't given you the wrong idea, calling him a recluse and all. He did seem nice, just very quiet, private I guess you could say. Now, his friends, it's always the same two individuals. The last time must have been a good three weeks ago."

"Did you talk to them?"

"Talk to them? No, I never have. As a matter of fact, the few times I saw them, we did nothing more than exchange the occasional polite nod." She sort of gazed off in the distance, remembering. "I had come up the stairs with two bags of groceries. To be honest, I was more focused on making it in here without dropping the bags. I was just back from Aldi, where I'd done my shopping for the next two weeks. I happened to see them just as they were stepping into his flat. But it was the same two gentlemen, I'm sure of that, always the same two. One has dark hair a bit long in the back and a ridiculous ponytail. His hair looked very greasy, I remember that. Honestly," she said, shaking her head. "The other gentleman was a large man, a very large man. Umm, not what one would call attractive. He had a shaved head and one very large, bushy eyebrow that ran all the way across. Almost frightening. Oh, and a mustache. The few times I've seen them, they've always been casually dressed, you might almost say work clothes, but nothing crazy, thank God."

"Do you know if they drove a car here?"

"Oh, I really have no idea."

"You've not seen them recently?"

"No. Like I said before, the last time was maybe three weeks ago. Could be even longer. I just can't be sure."

"You wouldn't happen to have the phone number of your landlord handy, would you?" Dillon said.

"My landlord?"

"We can look him up if it's a concern. I'd just like to call, make sure there's not a problem from their end. I would certainly keep our conversation private, not let him know we've interacted in any way."

She seemed to consider that for a moment, then picked her cellphone up from the coffee table, swiped the screen, and a moment later looked over at Dillon. "Ready?"

Dillon picked up his small notebook and pen from the coffee table and nodded.

She gave him the phone number, speaking slowly, making sure he wrote it down correctly. "They live over in Killester or Clontarf," she said more as an after-thought.

Dillon smiled, nodded, then raised his eyebrows at Suel.

Suel gave an almost imperceptible nod, and Dillon said, "When we get back to the station, we're going to do some immediate checking and find out why, exactly, your initial phone call seems to have fallen through the cracks. My apologies again for that happening, Noreen, that should not have been the case."

"I should say not. What if it had developed into a real incident? I'm not sure what was going on, and I suppose I'll never really know, but at least it's been quiet since that night. As I mentioned before, your man, this Mr. Schmidt, you said, he apparently likes to keep to himself."

Dillon smiled as he rose to his feet. "Thank you again for your time and concern. This has been most helpful."

As Suel rose from his chair, Noreen said, "Another chocolate biscuit, Detective?"

"No, thank you. They were wonderful, but two's my limit."

"Then you've more than exceeded your limit," she said with a smile. "Now, if I can be of assistance in any way, please, don't hesitate to call." She flashed a large smile at Suel, all white teeth and deep brown eyes, then reached for her purse on the floor, opened it and pulled out a card which she handed to Suel. "Don't hesitate," she said and flared those brown eyes again at Suel while he stood staring for a very long moment.

"Thank you again, Ms. O'Bannon," Dillon said as he headed toward the door.

Suel seemed to linger for a moment, and Dillon had to wait out in the hall until Suel hurried out and quickly headed down the stairs. Noreen stood in the doorway, watching Suel, then closed the door, and Dillon heard the lock snap.

He caught up to Suel at the front door.

"What do you think?"

"I think she could be a really fun time, and I intend to take her up on her offer and give her a call," Suel said, waving her card in the air.

"I was talking about the things she said about Matthew Schmidt, not her, you pervert."

"Oh, that. I think you should let me go grab my toolkit from the car and we can see if anyone is home in that flat. Wait for me here, and you can let me back in."

"Take your time," Dillon said.

"I intend to," Suel said.

THIRTY-EIGHT

Dillon remained on the stoop, leaning against the open front door, watching Suel as he walked down to the end of the block to grab whatever tools he needed out of his car and walk back. He appeared to be empty-handed as he returned to the steps leading up to Dillon, waiting at the front door.

"You get what you needed?"

Suel tapped the breast pocket of his coat and smiled. "Best slip your gloves on when we get up there, and let's not have Noreen hear us."

Dillon nodded, and they quietly climbed back up to the third floor. Suel gave a quick glance at Noreen O'Bannon's door, placed a finger to his lips, reminding Dillon to remain quiet, then hurried past. He knocked softly on Matthew Schmidt's door, then placed his ear up against the door in an attempt to hear any noise from inside. After a good minute, he shook his head, slipped on a pair of latex gloves, then reached inside his coat and pulled out a thin leather case. He flipped the case open, revealing a number of long, lean metal items that looked like a cross between knitting needles and dental picks.

He chose one, inserted the tool in the lock, rummaged around for no more than half a minute before Dillon heard the lock click open. "There you go. So much for security," Suel said with a broad smile and opened the door.

"Where did you learn how to do that?"

"I'm a man of many talents," Suel said then put a finger to his lips, and stepped inside the unit. Dillon followed, and Suel quietly closed the door behind them. They both remained still, scanning the room with heads slightly cocked in an effort to pick up the slightest noise.

Suel tapped Dillon on the shoulder, pointed to Dillon and himself, and moved his index and middle fingers back and forth, indicating they should walk around.

Although the unit appeared to be the same layout as Noreen O'Bannon's, the rooms were substantially smaller. The room they were currently standing in did not have a fireplace, nor did it have any of the elegant cornice and crown plaster molding. It was also devoid of furniture with the exception of a wooden chair on the floor lying on its side. The back legs on the chair appeared to be broken. Suel pointed to the chair, then headed for the bedroom.

A single twin mattress was on the floor in the corner of the small windowless room. Set mouse traps were on the floor next to the head and foot of the mattress. A rumpled blanket appeared to have been thrown on the end of the mattress. There were no bedsheets. Four brown paper grocery bags lay on their side in the opposite corner of the room. The bags were filled with socks, underwear, t-shirts, and jeans, respectively. No closet, no dresser. Dillon stepped over to the bags, rummaged through them one at a time, shaking his head as he returned each bag to the floor.

The bathroom, complete with traces of black mold on the walls and ceiling, wasn't quite large enough for the two of them, forcing Suel to stand in the open doorway. The floor was an ancient grey linoleum that curled up and away from the four walls. Even though he wore latex gloves, Dillon reflexively crossed his arms so as not to touch anything.

A small, metal shower just big enough for someone who wasn't too large took up a quarter of the room. The floor and walls of the shower stall appeared to have been painted at some point, although the paint on the lower portion of the walls and the shower floor had largely peeled off, making a bad situation appear even worse.

The dingy porcelain sink looked close to a hundred years old and had slightly pulled away from the wall. The sink had two chrome handles and faucets, one for hot and one for cold water. The chrome was partially worn off both handles from decades of hands rubbing against them, exposing the brass substrate. A razor and toothbrush along with the remnants of a bar of soap, were wedged behind the faucets. A long brownish stain below each faucet led toward the drain. Dillon turned the cold water faucet on and watched as rust-colored water slowly flowed out, gradually clearing up over ten or fifteen seconds. What passed for a bathroom mirror hung above the sink. The lower right-hand corner of the mirror was gone, leaving a sharp, jagged edge quite capable of cutting a finger or hand. The mirror simply hung from a nail driven into the wall. There was nothing like a medicine cabinet in the bathroom.

There was a toilet next to the sink with a seat to sit on, but no lid to cover the seat. A half-used roll of toilet paper sat on the floor next to the toilet. A greyed washcloth hung from a rusty nail embedded in the wall above the toilet.

They went into the kitchen. Again, the room was substantially smaller than Noreen's, barely the size of a walk-in closet with a two-burner stove similar to the one in Jasper Akintola's flat. The top of the stove and the wall behind it glistened with a thick coat of grease. A small saucepan sat on the burner filled with what looked like greasy water. The small, one-basin sink held three plates, glasses, and forks. There was a small cabinet above the stove that Dillon opened, revealing a single plate. Two Guinness pint glasses probably taken from a pub somewhere sat on a shelf above the plate, along with another fork and a carving knife.

A small kitchen window looked out onto an alley. An empty bottle of Paddy's Irish Whiskey and an empty glass sat on the windowsill. Dillon noticed that the window had been screwed shut.

The refrigerator was small enough to fit under a standard-sized desk. Suel opened the door and wrinkled his nose as the smell of what looked like a spoiled plate of chicken, an old pizza, and something in a dish with a furry green mold covering drifted out of the refrigerator.

"How the hell could you live like this?"

"Maybe he didn't," Dillon said. "Maybe it was like a safe house, a place to land if things became too hot elsewhere."

"Safe house? God only knows what terminal disease you're liable to catch in here."

Dillon stepped back into the main room. It had the same wood floor as Noreen's flat, but this was worn from decades of heavy traffic. There were two trails ground into the floor, one leading to the kitchen and the other leading to the bathroom. Dillon went over to the broken chair on the floor and looked at the back legs. What appeared to be traces of blood ran along one of the legs. Further along the floor were more drops of what looked like blood and above that, at maybe eye level, was a large splatter on the wall.

"We'll have to get a team in here to go through the place, hopefully, tomorrow. Just a guess, but try this on for size," Dillon whispered. "He gets cracked over the head with that chair, and he's bleeding, maybe even knocked unconscious. That's the noise Noreen O'Bannon heard, Matthew Schmidt getting hit over the head with this chair, maybe bouncing off the wall or dropping to the floor." He indicated the blood splatters on the wall as he spoke.

"And someone, maybe his two good friends, came in here more than once and did what? Clean up? They missed the damn refrigerator. There's no furniture. Probably afraid to go in what passes for the bathroom in this dump. If you were searching for something, drugs, money, jewels, it would take about ninety seconds to go through the place. I don't know. Maybe we should just get the hell out of here."

"You ready to go?" Suel said.

"Yeah. We can get a team over here tomorrow and have them go through the place, check for fingerprints, analyze the blood. I want them to check out the items in the kitchen sink, see if we can get a handle on the two *friends.*"

They headed for the door. Dillon stopped and listened for any noise out in the hall before he cautiously opened the door, just a crack, and checked the hallway. It was empty.

On the way out, Suel snapped a button on the doorknob, which left the door unlocked. "Just making it easier for the forensics team tomorrow."

The two of them tiptoed over to the staircase, then quietly went down the stairs and out the front door.

THIRTY-NINE

Back in the office, Dillon called Doherty Unlimited, the landlord for Noreen O'Bannon's building. A woman answered on the fifth ring.

"Hello."

"Is this Doherty Unlimited?" Dillon said. He could hear a small child crying in the background.

"I'm sorry, you must have the wrong…Oh, wait, sorry, yes, yes it is. That's my husband's dealings. I'm afraid he's not here just now. Can I take a message?"

Dillon left his name and number, didn't mention he was with An Garda Síochána, and hung up. Mr. Doherty would find out when he called back, and it might add a little pressure.

He Googled Doherty Unlimited. All that came up were two ads listing flats for rent, both at 85 North Circular Road. Both ads were dated early 2016, almost two years ago.

He phoned Aileen Murray next. A woman he'd worked with some months back on a case involving the shooting and death of an American college student in Dublin's city center. They'd gone out a couple of times. Nothing special, a rugby match that was Dillon's idea, a play that had been hers, and one night just for drinks where everything was supposed to fall into place, only it didn't. His physical attraction had been tempered by her political activism on every subject, from water charges to the internet stealing business from small shopkeepers.

His call was dumped into her message center, and he wondered for a moment if she'd recognized his number and didn't answer. Anyway, he ended up leaving a message on her voicemail. He did a reverse search on Google and got the address for the Doherty Unlimited phone number, then did a search with the address on Google Maps and looked at the image online.

The home was located in Killester, a largely residential area on the north side of Dublin, near Clontarf. The structure was a two-story attached house, the second of four, with what looked like a pebble and dash stucco exterior just like thousands of similar homes across Dublin. The image showed a trimmed hedge and what looked like daffodils along the front of the house. A nondescript grey or silver car with the license plate blurred out was parked in front of the house next to a garden.

He went into the break room, paid two euros for a candy bar from the machine that he remembered paying twenty cents for as a high school kid. The coffee pot had barely a cup left in it and looked to have been sitting on the burner for the past nine or ten hours to the point where just now it would probably melt right through the bottom of his coffee mug, so he decided to take a pass.

He was back at his desk, reviewing the medical examiner's report on Matthew Schmidt for the umpteenth time and in the process of cramming the second half of the candy bar into his mouth when his phone rang. Not thinking, he made the mistake of answering.

"Mmm-mmm, murmph, humph," Cough, swallow, choke, then finally a gasp before he mumbled, "Hello," followed up with another round of coughs and gasps.

"Dillon?"

He took a moment to swallow and clear his throat. He coughed a few more times before he was able to groan out, "Aileen?" then had to take a couple of deep breaths to settle down.

"Are you okay? For God's sake, it sounds like someone's strangling you at your desk. You must have done something truly dreadful this time if they're willing to risk having an office full of witnesses right there watching the entire event. Of course, on the other hand, maybe there's a long line of folks just waiting to get a shot at you."

"Oh, nothing like that. I just managed to choke on half of a candy bar. Fortunately, I don't think anyone has caught on yet to all the other dreadful things I've done."

"Oh, I wouldn't be too sure on that count, I've heard all sorts of rumors, seen a thing or two written on the wall in the ladies' loo. God, you're to the moon, Dillon. So, you called earlier. Sorry, I was away from my desk."

"Yeah, thanks for returning my call," Dillon said, then went on to give a brief summary of the Matthew

Schmidt murder investigation. He failed to mention the headless corpse. He skipped over the hands being found in a bag on the beach, although she was most likely aware of both those facts. He made no mention of the fact that he and Suel had been in the apartment on North Circular Road earlier that same day. He did tell her that he'd called the landlord at what appeared to have been a home number and left a message.

"Based on that call, it would seem to suggest they may only own the one building with ten flats as opposed to being in the rental business full time. It's an old Georgian structure. So, I'm guessing the place is a mess inside, not from the tenant necessarily, but just in general, outdated fixtures, bad heat, that sort of thing," Dillon said, then conjured up the unpleasant image in his head of the small, grimy bathroom.

"Could be, although there are the beginnings of some restorations going on in that area, but probably not in a place with a bunch of flats. What, exactly, would you like from me?"

"Can you confirm my suspicion that it's the only property the landlord has, and then if that's the case, what does the landlord, James Doherty, do for a full-time occupation? Or, for that matter, his wife? I'm presuming it was a wife who answered the phone. I want to send a forensics team in there tomorrow, if possible. It would avoid some potential headaches, not the least of which would be time, if I could get their permission rather than have to go and obtain a warrant."

"I guess I can see what I can find out. It's going to cost you though since it sounds like you're over the proverbial barrel in this investigation," Aileen said. She sounded like she was half-joking, but only half.

"Cost me?"

"Yes. There's a new Thai place that opened up, not two blocks away. They do lunch and dinner." She let that last word, dinner, hang out there for a long moment. "I've only heard good things about the place. I'm thinking it would be the perfect place for you to take me one of these next days. I'd have a long, leisurely meal with a starter, a dessert, and your undivided attention."

"I think that can be arranged," Dillon said, actually liking the sound of the idea. "Would dinner be more to your liking? We could consider a bottle of wine along with that starter and dessert."

"Yes, dinner would be perfect. You're getting the idea. How long are you going to be at your desk?"

"Another hour or two, unless something pops up."

"I should have something for you before you leave. Let me get on it. Oh, and stay away from the candy bars, be a shame to have to call 999 for an ambulance and list candy as the cause of your death. Besides, if you up and died, who would take me to dinner?"

"Not to worry, I've learned my lesson about shoving half of one into my mouth as I'm about to answer the phone."

"Half? Good lord, Dillon, you're absolutely incorrigible. Goodbye," she said and hung up.

Dillon's phone rang forty-five minutes later. "Jack Dillon."

"Before I pass on this top-secret information, are we still on for dinner in the near future?"

"I'm looking forward to it, Aileen. In fact, it's the only thing I've thought about since last we talked."

"You're impossible."

"Were you able to find anything out?"

"A little bit. Your hunch appears to have been correct, 85 North Circular Road is the only rental property James Doherty owns. His private residence, along with his wife Kira and three children, is located in Killester."

"I Googled the home address and checked out an image online. It looks pretty standard. A two story attached house, pebble and dash with a nice front garden. If I had to guess, I'd say three bedrooms and a bathroom upstairs, kitchen, dining area and a sitting room on the first floor," Dillon said.

"Sounds right for the area. The North Circular Road property was inherited from Mr. Doherty's father, Thomas, deceased as of 1998. Thomas held the property for eighteen years, purchasing it in 1980 for the princely sum of sixty thousand punt."

"What would it go for today?"

"Today? Mmm-mmm, this is just a guess," Aileen said. "But you could be looking at something in the neighborhood of at least nine hundred and fifty thousand euros. Then again, ten units could have it going for substantially more. You said you thought it might be in rough condition?"

"That's my thought based on the area. It looked like a lot of attached Georgian homes with anywhere from four to maybe a dozen flats. There were ten flats in Doherty's number 85. As I said before, I've not been inside, so it's just a guess," Dillon said, adding that last bit just to cover himself.

"The price could start at nine-fifty and go up from there. Housing prices are rising all over the country, but especially here in Dublin, where they're up ten percent over last year. I think I read somewhere that there's twenty thousand people looking for a place to live and only ten thousand units available, so it's definitely a seller's market. I fear we're on the verge of another bubble thanks to our illustrious plonkers in Dáil Éireann. God save us. It's all enough to make one want to scream."

Dillon suddenly recalled that Aileen's constant political rantings were one of the reasons he had drifted away after just a few dates. "So this is the only building Doherty owns?" he said in an effort to get back on track.

"It would certainly appear that way. His wife's name is Kira. I didn't find any properties listed to her."

"What's his daytime job?"

"Works for Fingal county council, in the parks department."

"Anything else you found?"

"Not really. No emergency calls to number 85. The building was last inspected in 1997."

"I thought that was supposed to happen every few years, an inspection?" Dillon said.

"You're right, it's supposed to be that way, but your man works for the county council. This is Ireland, Dillon. It's who you know, the laws on the books be damned. While the rest of us have to play by the rules, the wankers in the county council, Dublin city or Dáil Éireann, are all apparently above the law. It's enough to make one want to scream.

At this particular moment, Dillon could suddenly identify with that desire. "Thanks, Aileen. Let's look at sometime in the near future for that dinner. I'd love to catch up."

"And I'd love for you to pay for that dinner. I'm usually open, so give a call when you're able," she said and hung up.

Dillon pushed the idea of dinner out of his mind and thought for a moment. No inspection in over twenty years. Good to know in the event he needed some additional leverage.

He placed his desk phone on message, then went down to his PT Cruiser and drove home.

FORTY

He parked the PT Cruiser on the next street over and walked the block home, hoping to avoid the potential for another bombing incident, this time from someone with a little better information.

A new front window was already set in place next door at Deitora's house. A Garda car was parked just down the block, facing her house. Dillon walked down toward the car. The driver's door opened when he was about twenty-five feet away. He recognized the officer climbing out from behind the wheel, but couldn't recall his name.

"So, who did you piss off to get this job?" Dillon said as the officer groaned coming out of the car.

He was young, almost baby-faced, with freckles and red hair. He stood a good five or six inches above Dillon, with bulging arms, a muscular chest and flat stomach. "Who did I piss off? The list is so long, Marshal, I'm not sure where to even start."

"How long are you stuck out here?"

"I'll be here until about sunrise unless someone makes a mistake and shows up early to relieve me."

"Thanks for being here. I know it's not fun, but it certainly calms the neighbors, not to mention me."

"Not a bother, sir. We wouldn't want another incident like last night, now would we?"

"No, that's for sure. You need some dinner?"

"Thanks, but I'm taken care of."

"Can I at least get you a mug of tea, and maybe some biscuits?"

"I could be talked into that if it's not too much trouble."

"I'll have it out to you in just a couple of minutes. Milk or sugar?"

"Both, if you wouldn't mind, sir."

"No problem. Is it Kevin?" Dillon asked, taking a wild guess.

"It is, sir. Nothing wrong with your memory," the young officer said and flashed a big smile.

"Thanks, Kevin. Let me get you that tea. You need the bathroom or anything, feel free to ring the doorbell anytime."

"Thank you, sir." He nodded.

Lucifer was waiting just inside the door when Dillon opened it. He stepped out onto the front stoop, then looked over his shoulder and gave Dillon a questioning look.

"I parked on the next street over. We don't need another attempt tonight, or ever again for that matter."

That seemed to satisfy the dog's curiosity, and he hopped down the steps and onto the grass to do his business. Dillon stepped into the house, first checked the sitting room and then the kitchen in search of whatever Lucifer had destroyed today. Amazingly he didn't find anything. He set the kettle on to boil, placed a half-dozen tea biscuits in a plastic bag, then placed a tea bag in a large travel mug. Once the kettle went off, he poured the water into the mug and went upstairs to change.

He was back down in two minutes. He took the teabag out of the travel mug, added milk and sugar, screwed the lid on, then brought the mug and biscuits out to Kevin sitting in the car. Kevin jumped out again as he approached.

"Here you go, Kevin. No complaints now about the quality, but the price is right."

"I'm sure it'll be just fine," Kevin said, then slurped some tea. He didn't grimace, so Dillon figured it must be at least passable.

"You see anything from my neighbor next door?"

"The woman's house where the bomb went off?"

Dillon nodded, then glanced in the direction of Deitora's house.

Kevin took a short, slurpy sip and said, "She was out there late in the afternoon when I arrived, working in the garden, trimming what was left of that rose bush. I walked over to chat with her, but she seemed more interested in the bush than conversation. Maybe an hour later she was outside with a suitcase. Someone picked her up, and they drove off just before you arrived. I'd guess she might be spending the night somewheres else."

"Can't say as I blame her," Dillon said. "Now, don't forget, you need anything, just ring the doorbell, anytime."

"Thank you, sir."

"I'll bring you out another tea before I go to bed."

"That would be most kind."

It was almost ten when Dillon's cell signaled a text message coming through. He'd been reading, stretched out on the couch in the sitting room. He clicked on the message. *You available to take a call at this number? G*

Gino Andretta in New York. Dillon typed a quick *yes* and sent the message, then waited for what seemed like an hour before his phone rang.

"Dillon," he answered.

"Free to talk?" Andretta said.

"Yeah, I'm at home, all alone, I might add."

"Why should it be different than any other night?" Andretta chuckled. "Hey, I got a message from a contact in the politsiya."

"The Russian police?"

"Yeah," Andretta said, maybe sounding a little surprised that Dillon knew what he was talking about. "Remember the woman you told me about, actually the address tag that listed the town of Samara?"

Dillon quickly sat up. "Yeah, Sokolov, what was the first name? Almyra?"

"Close but no cigar. Alyona, Alyona Sokolov."

"I didn't know anything about her other than her name was on the address tag on an athletic bag. Did they talk to her, the police over there?"

"They couldn't."

"Couldn't?"

"She's dead."

"What?"

"Yeah, killed in a hit and run. Someone nailed her in a crosswalk and just kept on going. Threw her into an oncoming bus. If she wasn't dead from the first vehicle, I guess the bus really finished her off."

"When the hell did this happen?"

"Maybe forty-eight hours ago."

"Forty-eight hours ago? That seems like too much of a coincidence not to be related to what's going on over here."

"Sounds like just one more chapter in your book of international intrigue. What's the latest with your investigation, Jack? Anything happening?" Andretta asked.

Dillon didn't want to tell him about the bomb blast last night, so he focused on the present. "I think it just got a little tighter with this information. Not sure how it fits in yet, but something seems to be up. Shit. You got anything else for me, Gino?"

"No, at least not at this time. Anything comes through, I'll let you know. I asked my Russian contact about next of kin. It would seem to be a logical question. Someone in Dublin calls a hit on the Sokolov woman? I didn't think it would be that far-fetched."

"What'd he say?"

"Said he didn't know, but he'll check."

"You believe him?"

"Maybe. If it's in their interest, I'll hear something."

Dillon thought about that for a moment, then said, "Okay, you take care and feel free to call me anytime, day or night."

He went into the kitchen, made another tea for Kevin, put another half dozen tea biscuits in the bag, and walked out to the Garda car.

FORTY-ONE

Dillon lay awake in bed, thinking random thoughts for the better part of an hour. The only sound at this hour was Lucifer half-snoring on the pillow over on the far side of the bed. The names Matthew Schmidt and Alyona Sokolov, along with a recurring image of the three guys taking his sunglasses while laughing all the while, kept bouncing around in his head until he finally rolled over and squinted at the digital clock on his dresser. It was barely after four in the morning, and he was wide awake.

He looked out the bedroom window. The Garda car was still parked right where it had been when he'd arrived home. He walked into the bathroom, turned on the light, then waited a long moment until his eyes adjusted before he turned on the shower, and stepped in.

He got dressed, then made a tea for Officer Kevin, put the last of the tea biscuits into a bag, and carried them out the door.

Kevin slowly climbed out of the car as Dillon approached. He stretched and cracked his neck from side to side, gave a slight groan and said, "You're up early, sir."

"More a case of no rest for the wicked. I'm going in early. You have to use the loo before I leave?"

Kevin gave a sheepish grin, then said, "Not a bother, sir." Meaning, he'd apparently relieved himself in someone's front garden. Probably more than once. Dillon noticed a pizza box on the back seat of the car. A large soft drink cup lay on its side on top of the box. Dillon traded the fresh tea for the empty travel mug, chatted with Kevin for a moment, then carried the travel mug back into the house. He stepped outside a moment later, locked the door, gave a wave to Kevin, and headed up the street and over to the PT Cruiser.

There was a neatly-written note on the windshield of the car. *This parking place is reserved for residents of this street. Please don't park here again.*

Charming, Dillon thought. For a moment, he felt tempted to leave the car there all day and just taxi into the office. Instead, he climbed into the car, started it up, resisted the urge to lean on the horn, and drove off.

The streets were virtually empty, and he made it into the parking lot in record time. Just a few dim lights were on in the office, and the room appeared to be empty. Dillon poured the remnants of the coffee pot into the sink and made a fresh pot. He waited while the first cup brewed, filled his mug and headed back to his desk.

The message light on his phone was blinking. He took a healthy sip of coffee as he listened to the message.

"Oh, umm, this is James Doherty returning your call. You left a message this afternoon. If you're looking to rent a unit at 85 Circular Road, I don't have anything available at this time. I'll make a note and contact you should something become available. Ummm-mmm, well, thank you," Doherty said and hung up.

Dillon thought he could detect tension in Doherty's voice. That was good. An early morning call would hopefully do the trick.

At twenty-five minutes after seven, he was on his fourth cup of coffee when he made the call. The phone rang seven or eight times before a raspy male voice answered.

"Hello."

"James Doherty, please."

A throat was cleared, and then in a little deeper voice, "Speaking."

"Mr. Doherty, sorry to be calling so early. This is United States Marshal Jack Dillon, I'm working with An Garda Síochána and wanted to catch you before you left for work at the county council. I don't like to bother people at their place of employment if I can help it."

"Oh. I left a message last night, did you get it?" The voice now sounded slightly perturbed. "I'm sorry, I've nothing available just now. I'll keep your name on file and should something—"

"Actually, I'm not looking to rent."

"Oh?"

"I'd like to meet you this morning at your building, number 85 on North Circular Road. We're involved in a murder investigation, and we're going to need to search and examine—"

"Murder?" Doherty half shouted.

From somewhere in the background, a female voice said, "Who is it, Jimmy?"

"What's this about? Was someone killed there?" He suddenly sounded desperate.

"That's exactly what we need to determine," Dillon said and took a long sip of coffee, letting the idea sit rattle around in Doherty's mind for a moment. "I can get a warrant, and we'll get in there, but time is really of the essence, and the sooner we can get started, the better for our investigation."

"But who? When did this happen?"

"The victim is Matthew Schmidt, an American. He's been renting number nine up on the third floor."

"Schmidt? Number nine? That's, that's my corporate client. The, ahh, the name is, oh God, I can't think of it off the top of my head. If you can hang on a minute, let me just go into my office and…." Definite stress in the voice.

The female voice in the background was calling, "Jimmy. Jimmy, damn it, who is that?"

"I can save you the trouble. The renter is officially listed as Sysdigi, Incorporated. They're an American company."

"Yeah, right, that's it, but…."

"I'd like you to meet me at the building at nine this morning. Do not go in the unit. We'll be fingerprinting, running DNA testing, and if you enter the unit, you're liable to end up on a suspect list, and well, I can assure you, you certainly wouldn't want that."

"No. I mean yes, yes I'll meet you there. Nine o'clock you said?"

"Yes. I'll see you there, and remember, please don't enter the unit."

"Not to worry. Nine o'clock. Ummm, thank you for the call," Doherty said.

As he hung up, the female voice in the background started in again.

Dillon dialed an extension and requested an examination team. He left a message on Suel's phone, updating him, then hurried down to the motor pool to exchange vehicles.

"Well, if it isn't Marshal Dillon. And how did the PT Cruiser work out? Was it to your liking?" Sergeant Bourke said. He remained seated at his desk, busily dipping a chocolate-covered biscuit into his tea mug. He crammed the entire biscuit into his mouth, then rubbed his hands together and brushed crumbs off the desk and onto his lap as he rose from his chair.

"The purple Cruiser was wonderful. I had all sorts of women flocking to me and begging for a ride."

"Were they talking about the car?" Bourke said, then laughed out loud at his own joke.

Dillon slid the PT Cruiser keys across the desk and said, "What will I be blessed with today?"

Bourke turned around and glanced at maybe a dozen clipboards hanging on a rack. He pulled one from the middle, placed it on the counter in front of Dillon and said, "Initial the three areas highlighted in yellow. Sign your life away on the bottom line, and you'll be blessed with an Ecosport for the day."

"What's an Ecosport?"

"A Ford. We thought you'd be happy with a car from an American company. It's in parking spot seventeen,'" he said, taking the clipboard back once Dillon had initialed and signed. Bourke slid the keys across the counter, gave a sly smile, and said, "Hope you enjoy." But the way he said it, followed up with a devilish grin, made Dillon wary of the vehicle before he'd even seen it.

FORTY-TWO

It was a fifteen-minute drive from the office to 85 North Circular Drive. By the time he arrived, he'd been honked at innumerable times, given the finger twice and almost broadsided when the Ecosport stalled in the middle of an intersection. The car had to be someone's idea of a joke. Maybe Ford's. Dillon figured Sergeant Bourke was probably laughing at his desk in between cramming chocolate-covered biscuits into his mouth.

The car was officially classified as a mini-SUV. Not that Dillon found any comfort in the fact. It was a bright blue color, reeked of something unpleasant he didn't care to contemplate and felt like he was driving on concrete tires. It made a grinding sort of groan when he shifted from second to third gear, and had an apparent tendency to stall at the worst times; the middle of intersections, and every second stoplight. The interior looked like a throwback to 1960, complete with torn front seats. The radio didn't work, the passenger side headlight was out, the entire vehicle creaked and groaned, had trouble keeping up with thirty-mile-per-hour traffic, and the brakes squealed loudly.

Amazingly he made it to 85 North Circular Road ten minutes before the appointed time. He pulled up onto the boulevard, thanked God for having made it all the way in one piece, then turned the ignition off. The engine continued to run. He looked at the ignition, thinking maybe he'd neglected to push a button or something, but the key was in the off position, and the engine still continued to run.

Dillon attempted to remove the key, but he couldn't pull it out of the ignition. He switched it back into the start position then back to the off position— nothing. He checked the steering column, hoping to find some sort of button he was supposed to push, but couldn't find anything. He moved the key forward, past the start position. The ignition groaned loudly. He moved the key to the off position then back to start four or five times with no result. On the sixth try, the engine shuddered for a long moment, coughed a large black cloud of exhaust, then groaned and finally shutdown.

Dillon was able to pull the key out of the ignition, climbed out of the car, glanced at the cloud of exhaust seeming to hang in the middle of the street, and watched as a delivery van drove through it. He stuffed the keys in his pocket, gave a vicious glance at the vehicle, then walked through the front gate, hurried up the steps, and waited at the front door of number 85.

He was ten minutes early, and he placed a call to Paddy Suel.

"Did you get my message?" he said once Suel answered.

"The one where you were going to 85 North Circular Road and had a forensics team scheduled to be there at half nine? No, I didn't get that message."

"Can you join me?"

"I can. Just tying up a loose end here before I'm on my way."

"Anything on the ATMs?" Dillon asked just as a black BMW pulled onto the boulevard and parked behind his car.

There were two individuals in the front seat. The driver appeared to be maybe sixty, bald with a grey fringe around the side of his head. He was wearing a dark suit coat and a light blue tie. His passenger looked to be substantially younger, maybe mid-thirties. He had brown hair, neatly trimmed, an open collar shirt, and a blue jacket with a Dublin logo. The driver sat behind the wheel talking, and gesturing with his hands. The passenger nodded throughout whatever was being said. Dillon thought James Doherty was most likely the passenger, and since his father had passed away, the driver was most likely Doherty's lawyer.

After a minute or two, they got out of the car. The older gentleman kept his eyes focused on Dillon as they approached the steps, the younger man glanced at Dillon for just a second, then focused on the sidewalk. He stopped at the line of trash bins just inside the gate and realigned two of the bins, then hurried to catch up.

"Officer Dillon?" the older man said and smiled as he started to climb the steps, never taking his eyes off Dillon. Halfway up the steps, he extended his hand.

Dillon stepped forward and shook hands just as the man reached the top. "Jack Dillon, very nice to meet you. Are you James Doherty?" he asked, already knowing the answer to his question.

"No, I represent Mr. Doherty. My name is Seamus Riley. This is Mr. Doherty." The man took a half step closer to Dillon and gracefully waved his hand toward the younger man behind him.

Dillon extended his hand. "Thank you for coming, Mr. Doherty."

"Please, just call me Jimmy."

"Nice to meet you. Sorry this is such short notice, but we—"

"You're with An Garda Síochána?" Riley asked.

"Yes, I am."

"Forgive me, but is that an American accent I'm hearing?"

"Yes, it is. As I mentioned to Mr. Doherty earlier this morning, I'm with the US Marshals Service serving with An Garda Síochána. I'm in the special investigations unit," Dillon said and smiled, knowing where this was going.

"And you would like access to the building?"

"Yes, I would."

"On what grounds, exactly?"

"We believe the tenant in unit 9 was a gentleman by the name of Matthew Schmidt, an American."

"We checked this morning before we came over. That gentleman's name is nowhere on the lease."

"That's correct. As I explained to Mr. Doherty this morning, I believe the name on the lease is probably Sysdigi Incorporated. I believe a monthly rent payment arrives promptly from a bank in Grand Cayman, Virgin Islands, and I'm guessing the unit remains vacant for some fairly lengthy periods of time."

"And that's all perfectly legal," Riley said.

"Yes, it is," Dillon said, and glanced down the street. A large, industrial-sized, white van with police flashers mounted on the roof was heading toward them. The flashers were off, but even from this distance, Dillon could see it was the Technical Bureau team heading toward them.

"I think we're within our rights to ask to see some identification," Riley said.

Doherty kept his eyes focused on the ground.

"Not a problem," Dillon said and pulled out his warrant card along with his An Garda Síochána badge.

"And you wish to *investigate* the premises on your own?" Riley asked, suggesting by his tone that the idea seemed questionable.

"On my own? Oh, no, not at all. I'll leave that up to the crime scene investigation team. Look, if there's a problem, we can get a warrant. I was hoping to avoid any problems for Mr. Doherty here, but maybe I misjudged. I can go get a warrant and, well, since there hasn't been a building inspection here since 1997 I might as well inform Dublin City Council of that, and they can inspect the rest of the building while we're doing the crime scene investigation in number nine."

Doherty grew wide-eyed and, for the first time, actually looked at Dillon for more than half a second. "No. You don't have to do that. Let him in to number nine, Seamus. It's not a bother. Honest."

Riley looked surprised for a brief moment then recovered, and handed back Dillon's warrant card and badge. "There you have it, Officer. Just wanted to make sure you weren't pulling our leg. One can never be too careful."

"Certainly not. I'm wondering if we could have access to the images on your security camera," Dillon said, then indicated the camera mounted up on the second floor focused on the front stoop.

"Oh, umm, well that's sort of just for show. I mean, it isn't wired or anything, it pretty much doesn't operate. I, ahhh, got it from a building at an abandoned construction site back in 2009," Doherty said, then shot a quick glance at his lawyer and stared at the ground.

"Too bad, it would have certainly helped," Dillon said, then addressed Riley. "Like you said, one can never be too careful."

Doherty turned to climb back down the steps, anxious to get as far away from Dillon as possible. "I wonder if you'd have a set of keys you might leave with us," Dillon said. "I'd gladly drop them off later today at your home, we're liable to be awhile, and we can't have you enter the scene. No telling how long we might be. No problem for me to run them over to your home in Killester."

At that moment, the large white van pulled across the road, against traffic and up onto the boulevard, parking in front of Dillon's car. Large blue letters along the side of the van spelled out "TECHNICAL BUREAU," and then below that and slightly smaller, the words "Crime Scene Investigation."

"Ahh, perfect timing, here's the team now," Dillon said. "If I could get those keys from you, Mr. Doherty, I don't want to take up any more of your day. Nice to meet you both," he said, flashed a fake smile and held out his hands for the keys.

Doherty dropped a set of keys into Dillon's hand and hurried down the steps, almost running back to Riley's car.

"Nice to meet you. It's been— unique," Riley said and followed Doherty, although at a much slower pace.

"The pleasure was all mine," Dillon called after him.

They climbed into the black BMW. Riley sat behind the wheel for a moment, shook his head with a disgusted look on his face as he said something unpleasant to Doherty, then looked at Dillon and flashed an insincere smile. He backed the car up a few feet, then waited a moment for another vehicle to pass. Instead, the car slowed and cautiously climbed over the curb behind them. As they pulled out onto North Circular Road and drove off, Suel pulled into the space they had just vacated. Dillon watched them drive down the road until they were out of sight.

He examined the keys, which were brass and looked identical. He inserted one of the keys in the front door lock and attempted to open the door, but the door remained locked. He inserted the second key, and the lock clicked when Dillon turned the knob.

FORTY-THREE

Suel climbed out of the car, gave Dillon a wave, and headed over to the Technical Bureau van. Whatever he said by way of a greeting brought roars of laughter from the three men climbing into hazmat suits at the back of the van. They chatted for a minute or two, then Suel said something else that brought more laughter before he headed up to Dillon, waiting on the steps.

"Please tell me you got keys to let us in," Suel said.

"That was the owner just leaving as you pulled in. I'm guessing not too happy."

"Problems?"

"Not once I explained the situation. Aileen told me the building hasn't been inspected in over twenty years. I casually suggested I could just get a warrant and might have to mention the lack of inspections to Dublin City Council. Suddenly the keys magically appeared in my hands."

"Amazing," Suel said and grinned.

The Crime Scene team walked into the front garden. All three were dressed in hazmat suits. Each man was carrying two five-gallon plastic pails loaded with various items. One of them had a camera around his neck and what looked like a collapsed tripod strapped to his back.

Suel grabbed a five-gallon pail from the first man up the steps.

Dillon reached for a pail from the second man, but he said, "That's okay, I got these. Maybe give Mr. Hollywood there a hand."

Dillon grabbed a pail from the man with the tripod strapped to his back, then inserted a key into the blue metal door and heard the lock click as he turned the knob.

Suel stepped in and held the door. "You lead the lads upstairs, Jack. I'll bring up the rear."

"The rear, I've heard that's the position you like best," one of the guys in a hazmat suit said, which brought more laughter as they headed up the stairs.

Up on the third floor, everyone set their buckets down while Dillon began to unlock the door.

"Go ahead and unlock the door, sir, but don't enter, just step aside, and we'll get a path established. Do you have an idea of the layout?" one of the hazmat suits said.

"Other than it's sparsely furnished and small, that from the landlord," Dillon lied. "I've no idea what it's like inside."

"You're to remain out here until we give you the nod," the hazmat suit said to Dillon and Suel as he rummaged in the plastic pail. "Don't touch a thing inside, and, of course, gloves on at all times. It's going to be a good half hour before we give you the go-ahead. Maybe go grab a tea or something."

"Come on," Suel said. "I've got a thermos out in the car."

"More of that poison from the break room?" Dillon said.

"No, I'd a feeling this might be the drill, and I stopped and got some on the way, along with a pastry or two if you've a hankering. Lord knows you could use a bit of sweetening."

"Sounds like a plan," Dillon said and followed Suel out to his car.

Suel pulled a small cardboard tray from the floor of the passenger seat, pulled a paper cup with a plastic lid on it out of the tray and handed it to Dillon. He tossed the tray back onto the floor and grabbed a white paper bag off the passenger seat. He thrust the bag toward Dillon. "Here, help yourself."

Dillon set his cup on the hood of the car, then reached into the bag and pulled out a sugar-covered jelly doughnut. He took a sip from the cup, tea with milk and sugar, lots of sugar, just the way Suel liked it.

Dillon gave an involuntary shudder. "God, I'll have to test my blood sugar when I finish this."

"Relax, you're anything but sweet," Suel said and laughed. "When we're finished here, I'd like to borrow you for maybe an hour."

"What do you have?"

"I've been thinking about what you said when we were watching the tape yesterday."

"Those three guys grabbing the ATM?"

"Yeah. For the sake of argument, let's just say they're the ones we're looking for. If they were on foot and felt comfortable enough to pull that stunt with you and the sunglasses, it could be a fair assumption they live nearby."

"Possibly," Dillon said, then took another sip and winced again at the sweetness.

"Once we finish up here, I'd like to canvas the shops and pubs along the street. I've got a stack of blurb images that won't be much help, but we can hand them out to shopkeepers and at the pubs. The blurb image, coupled with a description of the damage you did to those two plonkers, it just might jog someone's memory. At this stage, anything would help."

"Yeah, sure. Count me in," Dillon said. "I'd like nothing better than for your ATM bandits to turn out to be those punks. I'd love to nail their asses to the wall."

"If only it would be that easy," Suel said, then took a bite of his jelly doughnut, squirting jelly down the front of his shirt in the process.

FORTY-FOUR

It was the better part of an hour, and Suel had just suggested they might start canvassing the shops on North Circular Road when they got the okay to go back up to unit nine.

Two of the hazmats were in the kitchen area, having a tea and chatting about a soccer match while the third was in the bedroom, taking photographs of the mattress on the floor.

The broken chair with the blood on it appeared to be in roughly the same position as Dillon, and Suel had found it yesterday. The whiskey bottle and glass resting on the window sill had clearly been dusted for fingerprints, along with the plates in the kitchen sink. All the items were now lined up and resting on the floor in plastic bags near the front door.

Dillon headed for the kitchen. "What do you think?" he said to the two men in the kitchen.

One of them took a slurpy sip of tea and said, "I think it's pretty clear whoever lived here didn't have a woman in his life. Well, unless he was paying her by the hour. The damn place is depressing."

"Yeah, it is. Anything unique?"

"Yes and no. No, in the sense that it's down to the basics. A chair, a bath towel, a razor. One small mattress on the floor. Not so much as a radio, or a magazine, let alone a TV. That said, the few clothes in the closet have had all the tags removed. Nothing like a cigarette butt or an envelope addressed to the resident."

"What about those blood splatters on the wall?"

"Consistent with the broken chair. Someone gets hit across the head. We've got samples from the wall and the floor as well as the chair. My educated guess is they'll all be from the same individual. Given the pattern on the wall and damage to the back legs of the chair, it was a sideways swing as opposed to someone raising the chair over their head and bringing it down on the victim's head. Be like this," he said, then set his tea on top of the stove, pretended to hold the chair and swung his hands across his chest from right to left.

"There's a small dent in the plaster halfway up the wall. I'd say he struck your man a couple of times with the chair. Your man collapses there." He pointed with his right hand. "That would be consistent with the blood on the floor. The chair gets tossed over here. One of the legs on the chair bounces off the wall. You can see the remnants of paint and plaster dust on the leg."

"You think they might have killed him? With the blow to the head?"

"I doubt it. He might have been unconscious for a moment, but I don't think it was a death blow. We did find three different sets of prints from the plates and glasses. No telling if they were from the same incident or if they were here before or after the apparent assault. We might be able to learn a little more in the lab."

"Any sign of a woman?"

"No, at least not initially. We vacuumed the mattress and, well, if we can identify the fingerprints, it's conceivable they might be female. But nothing definitive at this point, no thongs, perfume or lipstick."

The guy next to him laughed to himself after that last line.

"How long do you think you'll be? No pressure, I'm just trying to organize the rest of my day."

"We're pretty much finished. Maybe an hour to button things up, haul our equipment out of here. Hollywood?" he called. "How much longer are you going to be taking pictures?"

"Thirty minutes should be more than enough time," a voice called from the bedroom.

Dillon looked at Suel. "You want to go? We can pass your fliers out to those shops for an hour and then come back?"

"We might as well," Suel said. "Thanks, lads. Appreciate you making time to fit this in."

"This is tied to your man from the Royal Canal?"

Dillon nodded. "Strange one. I mean, look around, who would live like this?"

"Doesn't look like anyone lived here. At least not day in and day out, maybe more of a temporary place.

Think maybe someone was smuggling illegals, and this was like a place they stay one night?"

Dillon thought about that for a moment and didn't think it fit with the DEA paying the rent. "I guess right now just about anything's possible. Thanks again, guys. We'll be back in about an hour. When do you think you'll have anything on those prints?"

"We'll have prints and blood type in twenty-four hours. Video and digital images will be filed later this afternoon."

"We'll try and be back before you leave," Suel said.

FORTY-FIVE

Dillon told Suel he wasn't comfortable driving the Ecosport, so they left it parked on the boulevard, and Suel drove down North Circular Road. Suel had a two-page flier of blurry images from the CCTV camera along with a description of the three individuals Dillon had confronted. He mentioned the possibility of one sustaining damage to his teeth and the other to his chin during an altercation but didn't comment beyond that. The flier had a line stating it was suspected the individuals spoke Russian or possibly Polish. A phone number was listed at the end to call and leave tip information, along with the line that stressed whoever called could remain anonymous if so desired.

They stopped at three separate commercial corners and left information in a number of locations; a couple of newsagents, three pubs, two hairdressers, two small grocery stores, a convenience store, a real estate office, four fast food takeouts, a drug store, and a wine shop. No one they spoke with was able to offer up so much as a hint of a clue.

"God," Suel said, driving back to number 85. "What happened to the good old days when someone committed a crime and then felt so guilty they turned themselves in the next day?"

"That really happened?" Dillon said.

'Well, no, now that you mention it, at least not as long as I've been on the force, but I'm sure if you checked the books it must have happened somewhere, sometime. Now, your deal, the American drug lads—"

"DEA, stands for Drug Enforcement Agency."

"Yeah. Bit of a dark operation, are they? Like your CIA and all that spy sort of mumbo jumbo you Americans are always spreading around the civilized world."

"Maybe a little. I mean, dealing with drug pushers and cartels, it's spooky just by the nature of the beast."

"Spooky," Suel chuckled and pulled in behind the Technical Bureau van parked in front of number 85. The three guys were just pulling their hazmat suits off and stuffing them into a blue trash bag as Suel and Dillon climbed out of the car.

"So did you solve the crime of the century?" the one they'd called Hollywood said. The other two laughed.

"No, more like we just went down another dead end," Suel said and shook his head.

"We'll get moving on this as soon as we get back. We'll drop this off with the lab, then where are we headed, Ballsbridge?" Hollywood said.

One of the others nodded. "A domestic with a good bit of drink involved. Imagine that. Looks to be a murder-suicide," he said and shook his head.

"Thanks again," Dillon said as the three climbed into the van, started it up and drove off.

"Jaysus," Suel said. "Not wishing you any bad luck, but you'll be lucky to see those results in a month's time. Bloody budget cuts, and then everyone wonders why crime is on the rise. Bunch of stupid plonkers."

"Think positive," Dillon said.

"Now that's mighty tough talk from someone who wants me to follow him back to the station because he's worried about the car he's driving blowing up, breaking down or both."

They went back up to the apartment on the third floor. Plastic tape with the words "Crime Scene Do Not Enter" formed a crisscross over the door. Dillon pulled the tape off one side of the door frame, then used the key to open the door and stepped into the unit.

"You have a look around, and I'll catch up with you in just a minute," Suel said. He stepped over to the door for number 10 and knocked. Noreen O'Bannon answered a moment later just as Dillon stepped into number 9 and pressed the button on the doorknob to stop the door from locking automatically.

The unit looked basically the same as before minus the broken chair, plates, kitchen utensils, the empty whiskey bottle, and the mattress from the bedroom floor.

Additional lab tests would be run on those items, although Dillon didn't hold out much hope for anything conclusive to turn up.

Tea mugs from the crime scene team had been washed and returned to the kitchen cabinet. For the first time, Dillon noticed that there was no overhead light in the ceiling of the main room, and he wondered if the assault with the chair had taken place in the dark.

Had someone been waiting in here for Matthew Schmidt to return? Or had they somehow snuck in while he was sleeping?

Dillon heard a voice out in the hallway, and a moment later, Suel stepped into the unit. "Anything?" Suel said.

"Doesn't seem to be, at least nothing that's yanking my chain. I'm afraid, at this stage, our only hope is a discovery from the lab, maybe fingerprints or a blood sample."

"Maybe whoever killed him will suddenly feel some remorse and want to confess," Suel joked.

"Don't hold your breath. How'd things go next door?"

"I'll let you know Saturday morning. I'm meeting her for a drink Friday night."

Dillon shook his head, then said, "Anything jump out at you?"

"No, other than this place is even less than the bare minimum. I've seen homeless camps in empty warehouses with more charm."

"Let's head back to the office. I wouldn't want to miss the opportunity to let McCabe know we've come up against another dead end."

"I'll leave you to your own devices on that one," Suel said and stepped back into the hall. He reattached the crime scene tape across the doorway as Dillon locked the door.

"I'll follow you," Suel said. "I just want to see if that rolling deathtrap makes it back. Take the next right from here, that's Annamoe Road. There's a lot less traffic, so if you do run into a problem, you should be able to just coast to the side of the road and not have some knacker in a rush plow into you."

"I just hope that bomb makes it back," Dillon said.

FORTY-SIX

Arkady Sokolov finished the conversation, "I'll be home in an hour. Give me another thirty minutes to get ready, and thank you for the invitation. It sounds like quite the party, and I wouldn't want to miss it." Then he disconnected the phone.

Yakov Gulin tossed his cellphone onto the passenger seat and waited. He'd told Arkady he had some great vodka and two young women lined up. They'd drink a toast to Arkady's sister, Alyona, killed the other night in a hit and run back in Samara.

Arkady hurried to his front window and looked out onto the street without touching the lace curtain. It looked clear, at least for the moment, but he'd have to hurry, aware he had a lot less time than an hour. It was the first ever phone call he'd received from Yakov where he hadn't called Arkady a stupid bastard. Arkady had only just learned of his sister's death that morning and hadn't told anyone. Peeking from behind the lace curtain, he wondered how Yakov had known, unless he and Alexei Bazanov had something to do with her death.

In less than fifteen minutes, Arkady had stuffed a backpack with a change of clothes, what cash he had stashed away, and the picture of him and his sister as small children. Looking at the photo, he vowed revenge on Yakov Gulin and Alexei Bazanov, kissed his sister's image, then stuffed a pistol into the small of his back and headed down the four flights of stairs.

* * *

Yakov tossed his cigarette out the car window, the third while he'd been waiting, and studied the front door of Arkady's building through his binoculars. The stupid bastard wouldn't have enough sense to flee out the back, and Yakov figured he would be able to calmly pull alongside and empty fifteen or twenty rounds into Arkady, solving any future problems. He'd just leave the body on Annamoe Road and calmly drive away.

* * *

Dillon listened to his brakes squeal as he slowed for three oncoming cars, then turned right onto Annamoe Road. The car began to cough and stall as he made his turn, but some quick footwork on the clutch had the engine groaning before it half exploded and came back to life. The car emitted a black cloud of exhaust that all but hid Suel's vehicle. Dillon glanced in the rearview mirror as Suel drove through the cloud, then turned his wipers on and squirted the windshield. Dillon gave the car some gas, causing the engine to sputter for a moment before it picked up speed. Suel remained close behind him.

* * *

Arkady peeked out the front door window and examined the street for a few long minutes, but saw no sign of Yakov. He eventually opened the door, hurried down the steps, out the front gate, and across the street. He took a right, heading down the sidewalk toward the train station. He'd take a ferry over to the UK tonight, and from there, a train would bring him onto the continent by this time tomorrow. He would be with cousins in Estonia in less than forty-eight hours.

Yakov watched through his binoculars. At no surprise, Arkady foolishly hurried down the front steps. He half-ran across the street, pulled the cap down on his head, then put on a pair of sunglasses. He headed off in the opposite direction and quickly made his way down the sidewalk, glancing nervously over his shoulder every few steps. He carried a black backpack slung over his shoulder, and Yakov made a mental note to grab it, no doubt it carried cash.

He'd cursed initially, hoping Arkady would have walked past his car, although on second thought, this was the much better option. Now he could pull alongside the fool from the rear, lower the passenger window, kill him and grab the backpack. No one was going to question someone with a weapon who obviously wasn't afraid to use it.

Yakov turned the key in the ignition and slowly pulled back onto the street, gradually coming up on Arkady. When he was no more than thirty feet away, he lowered the passenger window.

Dillon pulled up behind the SUV with the dark-tinted windows, then swore when he saw the brake lights come on. No doubt some fool blocking traffic while he called out to his friend on the sidewalk.

As the SUV pulled alongside, the friend hurrying along the sidewalk casually glanced at the vehicle. The color seemed to drain from his face as a stunned look washed across him. He seemed frozen in place for a brief moment as the vehicle ahead of Dillon came to a complete stop. Dillon heard a voice but couldn't make out what was being said. He leaned on his horn as his engine began to sputter, and his brakes squealed in his attempt to stop.

Suddenly the figure on the sidewalk leaped over the wrought iron fence behind him, followed by a spray of bullets from an automatic weapon. He was tangled in the hedge for a half-second before he dropped to the ground and disappeared. Bullets continued to spit out of the passenger window in the SUV.

Dillon's foot pushed the brake pedal to the floor, and the brakes squealed as the Ecosport rammed the SUV from behind, pushing it forward a few inches. The hood on the Ecosport buckled, and a cloud of steam rose from the engine block. The driver's door on the SUV opened, and a large, bald man with one massive bushy eyebrow stepped out of the car and pointed his weapon at Dillon.

Dillon dropped below the dash just as his windshield exploded. He pulled his pistol out from the small of his back and crawled across the front seat, over shards of shattered windshield, toward the passenger door. He heard a weapon firing from behind him and then the roar of an engine.

"Jack, Jack," Suel shouted, coming alongside the vehicle. He yanked the passenger door open and looked down at Dillon. "Jack?"

"What the hell was that?" Dillon shouted as he slid out of the car and onto the pavement. He crouched alongside the Ecosport and looked down the street. He couldn't see anything that looked like the SUV on the road. He cautiously shook shards from the windshield off his coat and trousers. The left knee on his trousers was torn, and the shoulder on his coat was ripped along the seam with white padding hanging out. Two fingers on his left hand were bleeding from glass cuts, which he didn't notice until he brushed his shirt and left a small trail of blood down the front. He examined his chest for bullet holes but thankfully didn't find any.

Suel had moved into the small front yard, just inside the gate where the guy had jumped. He had his pistol drawn and was pointing it in a two-handed stance toward the ground, shouting, "An Garda Síochána. Drop your weapon. Drop your weapon. I said, drop the fecking weapon."

Dillon hurried into the front yard next door and cautiously approached from the rear, pointing his pistol at the figure on the ground with his back to Dillon. His hair was long in the back and tied in a thin, greasy ponytail. The man didn't appear to be wounded. "Drop your weapon," Dillon shouted from behind. "Drop it. Drop the weapon."

The man half jumped, looked at Dillon, then back at Suel, seemed to think for a brief moment before he tossed a pistol five or six feet in front of him and stretched out face down on the lawn.

Suel nodded at Dillon. "Watch him," Suel said. He reached for the backpack, tossed it off to the side, then kicked the man's pistol away. He pulled a pair of handcuffs from a coat pocket, pulled one of the man's arms behind him, and cuffed it, then the other, cuffing both hands behind his back. He took hold of the man by the shoulder, rolled him over, and helped him sit up.

Dillon hopped over the three-foot brick wall, picked up the pistol, and then the backpack.

"What the hell was that all about?" Suel asked.

Dillon shrugged and said, "I don't know. That SUV slowed down and just started shooting."

"I thought he was going to come for you," Suel said. He shook his head and glanced nervously up and down the street, the aftereffect of an adrenaline rush just beginning. "Let me call this in," he said and walked out to his car.

Someone slowed down while an oncoming car passed by then lowered his window and started to yell at Suel. "You might think about moving the damn car and...." He stopped, focused wide-eyed for a brief second on the pistol Suel still carried, then sped off down the street.

FORTY-SEVEN

Dillon sat in the interview room with Arkady Sokolov, where they'd been for the past three hours. Arkady's hands were still cuffed, only now they were resting on his lap and attached to a chain that was embedded in the floor. Dillon was marveling at the small world aspect of things. Just trying to make it back to the office, and they run into Arkady Sokolov. Who knew? He stared for a long moment at Arkady's greasy hair and his ponytail, remembering Noreen O'Bannon's description of the "friends" visiting Matthew Schmidt. An unattractive, very large man with a shaved head, a mustache, and one massive bushy eyebrow, the other with a greasy looking ponytail.

"It's a pretty sure bet they murdered your sister and tried to make it look like a hit and run. As for you, they simply don't care, they were going to shoot you down on the street like a dog and just leave you there. So what do you hope to gain by remaining quiet? If you think they're going to post bail and get you out of jail, you're mistaken. Well, unless they do that and then murder you, they might try that."

Arkady continued to stare back and not say a word.

"I see you went to college," Dillon said, nodding at the gold ring with the bluestone on Arkady's left hand.

"I smart man."

"You must be. Northwestern University, class of 2004, impressive. How'd you like the States?"

Arkady appeared confused for half a second, then returned to his expressionless face.

There was a knock on the door, and Suel stepped into the room with a sheaf of papers and handed them to Dillon. On top of the sheaf of papers was a note that read, *"Go along with me."* Dillon looked up at Suel and nodded.

"Nothing on his fingerprints. No outstanding warrants. I think we should let him go," Suel said. "With all the budget cuts we can't afford to keep him."

Arkady smiled, and for the first time since his initial arrest, he said something. "You should deport me, send me back to Russia. I do not deserve to be in your country. This would be best for you, no?"

"No," Suel said. "We're going to let you just walk out the door. You can go back to your flat on Annamoe Road. Sorry for any inconvenience we may have caused you. You said you have no idea who that was or why someone would want to shoot you. Okay. Nothing we can do about it. I've put out an APB on the vehicle, but with no license number, just the briefest of descriptions, it's best not to expect any results. Probably just some bollocks thinking it would be funny to scare an innocent man such as yourself. You'll be free to leave in just a few minutes."

The color seemed to drain from Arkady's face. "No, wait, you can't do that. You must deport me tonight, send me back to Russia. I—"

"We don't have the budget for that sort of thing. Not to worry, I'm sure your friends will be able to help. It will be on the news that someone tried to kill you, Mr. Sokolov, and I'm sure they'll all want to help."

"No, no, you can't do this. I—"

Suel pulled him to his feet, then reached into a pocket, took out a key and removed the handcuffs from Arkady's wrists. "I'm afraid we'll have to hang on to your backpack for a while. Shouldn't be more than a week, maybe two. Well, that is provided everything goes smoothly. You didn't have any illegal drugs in there, did you?"

"No, no drugs."

"Then there shouldn't be a problem. You can fill out the paperwork on the way out. They'll have you list the contents, so it's all there once you're able to pick it up."

"But my money—"

"Your money?"

"Yes, it is all I have."

"Well, that shouldn't be a problem. Just let them know the amount. Show them the bank receipt or a letter from your bank if you don't have the receipt, and they'll—"

"It was not in bank."

"Not in the bank? How much are you talking? A couple hundred euros?"

"No. It was everything I have. All of it. I save for years. Ever since I come here to your country."

"Not a problem, like I said, a letter from the bank where you kept the money and—"

"It is what I just said, I had it at all times. I don't trust the bank."

"Mmm-mmm, now that *is* going to be a problem."

"But it is my money."

"Sure it is," Suel said, then paused for effect. "If you could let us know who your employer is or was, we can check with them and get this cleared up. Your tax records would help."

"I don't pay the tax," Arkady said, then swore something in Russian. His voice had suddenly become shrill, and his face flushed as he half yelled, "It is my money, and I want it. I need it."

Suel calmly smiled. "I'm sure you do, and we'll get that to you just as soon as possible. You'll just have to be patient for a week or two…maybe a little longer."

"Do you listen? I need money now."

"First of all, please don't raise your voice, Mr. Sokolov. I understand you're upset, what with your sister's untimely passing and now this assault. At least you're safe in here, well, except we're about to let you go. You're wearing a class ring that belonged to a murdered American citizen and your blood type matches that found in a plastic bag containing a pair of hands. Just a coincidence, I guess. I can promise you, the moment we have answers to our questions, you'll be able to claim your money and go wherever you want. Now." Suel took hold of Arkady's arm. "Let's get you downstairs to fill out that paperwork. The sooner we get the paperwork filed, the faster things will go. Like I said before, just a week, maybe two, and once everything checks out, you'll have that money back in your hands."

Suel began to lead Arkady around the metal table bolted to the floor. They'd taken just four or five steps. Dillon was about to put a halt to their leaving the interview room when Arkady locked his knees and yanked his arm away from Suel's hand.

"You can't do this. They'll kill me."

"Relax. No one will do that," Suel said. "It's against the law."

FORTY-EIGHT

Interview room three was a little more crowded now. Arkady Sokolov was in the process of inhaling a large order of fish and chips, which did nothing to add to the air quality in the enclosed room. In an attempt to circulate the heavy air, a large fan had been brought in and positioned in a distant corner, but since the room was windowless and the door remained closed, it left one with the effect of a windy day in the confines of a garbage pit.

McCabe had joined Dillon and Suel and was now leading the questioning. The three of them sat across the steel table from Arkady Sokolov. McCabe's boss, Dermot Garrigan, a humorless, bald bureaucrat who hadn't seen street duty in over a quarter of a century, sat in a chair behind them. Next to Garrigan and wishing she was somewhere, anywhere else, sat a red-headed solicitor assigned to the department, Colleen McHugh. Just off to the side of the steel table, essentially between DCI McCabe and Arkady Sokolov, was a Russian translator whose name Dillon couldn't pronounce and had promptly forgotten anyway. Some guy Dillon knew as

"Chuckles" from IT was standing behind everyone, recording the interview on an ancient video recorder mounted on a tripod as well as two separate computers.

"What you need to understand, Mr. Sokolov," McCabe said, "is that in order for you to receive immunity you're going to have to provide us with information that makes it worth our while to grant you immunity." He paused and waited for the translator to relay the message.

Arkady Sokolov swirled a length of deep-fried battered fish through a mound of mayonnaise, took a large bite, then nodded before he responded in Russian. As he spoke, bits of fish and mayonnaise sprayed out of his mouth, covering the steel table and causing McCabe to reflexively pull his hands back.

The translator half turned on the plastic chair, faced McCabe, and repeated Sokolov's response in English. "We all know how unsuccessful you have been in arresting Alexei Bazanov. I have information for you that will finally bring him to the justice you seek. What I need from you is protection and the guarantee that you will provide me with safe passage back to Russia along with the return of the funds you confiscated from me."

"We may be able to do this," McCabe said. "But we need an indication of the quality of the information you have. We are all aware of Bazanov's dealings in illegal drugs as well as women being brought into our country for the sole purpose of prostitution and sexual slavery."

Sokolov rolled his eyes and gave a short laugh when he heard the translation. He responded in Russian, then sat back with a smile on his face and crossed his arms.

"What about the murder of an American agent here in Ireland," Sokolov said in heavy accented English, holding up his left hand and flashing the gold Northwestern University class ring. "Or maybe the robberies you've been helpless to prevent in your stores?"

Dillon leaned forward. "What do you know about the murder of Matthew Schmidt?"

At the sound of Schmidt's name, Sokolov's eyes quickly focused on Dillon, and he flashed a quick smile then quickly returned his gaze to McCabe.

"A little restraint, please. DCI McCabe is in charge here, Marshal Dillon," Dermot Garrigan said from the back row.

Sokolov smiled.

"Please tell us what you know. Help us with our ongoing investigations," McCabe said.

Sokolov seemed to think for a long moment after he listened to the translation, then said in English, "The next taking of the ATM will happen in just a day or two."

"Where?" Suel half-shouted.

"Gentlemen, the both of you, another outburst, and I'll see the two of you out of here," Garrigan said.

Suel ground his teeth and scratched the back of his head.

Sokolov crammed the last of the batter-fried fish into his mouth, chewed, gave a loud belch, then sat back, folded his arms again, and smiled.

"Do you know where this robbery will happen?" McCabe asked.

Sokolov just continued to smile.

Garrigan leaned forward and said, "Mr. Sokolov, it would be very helpful to your situation if you could tell us where and when this would occur. It would demonstrate your intent to work in conjunction with us, and at the same time, indicate a level of information that might make it worth our while to agree to your— requests."

Once the translator spoke, Sokolov didn't so much as blink, and everyone in the room remained quiet for the next few very long minutes.

Eventually, McCabe began to say something, but Garrigan leaned forward and placed a hand on his shoulder. "I'll take things from here, Detective Chief Inspector. Mr. Sokolov, we've attempted to work with you to ensure that your rights are protected, and we've asked for a modicum of support from you. I feel as though just the opposite is happening, and at this point, I'm going to terminate our discussion. When you are ready to cooperate, please let one of us know, and we'll be happy to sit down and discuss options with you. Until that time, you will be held for a period of forty-eight hours under Section four of the Criminal Justice Act of 1984. If, at that time, you choose to continue to remain uncooperative, you will be released." Garrigan turned to Chuckles from

IT and said, "That will conclude the interview. Please turn off all recording equipment."

"We usually wait until the suspect has been led out of—"

"I know when the equipment should be turned off. Now, I'm Chief Superintendent, and I want it off now, damn it. Turn it off now," he shouted.

Chuckles hit a button on the antique video recorder and then quickly typed something on the keyboard of both computers. Once finished typing, he looked up and nodded, wide-eyed, at Garrigan. "Everything's off, sir."

"Everyone out please," Garrigan said.

McHugh, the solicitor, was up and out of the room in a second or two. The translator quickly followed. McCabe gave a look that Garrigan didn't catch, then followed McHugh out the door.

"I've to put the equipment away, sir," Chuckles said.

"Out, now," Garrigan said, pointing toward the door, and Chuckles hurried out.

Dillon and Suel weren't sure what to do.

Garrigan ignored them, stood and leaned across the table so that he hovered over Sokolov. "In forty-eight hours, if you don't tell me where the next ATM robbery is going to take place, I will personally see to it that the full weight of our judicial system crushes you." He turned to Dillon and Suel and growled, "Get this despicable individual out of my sight."

FORTY-NINE

Suel downed the remainder of his Guinness and signaled the bartender for two more. "I say we go back and beat it out of the bastard." Since the Ecosport had to be towed away after the shooting incident on Annamoe Road, they were seated in the Autobahn pub, which was within walking distance to Dillon's place.

"If only it was that easy. God, I could see the bastard beginning to weigh the options and consider talking, you could see it written all over his face, and that idiot Chief Inspector Garrigan decides to call it quits. What? Did he have a golf game he had to get to? A meeting with the in-crowd somewhere?" Dillon said. He was still wearing his shirt with the blood streaks but had left his suit coat with the torn shoulder in a wastebasket back at the office.

"The last time that plonker got his hands dirty in any street work, we were still patrolling on horses," Suel said.

"I don't know, maybe a night or two in a cell will loosen Sokolov's tongue."

The bartender gave Dillon's shirt a quick glance, but didn't say anything. Suel nodded thanks as he slid two fresh pints of Guinness across the bar. Suel passed one over to Dillon, then gulped down the top third of his pint. "Arkady Sokolov could probably do ten years standing on his head. Our jails here, they're like a big country club to these bastards. A right disgrace is what it is."

"What if we just haul his ass back to the interview room and tell him it's now or never?"

Suel shook his head. "After the excellent job our chief inspector did, your man knows he's got us over a barrel. His bargaining position will only get stronger if he keeps his lips buttoned until the next ATM robbery. The thing is, he may not even know when it's going to happen, but if it does occur in the next few days, he's got us believing him, and then we're just plain fecked." Suel shook his head, drank another third from his pint glass, and said, "I've got an early day tomorrow, so I better be off."

"One more pint? I think it's my turn to buy."

"It is, and you can save it for another time. I'd best be off." He slid off his barstool, downed the rest of his Guinness, then waved a finger at Dillon and said, "See you in the morning. I'll pick you up about seven-thirty."

"Thanks for the warning. See you then," Dillon said. He sat at the bar by himself for no more than five minutes, then walked home. The lights were off at his next-door neighbor Deitora's home. Apparently, she was already in bed or still at some other location where she felt safer than next door to Dillon. There was no Kevin, or for that matter, any Garda vehicle to be seen on his street. So much for protection.

He unlocked the door, let Lucifer out, then walked into the kitchen and got the coffee pot ready for the morning. He let Lucifer back in, locked the door, and followed the dog upstairs to the bedroom. He tossed his shirt and trousers onto the growing laundry pile in the corner of the room, then walked into the bathroom and brushed his teeth. He turned the bedroom light off, then walked down the hall and slept in the guest room just to play it safe. He woke just before six the following morning.

He was on his third cup of coffee when Suel pulled up outside. "What time did you get out of there last night?" Suel said as Dillon opened the passenger door.

"I was probably home and asleep before you were out of the car, left just a few minutes after you."

"Humpf," was the extent of the conversation for the rest of the drive.

FIFTY

Dillon was on his phone. He'd been on hold for the past seven or eight minutes, waiting for someone in the medical examiner's office to pick up. Each minute seemed like an hour.

"Bloody hell," Suel suddenly yelled from his desk and slammed his phone down.

Dillon hung up and hurried over. "What's happening?" he asked a red-faced Suel, now in the process of pulling on his suit coat.

"Another ATM hit, down in Cabinteely."

"Never heard of it," Dillon said.

"Dún Laoghaire - Rathdown. You want to come along? It should prove to be special, this time there's a fatality, for Lord's sake."

It was a twenty-five-minute drive with the siren blaring and lights flashing. When they arrived a half-dozen Garda vehicles were parked at various angles around the convenience store located at one end of a small commercial corner. There were four gas pumps in front of the store, but the parking lot and refueling area had been sealed off. A technical van, different than the one that had gone through Matthew Schmidt's apartment on North Circular Road, was parked alongside the store. Three uniformed officers were out in front of the building, examining the shattered window and the two-foot-high brick wall that the vehicle had smashed through to get to the ATM. If it wasn't the same crew as the earlier robberies, Dillon thought it had to be a very good copy-cat.

Just like the previous robberies, the vehicle had smashed through the front window. If they were lucky enough to have functioning security cameras, they'd see two guys wrap a chain around the ATM, yank it from the base bolted to the floor, hoist the ATM into the back of the vehicle and be on their way in just over one minute.

Suel flashed the ID he had hanging around his neck as he stormed into the convenience store. There were more officers inside, including two guys in hazmat suits. One was in the process of dusting for fingerprints along the side of a shelving unit next to the empty space where the ATM had been. Another was filming the area where the vehicle had come through the front window, now just shattered glass and bricks scattered for about twenty feet in all directions. Suel headed toward two officers in plain clothes with ID badges hanging from their necks. One of them looked up and shook his head as Suel and Dillon approached.

"Hi, Paddy. Figured we'd see you here. This has all the earmarks of the same bunch you've been tracking. They got 'em on tape, for all the good it'll do. In and out in little more than a minute. Vehicle was reported stolen about an hour after the robbery."

"Sorry to see you dealing with this, Dennis. There was a fatality?"

"Yeah, unfortunately. Elderly woman, a regular, apparently lives just around the corner. Someone's at the home now, God bless. She was headed over there," he said, pointing toward a shelving unit loaded with bread and pastries. "Appears she turned and hurried back here like she might have forgotten something, which put her just about at ground zero when the bollocks barged through the front window. Not a chance in hell, poor soul."

"You said they've got a tape. Have you seen it?"

"Yeah, leastwise what there is to see. They're running it back in the office. Go on back and have a look. Any input you might have can only help. Casey's back there."

"Jimmy?"

"Mmm-mmm, he was first on scene, so he'll be your point man."

Suel and Dillon walked back past the shelving with the bread and pastries, then past coolers holding various milks, cheeses, and packaged meats toward an unobtrusive swinging door in a far corner that led to the back of the building and a loading dock. Just a few feet beyond the swinging door was a small room with a desk and a fairly large computer screen. Someone was seated at the desk, wearing a white baseball cap with the store logo, presumably the store manager. Four others in shirts and ties stood around him. All eyes were focused on the computer screen.

"Speak of the devil, here he is now," one of the four said. He looked relatively young with a full head of curly white hair slicked back and in need of a shave.

"Hiya, Jimmy," Suel said. "You've a tape, fantastic."

"Not much to see. Run it again for us if you would, Tommy," he said to the man seated in the chair.

The man in the chair clicked a couple of keys on the keyboard then waited while Suel and Dillon crowded into the room. "All set?" he said, then clicked a couple more keys without waiting for an answer, and the tape started. What they saw was more like a black and white film than the jerky image every five seconds, and it was certainly better than the previous security tapes Dillon had seen. That said, it appeared to be the same crew. The elderly woman walked into the camera area for just a brief second or two before the vehicle smashed through the window and into her, sending her flying off-camera. Neither individual jumping out of the vehicle appeared to notice her. One of them hoisting the ATM up into the back of the vehicle had a nose splint taped to his face, and his lips appeared swollen and black and blue. His partner wore a balaclava, so his face was completely hidden, but he appeared to be the same size as the one Dillon had hit on the chin with the hurley a few days ago.

"Freeze that image, please. I'm pretty sure that's them, Paddy, the guys who took my sunglasses. Look at the lips on that fuck."

"And maybe that means that bastard Sokolov really does know where they are. Can you send me a copy of this tape?" Suel said, tossing a business card onto the desk.

"I should be able to," the guy at the desk said.

"You know who these bastards are?" Casey asked.

"We might have a line on that one, Jimmy. We've got a guy cooling his heels in a cell," Suel said, pointing at the figure with the nose splint. "We'll see how 'accessory to murder' appeals to him. Thanks. I want to get back there and read him the riot act. Anything you need from me?"

"Just these bastards' heads on a platter," Casey said.

They had the siren blaring and lights flashing, racing back to Arkady Sokolov just a couple of minutes later.

FIFTY-ONE

Dillon and Suel were waiting for Sokolov to be brought into the interview room. They were in interview room one today, only because when they stuck their nose into number three, it still seemed to have the lingering scent of yesterday's fish and chips Sokolov had eaten. Interview room one simply reeked of sweat and fear, like it was supposed to.

Chuckles from IT was there and had just finished copying the file of the morning's security tape the store manager in Cabinteely had sent to Suel. He was in the process of setting up the ancient video camera on the tripod when there was a knock on the door.

"Come on in," Suel called as the door opened, and a handcuffed Arkady Sokolov flashed a broad smile as he was led toward the steel table.

"No fish today? I was so looking forward," Arkady said, then laughed.

"Set him in that chair," Suel said to the guard. They waited while the guard locked Arkady's handcuffs to the chain attached to the floor. "Thanks. We'll call you if we need anything," Suel said once the guard had finished.

He nodded and left the room.

Arkady leaned back in his chair and smiled like he had all the time in the world. "So, what is it I can—"

Suel held up a hand, stopping him in mid-sentence. "You got that first clip ready?" he said to Chuckles.

"Yes, sir, just hit return on the computer, and it should come up. I've cued the tape to play immediately. You might want to turn the screen toward, him so he doesn't miss anything."

Suel spun the laptop around to face Arkady, then hit the return key. Yesterday's tape of Arkady in interview room three immediately began to play. It was his voice, speaking in heavily accented English. "The next taking of the ATM will happen in just a day or two."

Sokolov grinned, exposing yellow-brown teeth the color of stained oak. "So, I'm guessing it has happened, and now you are ready to bargain. I warned you, but you would not listen. You thought you knew better. Now you know what happens when you think you are so smart."

Suel had turned the computer back around and, using the mouse, paused the tape. "That's what you think? That the robbery has already happened?"

"We both know it has. It was this morning. I could tell you where, but why? You already know. How successful were you in stopping them? Let me answer for you. You weren't. I lose track. This is now the sixth or seventh robbery? And you, with all your resources, are powerless to stop them. So, how does it feel?" he half laughed. "Maybe now you'll realize what I can do for you, and we can work together. I need only safe passage back to Russia and, oh yes, my money that you took from me."

Suel nodded at Chuckles, then said, "I think what you're going to need, Mr. Sokolov, is good representation."

"I'm not understanding."

"It's all set to go," Chuckles said to Suel.

"You're in big trouble. Here, have a look," Suel said, then spun the laptop around so that it was facing Sokolov again. He reached over and pressed the return key as Sokolov focused on the screen.

The grin from Sokolov's face quickly disappeared as the vehicle crashed through the window, and the elderly woman disappeared off camera. Suel let the tape run for a few more seconds before he spoke, never turning off the tape.

"What you just saw at the beginning of that tape, the elderly lady hit by the vehicle when it crashed through the window, she's dead. Died instantly. An upstanding citizen, active in her church, and she was murdered by the crew who made off with the ATM."

"That was not supposed to happen. They—"

"Shut the fuck up. It doesn't matter, Arkady. She was murdered in the commission of a crime. That's the way the court is going to look at this. Oh, and by the way, since you had knowledge of this prior to the incident, you're an accessory. That means you're going to face a murder charge, too. All bets are off. We're not going to help. You're going to prison for life. You will be locked up until the end of your days."

"But I, I didn't really know, I only thought they might do it again. I didn't know where or even when."

"So you say, but, well, I suppose I could play that tape from yesterday for you again. There were five, no wait, six of us in the room who can attest to you making the statements. You indicated you knew where and when the next robbery would occur. You even told that to Superintendent Garrigan, told him you knew, but you weren't going to let us in on your little secret."

"Chief Superintendent Garrigan, he has a lot of power," Dillon added.

"Yeah, doesn't get much higher than that, kind of like me lying to your man Putin and thinking I can get away with it. I'm afraid it's just never going to work out well for you."

"But, I didn't know, you must believe. I did not know, I was only making the buff," Sokolov said, looking back and forth, from Suel to Dillon.

"You mean bluff? Yeah, maybe, but then again, you sure sounded pretty real to me."

"Me too," Dillon said.

"Right now, I'm trying to think, should we charge you with murder or just gift wrap you and drop you off at Alexei Bazanov's house?"

At the sound of Bazanov's name, the color visibly drained from Sokolov's face.

"Here's my thought, a trial, solicitors, a judge, the jury, court costs you'll be unable to pay. It's going to go on for a couple of weeks, and then you have to figure once they find you guilty, oh, and they will, by the way. You're guilty as sin, you asshole. But once they find you guilty, we'll have to pay to feed you everyday for the rest of your life. Doesn't seem very fair to me. I think with all our budget cuts, and we're short on staff, I'm thinking Alexei Bazanov just might be the best choice."

"You know, if we could tape it, catch them killing him," Dillon said. "We could nail Bazanov at the same time."

Suel seemed to think, then slowly nodded. "I like it. Two birds with one stone sort of thing."

Sokolov looked from one to the other, shaking his head back and forth, muttering, "No, no, no."

"Actually, it's yes, yes, yes." Suel turned to Dillon, "We'll be heroes, saving the country all sorts of money, plus getting Alexei Bazanov. They're bound to give us both a promotion."

"No, wait, wait. You haven't caught them yet, have you? The robbers. The ones in your movie?"

"Well, no, but didn't you just get done telling us you don't know where the next—"

"I don't know where the next robbery will be, but I, I can tell you where you can find them. Not far from where you save me. Remember, you save me, from Ya-kov. He is man for Alexei Bazanov. I can tell you where the robbers are and, and it was Yakov who killed the American," he said, looking at Dillon.

"Matthew Schmidt?" Dillon said.

Sokolov nodded, frantically looking back and forth between Dillon and Suel. "Yes, yes, that's him. The body with no hands and head. He did that, Yakov did in a warehouse Alexei Bazanov owns. I told him not to, but he was going to kill me, too. You saw, you were there, you two stopped him from shooting me. He is the madman. Crazy. Yes, a crazy Russian, this is what he is."

"Where are the robbers?" Suel said.

"I can show you. I don't know what the address is, but I can show you the house, where it is. They rent a house, the three of them together."

"And were they beaten the other day?"

"Beaten? Yes, but how do you know this?" Sokolov said and looked surprised. "Some crazy man with a club jumped out at them on the street."

"Yeah, some crazy man is right," Suel said.

"They swear to kill him," Sokolov said.

"We'll see about that."

FIFTY-TWO

Number sixteen Black Street was the fifth house from the corner. Single-story attached homes for the length of the block, all built around 1880. The home was small and featured a window on either side of the wooden front door.

The shades were drawn over both windows at number sixteen, and what looked like an envelope hung partially out of the mail slot in the lower portion of the door. Most of the fronts were white or grey stucco, although the front of number sixteen was covered in fake stone. The location wasn't more than a ten-minute walk from the corner where Dillon had attacked the guys who'd stolen his sunglasses.

"That's it there, with the stone," Sokolov said, looking out the window of the black unmarked van. Dillon was driving. Suel sat in the passenger seat. Sokolov was on his knees in the back, chained to the inside wall of the van. A vehicle with four gardaí waited around the corner at either end of the block-long street.

"You're sure that's the place?" Dillon said.

"Yes. I've been there. Yakov, brought me there the night he killed the American. I remember it because they had the trays from the machine sitting on the floor."

"Trays, from the ATM?" Suel said.

"Yes. They were saving them for a party."

"How many in there?"

"Just the three, no one else."

"They have people over? Friends?" Suel said as Dillon turned the corner and drove slowly down the next street.

"No, no one is there this time of day except Yakov sometimes, but his car, the big black one, is not there. They sleep during the day, pay for a woman, and party at night."

"Nice work if you can get it," Suel said.

They drove the length of the block, then pulled around the corner and talked by radio with the crews at either end of the street, then waited for the delivery of two key pieces of equipment. Twenty minutes later, a pickup truck came around the corner with two aluminum ladders stacked in the back. Two of the gardaí, dressed in jeans and t-shirts, climbed into the back of the pickup and drove down the street. One man got off the truck with a ladder and a bucket about four doors before number sixteen. The second man climbed out of the pickup a few doors past number sixteen.

Both men leaned their ladders up against a house and quickly climbed up onto the one-story roof carrying a bucket. Once on the roof, they pulled a small, automatic weapon from the bucket, then carefully made their way along the peak of the attached roofs toward number sixteen. As soon as they were in position, they gave a wave to Suel, who then gave both groups the go-ahead over the radio.

Both groups hurried along from either end of the street, converging on number sixteen. Armed men quickly stood back from the two front windows with the shades drawn as Suel approached the front door. He knocked softly on the door, holding his pistol in his right hand, just behind his back.

He waited no more than a few seconds before he waved the man with the red battering ram over. One solid swing, landing just next to the brass doorknob, sent the door flying open and bouncing off an inside wall.

"Police. Hands up. Hands up," Suel shouted as he charged in through the open door followed by a half-dozen armed men and then Dillon bringing up the rear. From somewhere inside, a woman screamed. A shot was fired and more yelling, "Hands up. Hands up."

It was all over in less than a minute, voices now calling, "Clear," coming from two rooms in the rear of the house.

As Dillon entered, he kept his pistol held at arm's length, half crouched as he moved down the narrow hallway. The room to his right was small with dingy grey walls. Two gardaí were in the process of handcuffing a naked man lying on the floor. A third officer stood on the bed, keeping his weapon trained on the man being handcuffed. Blood was on the floor and seemed to be coming from the man's shoulder. A naked woman stood facing the far wall with her hands raised over her head. She had an orthodox cross in blue ink tattooed on her back and was crying softly.

Once the man on the floor was cuffed, the officers rolled him over. The wound was on his shoulder and didn't appear too serious, although Dillon's eyes were focused on the nose splint the man was wearing. As they sat him up, the man grimaced, exposing a large space in the front of his mouth where a number of teeth had been knocked out. The area around his mouth was still swollen and black and blue. Dillon resisted the urge to comment or introduce himself.

He strolled back down the hall toward Suel, who was on the radio calling the medical unit, telling them there was one wounded individual with a non-threatening gunshot wound. He nodded at Dillon, then stepped outside and gave the all-clear to the two officers up on the roof.

One of the officers led the woman, now with her hands handcuffed behind her back, onto the couch in the front room where she sat, semi-curled up, in an effort to hide her naked body, and failing miserably. Two men lay facedown on the floor. They were handcuffed, and two gardaí stood next to them, a right foot was planted between each man's shoulders.

Suel came back in through the front door just as an officer stepped into the hall from a back room and called, "Detective, we got it, money still in the cash trays and a lot more in a trash bag under the bed."

FIFTY-THREE

S uel was in the process of interrogating two of the men they arrested in the raid just a few hours ago in interview rooms one and two. The third was still being treated in the hospital for the wound to his shoulder, although they expected him to be delivered into their custody sometime in the next few hours. The woman had been issued some sort of smock and, at the moment, was cooling her heels in a holding cell.

"Please. You must send me back to Russia now, to-day," Arkady Sokolov said. He was in interview room three with Dillon. The room still held the unpleasant tell-tale scent of fish and chips from thirty-six hours earlier.

"And you have to tell me about Matthew Schmidt."

"I say to you before, many times. I will tell when I'm on planc to Russia. Not before. Here, I give you the robbers of the ATM. You had no idea. I show them to you and now you not send me back to Russia. It is crazy. It is stupid, not fair."

"You have to appear before the court first, that's to-morrow morning. We have to get extradition approval.

That's going to take time. You have to have legal representation appointed, so you are protected under the laws—"

"What is this representation? You just send me back to Russia, now, today, and I will cause no problem. The money you took from me use some to pay for my ticket. Yes? There, no cost to you and Ireland, and I'm gone and will not return, ever. So see, is good. Yes?"

"No. It doesn't work that way. We have to go through the court system to—"

"But we think the same, yes? You should send me back to Russia. I am the problem here, and so you can get rid of me."

"Much as I'd like to, we can't, at least not yet. I'm afraid that is the system here, and we have to follow it."

"It is crazy. Is shit. They will kill me as soon as they find out I was one that show you where they live."

"We're going to keep you in protective custody. You'll be safe."

Sokolov shook his head and said, "You do not know what you say. There is no safe place for me here. Only in Russia where I can hide will I be safe."

"And we'll get you there just as soon as we can. You just have to trust us."

Sokolov shook his head and muttered something in Russian.

"We're going to keep you in an isolated cell. No one will get to you. Your hearing is tomorrow morning at ten. You'll be driven down to the Criminal Courts building under a protective guard for a short appearance, then back here, all the while under Garda protection. Other than a handful of gardaí, no one even knows where you are. As far as they know, you left town and you're probably somewhere on the continent. They'll think you're down in Costa del Sol, drinking wine with a couple of beautiful women."

Sokolov scoffed, then shook his head. "You don't know."

"Let's get you back in that cell. You'll be safe there. I'll be on the team escorting you to your hearing tomorrow morning. You'll see. I think you're going to feel a lot better about your protection. We'll have a short hearing, and we can get things moving and soon we'll send you back to Russia. Okay?"

Sokolov shook his head again, then said, "I think it would be best now, to get me to my cell."

Dillon walked over to the door and gave a soft knock. It opened almost immediately, and he said, "Take the prisoner back to his cell. Absolutely no interaction with any other prisoner. I want him kept completely isolated."

The guard nodded, then walked over to Sokolov, removed the chain bolted to the floor from his handcuffs, then helped him to his feet. Solokov gave Dillon a long, sad look, shook his head then headed toward the door with the guard holding his arm. He had to take short steps because his ankles were hobbled.

Dillon watched him leave the room, then walked back to the table and glanced at the notes he'd taken. Sokolov had alluded to this Yakov Gulin person killing the American DEA agent Matthew Schmidt, but Sokolov seemed determined not to say anything more until he knew for sure he was going to be returned to Russia. Dillon stared off in the distance wondering what, exactly, were the chances he would be returned?

Suddenly, from out in the hallway came shouting, followed by what sounded like some vicious swearing. Dillon hurried to the door. By the time he looked out in the hall, Sokolov was quickly hobbling down the hall-way, glancing over his shoulder with a frightened look on his face.

The ATM robber Dillon had hit on the chin with the hurley a few days ago was held up against the wall by two gardaí, one of whom was holding a wooden baton across the man's throat. The man was red-faced, scream-ing something vicious sounding in Russian as Sokolov hurried toward the elevator just as quickly as his hobbled ankles would allow.

The door to the Interview Room One opened just as Sokolov hurried past, and Suel stepped outside to see what the commotion was. He looked at the prisoner pressed up against the wall with the baton held across his neck, then glanced over his shoulder at Sokolov hurrying as best he could toward the elevator.

"Damn it," Suel said. "I want that man in solitary. No interaction with other prisoners for seventy-two hours. And you," Suel said, taking a half-dozen steps toward the prisoner against the wall. "You'd better start to behave, or you'll find yourself in some very unpleasant circumstances."

That seemed to quiet him down, well, that and the fact that Sokolov was now around the corner at the end of the hall and out of sight.

"Take him down to solitary confinement. No interaction with any other prisoners for the next seventy-two hours."

FIFTY-FOUR

It was nine the following morning, and Dillon had on a bright green high-visibility vest over the olive-drab protective vest he wore. Two black SUVs were parked in the parking lot behind the building. Two men to each vehicle plus Dillon, another man and the driver in the third vehicle, which was a white SUV with reinforced door panels and bulletproof windows.

Arkady Sokolov's hearing at the Crimninal Justice Center was scheduled for ten o'clock. They would drive him to the building, bring him in the back way, immediately head to the hearing in a courtroom closed to the media and all but a half dozen individuals. They would avoid any interaction with other prisoners. Then, once the hearing concluded, estimated to last no more than fifteen or twenty minutes, they would whisk Sokolov off to Mountjoy Prison, where he would be held in solitary confinement until he was flown to Russia and turned over to the Russian authorities.

Dillon checked his watch. They wouldn't leave for another twenty minutes. There was no sense in prolonging their stay at the Justice Center. They planned to travel with flashing lights all the way to the hearing, avoiding any unnecessary stops. With any luck, Sokolov would be out of the country in seventy-two hours after providing detailed information regarding Matthew Schmidt's murderer, along with a laundry list of crimes that would bring Alexei Bazanov to justice and lock him up for the rest of his life. It all sounded so simple, which was exactly what had Dillon worried.

He pulled out his phone and called Suel, already over at the Criminal Justice Center.

"You're leaving?" was the way Suel answered his phone.

"No, not for another fifteen minutes or so. What's it like over there?"

"Not a bother. A banker due in on charges he was part of the Nama scam in 2011, so there's press and cameras waiting for him to show up out in front of the building. It will serve as a good diversion. I've got two men stationed out back where you'll be turning in. No one has been allowed in there for the past thirty minutes. We'll have armed guards watching the vehicles during his hearing. He'll be wearing a protective vest?"

"Yeah, probably putting it on now. I'll lead him out to the vehicle myself. I'm going to have him riding on the floor of the vehicle on the way over and on his trip to Mountjoy."

Suel gave a short chuckle and said, "Seems a bit excessive, but I get it. I'll be happy to see the backside of him in a few days."

"You're preaching to the choir on that. Once we're out of the hearing, we've a room lined up at Mountjoy to interview him and take his statements. Chuckles is over there now, setting up the taping equipment in an interview room. There are a number of people who want to question him."

"God, Chief Superintendent Garrigan isn't one of them, is he?"

"No, fortunately, he's *indisposed* down in Cork, addressing some pensioners meeting. If the truth were known, I think McCabe's been sitting on the paperwork and Garrigan's completely in the dark on any of this."

"Long may it last," Suel said.

"I'm going to go down to the cellblock and bring him out in a minute or two. We'll see you when we get there."

"Stay in the vehicles until you see me come out. I'll have two others with me and we'll all escort the bastard into the hearing room."

"See you there," Dillon said and hung up. He waved the six men waiting with the vehicles over to him. Everyone wore protective vests and carried an automatic weapon. They looked like they were ready to storm the Normandy beaches instead of delivering a criminal to a court hearing.

"I just spoke with Suel. They're all set for us at the Justice Center. We'll be driving with flashing lights, but no sirens. Radio silence along the way until we're approaching the rear of the Justice Center. You've done a communications check?"

"Twice," one of the men responded.

"Okay. Mount up. I want to put him in the white vehicle just as fast as possible. I'm going to have him ride on the floor. It's only a ten-minute drive. Questions?"

Everyone shook their head no.

"Good. I'll go get him and have him down here in a minute."

Dillon took the elevator down one level to the cell block. Sokolov was in civilian clothes, wearing a protective vest, sunglasses and handcuffs, no restraints around his ankles.

"Just need your signature on the paperwork, Marshall," a uniformed officer said, and handed a clipboard to Dillon.

Dillon initialed two areas highlighted with a bright green marker and signed his name at the bottom of the sheet, then nodded at the men on either side of Sokolov. They each grabbed an arm and helped him to his feet, not that he really needed any help.

They rode the elevator back up to the first floor. As the elevator doors opened, Dillon stepped out to make sure the hall was clear. No one was in sight, and he waved them out of the elevator. He had them pause at the door leading outside. He stepped out ahead of everyone, gave a cautious look around, then waved them outside, and they hurried toward the white SUV with both doors on the passenger side open. The roof lights were flashing on all three vehicles.

"You get in the rear seat, then down on the floor. It's a short drive to the Justice Center, and I want you on the floor the entire way."

Sokolov looked for half a moment like he was going to say something but then nodded, hurried to the SUV with a guard on either side of him and Dillon following behind, looking left and right.

Sokolov gave a slight groan as he turned around in the seat and settled onto the floor. One of the armed men in a protective vest was in the back seat, sitting behind the driver. He helped Sokolov get positioned on the floor and let him lean against his leg. Dillon closed the door, nodded thanks to the two guards, then hurried into the front passenger seat, and they were off with a black SUV in front and behind, Dillon, Sokolov, and two guards in the white SUV.

FIFTY-FIVE

In no time at all, they were turning onto North Circular Road. Two minutes later, they passed number 85, the building where Matthew Schmidt had lived. Dillon made a mental note to check with Gino in New York to see if he had anymore information on Matthew Schmidt, then wondered if Suel had gone out yet with the woman in number ten, Noreen O'Bannon. Five seconds later, they drove past the corner where Dillon assaulted the ATM robbers with the hurley, although he had no idea who they were at the time.

They made a left-hand turn off North Circular Road onto Infirmary Road, then drove three blocks, passing the old infirmary on their right side. Just beyond the infirmary, they slowed to turn into the rear of the Criminal Justice Center.

The radio suddenly chirped. "Two guards are waving us through into the rear area. All quiet up ahead."

Dillon responded, "Once we're in the rear of the building, first vehicle pull over to the right side, we'll pull in next to you, rear vehicle pull behind us, forming an 'L.' Leave the flashers on. Everyone out and keeping an eye peeled for anything unusual. We'll wait for Suel to come out, then unload the cargo and hurry into the building. It's a small area, but that should serve us well."

They headed down the two-way lane to the rear of the building. An eight-foot stone wall was on either side of the lane. They turned left into the small parking area, and the SUV in the lead pulled over to the right-hand side. The driver and passenger jumped out, armed and scanning the area. The second vehicle, with Dillon and Sokolov, pulled alongside. The third vehicle pulled in crossways behind them, essentially forming an 'L' just as Dillon had requested. Dillon watched in the side view mirror as the driver in the SUV behind him climbed out and took up a position. He waited a few more seconds, then saw Suel hurry out the door with two armed gardaí and said, "Okay, let's go."

Dillon hopped out of the passenger seat, gave a quick look around, then opened the rear door and pulled Arkady off the floor and up onto the rear seat. Arkady took a deep breath, smiled, slid across the seat and out the door into the tight parking area. He stood next to the SUV and seemed to smile at the protection.

"Come on, let's get you inside," Dillon said.

Arkady nodded, took a step toward the building, and his head suddenly exploded. The sound of a single gunshot seemed to echo off the side of the eleven-story building for a very long moment.

"Down, down, everyone down," someone yelled.

Dillon caught Arkady by the shoulders and slowed his fall, lowering him to the pavement, but he was already dead. There was a hole about the size of a nickel just above the temple on the right side of his head. The top and left side of his skull were splattered across the White SUV. Blood, bits of skull and brain matter slowly dripped down the bulletproof glass on the side of the SUV.

Dillon reflexively rubbed a hand across his eyes, and it came away bloody, although he didn't think he'd been hit.

"Where'd it come from?" someone yelled.

"Anyone see anything?"

One of men scurried from behind the SUV and ran in a half crouched position to the far wall. He looked back at the group crouched behind the vehicles and extended his arm in a questioning manner. No one gave a response. He slowly stood and cautiously peeked over the wall into the infirmary grounds.

"For fuck's sake, Dennis," someone shouted.

A four or five-story building on the infirmary grounds sat on a higher plot of land overlooking the small lot, and the shot could have come from one of the windows, maybe the roof, or any of a dozen other places.

Dillon heard one of the men shouting commands into the radio, but he couldn't make out what was being said. He stared at the body of Arkady Sokolov and his shattered skull, wondering if there was some way he could fix this, knowing all along there wasn't.

FIFTY-SIX

Alexei Bazanov grinned and said, "A little something for the guest of honor," He was barefoot, clad only in his blue silk dressing gown with the white silk lapels. He removed his arm from around the half-naked woman next to him and raised his glass to Yakov. "My friend, you are an excellent shot, and you are empty again. Fill him up, Katrin."

Blonde Katrin, naked except for her thong, stepped forward, took the bottle from the ice bucket, smiled, and poured chilled vodka into Yakov's glass until it overflowed. Yakov staggered slightly on unsteady feet, then attempted to down the glass. Half the contents ran down his chin as he wobbled back and forth. He wiped a hand across his mouth, belched and stood bleary-eyed, holding his empty glass out toward Katrin for another refill.

She refilled the glass then effortlessly ducked and spun around, avoiding Yakov's clumsy attempt to grab her. There were three other women in the room, making five altogether, all naked except for the small thongs they wore. Yakov had raped them all at one time or another, and Alexei had insisted they attend the event as a special gift from him to Yakov.

The women laughed nervously as Katrin ducked away from Yakov and strutted toward the women, teasing Yakov with a rear view of her attributes. One of them said something in Russian, and they all downed their shots. Katrin refilled their glasses as they slowly formed a rough circle around Yakov, all the while swaying back and forth to the music playing on the sound system.

One of the women, a brunette with bleached highlights and a large pair of angel wings tattooed on her back, strutted toward Yakov. He pretended to reach for her. She quickly stepped to the side only to have him wrap his massive arm around her, effortlessly lift her up off the floor and begin biting her on the neck, working his way down toward her breasts. He left red welts along her neck and on her shoulder in the pattern of his mismatched teeth.

She screamed and hit him repeatedly on the back of the head, but to no avail.

A woman downed her shot, then stepped forward and shook her chest from side to side in front of Yakov, daring him to reach for her as the brunette with the angel wings squirmed and kicked and eventually slipped down far enough to knee him solidly in the crotch. He gave a loud grunt as he let go, then grabbed for her as he dropped to his knees. He caught hold of her thong as she turned away, ripping the tiny garment from her hips. She took a step to the side, spun, and viciously kicked him in the face, landing a heel along the side of his nose.

His head jerked back as blood spurted down his chest. He groaned, then swore at her in Russian, although his words were so slurred they were unintelligible.

Alexei Bazanov set his empty glass on the corner of an end table, took the woman next to him by the hand and headed for the door. Just as he was about to open the door, he turned to the other women in the room and said, "Finish it, ladies, and clean up the mess."

Bazanov stepped into the hall, closed the door behind him, and slowly began to climb the stairs to the second floor, undoing the velvet belt that had been tied around his waist. He heard a shot, climbed two more steps, then heard a number of shots in quick succession. He smiled and thought to himself, *Problem solved,* then focused on the half-naked woman next to him as she grabbed his hand, kissed it, and followed him up the stairs, all the while quietly whispering, "Thank you."

FIFTY-SEVEN

Dillon and Suel were sitting in McCabe's office, presenting their plan on how to arrest Yakov Gulin. "He's the manservant to Alexei Bazanov," Dillon said.

"He's a heartless bastard, and we can personally identify him as the one who fired at Sokolov on North Circular Road and attempted to kill Dillon in the same incident," Suel said.

"Not if, but when we turn Yakov Gulin, Alexei Bazanov falls into our hands. Murder, prostitution, rackets, drugs, it would go a very long way in eliminating a number of problems."

"And you think Bazanov's servant will turn and give evidence?" McCabe said, sounding unconvinced.

"A lifetime to ponder life's inconsistencies from behind bars seems to provide a way of clearing one's thought process. Yakov Gulin could be an even better source than Arkady Sokolov would have been," Dillon said.

McCabe's phone rang at that moment, and he glanced at the caller ID, frowned then picked it up. "This is McCabe. What the hell. When? Oh really?" he said then glanced at Dillon and Suel sitting across the desk from him. "Tell me where, again," he said, grabbing a pen and writing something down on a pad of paper. "No, thank you. Yes, immediately," he said, then hung up the phone. He folded his hands as if in prayer and bounced his index fingers against his lips a half dozen times, apparently deep in thought, then gave an audible sigh.

"Everything all right, sir?" Dillon asked.

"Yakov Gulin, they've got him."

"Got him? He's been arrested?"

"No. They found him this morning, lock number seven along the Royal Canal. Dead. Shot and castrated."

The End

Thanks for taking time to read **Fair City Blues**. If you enjoyed the read please leave a review, I'm indie published and a one or two sentence review really helps. Don't miss the sample of the next Jack Dillon Dublin Tale, **Spade Work** on the next page.

PROLOGUE

The taxi driver pulled to the curb and said, "Fourteen euros."

"I got it. You okay, honey?" Joey said and looked over at the blonde in the sexy black dress.

She gave him the finger.

Not that he cared. Right now, he was just thankful for the silent treatment. At least she was done bitching. He wondered how long it would be before she said anything positive. It was a mistake to have brought her over in the first place. They were on a flight back to Boston in the morning, and he planned to ditch her at the airport the moment they landed. He tossed two twenty euro notes into the front seat. "Keep the change, pal."

"Thank you, sir," the driver said and smiled into the rearview mirror.

The blonde opened the passenger door without saying a word, stepped out of the back seat, and looked at the figure hurrying toward her.

"Joey Touhy?"

Bang, bang! Bang, bang! Bang!

ONE

US Marshal Jack Dillon pulled up and over the curb, parking his car halfway on the narrow sidewalk and halfway into the street, leaving enough room for another car to pass. He climbed out from behind the wheel and clicked the lock button on his key. The lights gave a quick flash as the doors locked, and the horn beeped. He looked up at the two-story attached house. It was light-colored stucco, with the exact same floor plan as all the homes in this Dublin housing estate.

He focused on the second-floor window, the master bedroom. Candlelight flickered from behind the lace curtains, and he smiled, pulled out his phone, and reread the text message from Brianna Fallon for the umpteenth time.

"Happy birthday, baby! Front door is unlocked. Incredible wonders await.

You've got thirty minutes to get here, or I'm starting without you.'"

He opened the front gate, hurried past her car and stepped in the front door. The house was dark except for a series of small, battery-operated vigil lights flickering on every other step leading up to her bedroom. He locked the front door then hurried up the stairs, taking them two at a time. The smile on his face turned into a wide grin by the time he reached the bedroom door.

The bedroom was illuminated by a half dozen candles, at least one of which was scented, since the room had a wonderful vanilla scent.

Brianna was naked, leaning against a pile of three pillows on the black silk bed sheet, sipping from a champagne flute filled with prosecco. She kept her dark hair in a pageboy cut, and it seemed to glisten in the candlelight. A silver ice bucket with a chilled bottle sat on the end table next to her side of the bed. She wore the pearl necklace he'd given her last Christmas and a smile. She slowly ran her tongue across her full lips and, with her free hand, began to play with her navel. Dillon focused on the sunburst tattoo surrounding her navel for a moment then watched as she slowly moved her hand lower.

"I was beginning to wonder, birthday boy," Brianna said. She raised her glass of prosecco in a toast. "Yours is waiting for you, just the way you like it." She nodded at the cut crystal tumbler with a healthy inch of Jameson resting on the end table next to the door.

Dillon hurriedly undressed, tearing the button off the cuff of his shirt in an effort to quickly get the thing undone.

She giggled and said, "Relax, bad boy. We've got all night, and I intend to put it to very good use."

That only seemed to make him more frantic. He kicked his trousers off, dropped his boxers, and half jumped into bed. He rolled toward her, gave her a long kiss, then picked up the tumbler of Jameson and clinked glasses with her.

She took a small sip, set her flute next to the ice bucket, said, "Let the games begin." She pulled the silk sheet up to Dillon's chest and then proceeded to slowly slip beneath the sheet, kissing his chest along the way.

Dillon placed a hand on her shoulder and began to pull her back up.

"No, you just lie back and sip that whiskey," she said. "I've been waiting very patiently, so I get to do whatever I want, and I intend to take my time." With that, she slipped back beneath the sheet.

TWO

The opening guitar solo to George Thorogood's "Bad to the Bone" slowly dragged Dillon from his sleep. He glanced over at Brianna just as she pulled a pillow over her head. He shook his head a few times in an effort to clear the cobwebs, then tried to locate his cellphone in the dark. He'd kicked his trousers off halfway across the room, which meant he had to climb out of bed to get to his phone. The guitar solo started up again. Brianna gave a sleepy groan from beneath the pillow, and Dillon stubbed his big toe against the bedpost. He pulled the cell out of his trouser pocket, swiped his finger across the screen to stop the noise, and limped toward the door.

"What the hell," he whispered out in the hallway. His big toe was throbbing.

"Wake you?" Detective Inspector Suel asked.

"What the hell time is it?" Dillon said as he limped down the hall, turned on the bathroom light, and closed the door behind him.

"Just a little after four. There's been a shooting."

"And?"

"Two dead, a third in critical condition. He's probably in the operating room at Saint Vincent's as we speak."

"Is he American?"

"No, a Dub, the taxi driver. But the two victims are American, a couple. You'd better get over here and have a look."

"Now?" Dillon didn't mean to sound like he was whining. On the other hand, he had a momentary thought about a breakfast rematch with Brianna, and since they were already dead . . . "How long will the crime scene be—"

"Dillon, get your ass over here. Chief Inspector McCabe will be here within the hour, and it would best for both of us, you and me if you were here."

Unfortunately, he knew Suel was right. "Oh, for Christ's sake. All right, all right, where, exactly, are you?"

"Clontarf, not far from the castle— Seafield Road, just in front of number eight as a matter of fact. At this hour, it shouldn't take you more than ten minutes to get here from your place."

Dillon saw no point in letting Paddy Suel know he wasn't home, and that, in fact, he was in Coolock. But the drive time would be about the same; ten, maybe fifteen minutes. "All right, let me get dressed, and I'll see you shortly."

"Much appreciated," Suel said and hung up.

"Great. Probably a couple of tourists," he said to his reflection in the mirror. That meant he'd have to be on the line later today, contacting some family member to ID the body. Not exactly the perfect end to a birthday. He tiptoed back into the bedroom and gathered up his clothes. He gave a longing last look at Brianna, the pillow with the black silk pillowcase still over her head and that wonderful, oh so talented body hidden beneath the duvet. He caught a glimpse of the pearl necklace she was still wearing and sighed. *Perfectly dressed*, he thought.

He quietly closed the bedroom door, dressed out in the hallway, then tiptoed down to the kitchen and wrote a quick note explaining the situation. He placed the note next to the tea kettle, where she was bound to see it. He quietly stepped outside, double-checked the front door to make sure it was locked behind him and hurried to his car.

He drove down St. Brigid's Road, which turned into Abbeyfield, from there over to Castle Avenue and down to Seafield Road. At this hour, he only passed two cars along the way, both taxis. As he turned onto Seafield, he saw the flashing lights from a couple of squad cars and an emergency vehicle up ahead. He thought the drive would take him fifteen minutes, but even after waiting for a red light, he'd made it in eight.

He parked behind Paddy Suel's car, a silver Omni. He tried to wipe the lingering image of gorgeous Brianna Fallon from his mind as he opened the glove compartment and pulled two latex gloves from the box. He sat

for a few seconds, then took a deep breath and climbed
out from behind the wheel.

THREE

White plastic tape with blue letters that read "GARDA NO ENTRY" was tied from the wrought iron fence on top of the short wall to one of the squad cars with the flashing lights.

Behind the fence rested a large, well-manicured lawn with neatly trimmed shrubs, a paved driveway, and a large, two-story white stucco home with a red tile roof. The front door to the home was positioned in the center of the structure with large, curved bay windows on either side of the door.

The house was dark, with the exception of a lamp in one of the bay windows. A man in a dark bathrobe stood in the windows, sipping tea, or maybe coffee from a white mug while he stared out at all the activity in front of his home. Dillon raised the plastic "GARDA NO EN-TRY" tape and ducked underneath. He walked toward a taxi blocking the sidewalk at an angle. The taxi rested up against the brick column that held the gate to the paved driveway. The engine wasn't running, and the lights were off.

The passenger door on the street side was open. A pair of female legs hung out of the door. The right foot, in a red stiletto heel, rested at an odd angle with the toe of the shoe wedged against the pavement. The left foot was bare. The stiletto for the left foot was maybe fifteen feet away, lying in the street. A number of brass cartridges were scattered around the stiletto. Little white plastic tent structures, six in all, numbered and maybe four inches high, had been placed next to each cartridge. A female technician in a white hazmat suit was crouched down in front of the open car door, taking photographs. Three other hazmat suits looked to be discussing something on a clipboard.

Dillon walked maybe five feet behind the technician taking pictures and peered inside the vehicle. The female wore a short black dress that rested above her thigh, revealing a black thong. Her body was positioned across the seat. Her left shoulder, left arm, and her head were hanging off the seat. What looked like a large diamond ring was on her left hand. The right wrist had a sparkling bracelet wrapped around it. More diamonds.

Her blonde hair appeared to be about shoulder-length and hung across her face, covering all but her chin. Two wounds were apparent. One, on the left side of her chest, looked like it could have hit her heart; the other had torn away a front portion of her throat. A pool of blood had collected on the floor of the taxi beneath her head. Based on the condition of her arms and hands, plus the little bit of chin he could see, she appeared fairly young; late twenties, maybe early thirties. She was large-breasted and looked to have been in fairly good shape. A stud earring, possibly another diamond, was in her right ear. A large pendant, again possibly a diamond, hung around her neck, and the one hand Dillon could see sported a fancy ring that appeared to be an emerald surrounded by more diamonds.

The second body in the back seat was that of a male dressed in a grey suit and an open-collar white shirt. It looked like he may have been neatly groomed, although what remained of the face and head after taking multiple rounds made that rather difficult to determine. He had grey hair, neatly trimmed. His right arm rested in a strange position, almost looking like someone had twisted it behind his back. The rear window and the passenger window on the far side of the interior were sprayed with blood, bits of skull, and brain matter. Dillon wondered if the couple might be a father and daughter.

"Not the best way to start our day, or for them to end their evening," a voice said from behind.

Dillon turned around, and there was Paddy Suel, sipping from a steaming paper cup. "Oh, and before I forget, happy birthday," Suel said, flashed a brief smile, then handed Dillon a paper napkin. "Jaysus, you might want to rub at least some of the lipstick off, ya gobshite."

Dillon smiled, took the napkin, and rubbed it across both cheeks.

"Back on the left side, closer to your ear. Yeah, okay, you got it. Who was he?" Suel said and grinned.

"No one who'd admit to knowing you. I'd just like to state for the record that I gave up everything I'd planned for later this morning just to come out here and join you tonight. You wouldn't happen to have another one of those teas, would you?"

"Yeah, waiting for your Lordship in the car. Come on, we might as well get comfortable until the tech team is finished," Suel said, then headed back across the street to his car.

Dillon took a moment to study the two bodies in the taxi, made some mental notes, then followed Suel.

FOUR

illon climbed into the passenger side of the car. Suel handed him a paper cup of tea from the console, then glanced back across the street at the taxi.

"What makes you think they're American?" Dillon asked then took a sip of tea. It was hot, and he'd been in Dublin long enough to not really mind it, the tea.

Suel continued to stare out the window at the taxi. "One of the techs told me. Apparently, there's a billfold on the floor of the backseat, a couple of hundred-dollar bills hanging out of it, and a driver's license from your state of Massachusetts."

"You get a name?"

Suel shook his head no, took another sip of tea, and turned to look at Dillon. "What do you think?"

"About the scene?"

"No, about the unfortunate woman you were sleeping with. Yes, about the scene."

"At least six shots, I'm guessing from a smaller-caliber weapon. Someone was pissed off. At first glance, given the location, the number of rounds, it certainly doesn't appear to be random."

"I wonder who in the hell they are?" Suel said and took another sip.

"Clothes look expensive. Hell of a rock on the woman's finger, plus a bracelet and a pendant. The guy's billfold is still in the taxi, so maybe robbery wasn't the primary motive. I'm guessing husband and trophy wife."

"Politicians? Business? Gangsters?" Suel said, almost to himself.

"Guess we'll find out soon enough," Dillon said, as a guy in a hazmat suit turned and began walking toward them. Suel drained his cup, Dillon took another sip, placed his cup back in the console and stepped out of the car.

"Inspector Suel, you can have at it. Need gloves?"

"No, I'm covered. Dillon?"

"No, I've got a pair," Dillon said, pulling the latex gloves from his pocket and slipping them on.

"Let's get to it," Suel said, and they headed over to the taxi.

They stopped by the red stiletto heel lying in the street. Dillon bent down and picked up one of the brass casings on the street. He reflexively smelled it, then looked at the end. The casing was small and stamped with the image of a hummingbird on the end. "Maybe a .22LR, long-range," Dillon said.

"Have a look," Dillon said, handing the casing to Suel.

Suel looked at the end of the casing, then placed it back down in the street, shaking his head. "Bollocks. Reloads?"

Dillon nodded and said, "At least that would be my educated guess." Dillon picked up the red stiletto. The name MANOLO BLAHNICK, in black letters on white, was delicately stitched on the instep of the insole. He flipped the shoe over. The beige leather outsole was stamped "Manolo Blahnick" along with the line "Handmade in Italy." The shoe size, 37, was stamped just after the name. The little bit of wear apparent on the sole suggested the shoe was barely worn, possibly new, maybe purchased within the past few days.

"These things probably go for a couple of grand a pair," Dillon said.

"For shoes? Humf, so much money they don't know what to do with it. I've gotten cars for less than that," Suel said and walked around to the far side of the taxi.

Dillon walked over to the woman's legs hanging out of the car. He lifted the toe of the shoe on the right foot and examined it. The red leather had been worn off when it scraped across the pavement, and the odd positioning of the taxi suddenly made sense. He stood, and noticed for the first time two blood-soaked twenty-euro notes on the console.

"So the driver pulls over, waits to get paid with his foot on the brake," Dillon said. "She climbs out or starts to, when someone runs up, puts two in her, three in your man next to her and one into the driver. The whole thing probably took less than five seconds. When the driver's shot, his foot comes off the brake, and the car rolls across the sidewalk and into the corner of the brick wall."

Suel didn't give a reaction. He cautiously opened the rear passenger door, ready to stop the male body from falling out of the vehicle, but the seat belt and what was left of the head, wedged in the corner of the seat, prevented it from falling out. Suel reached in, picked the wallet up off the floor, then gently closed the door.

"Half dozen credit cards, a couple of grand in euros, and—" He moved his lips, counting for a moment. "Twelve hundred in American dollars," he said, then looked up at Dillon. "I'm guessing they probably didn't fly economy-class." He turned the wallet to read the driver's license as Dillon walked around the back of the vehicle to have a look. "Yeah, Boston. Hmm-mmm, Marlborough Street, in Boston. Ever hear of it?"

"Marlborough Street? Yeah, about as pricey as it can get. One of those neighborhoods where if you have to ask, you can't afford. Couple of million easy. What's the name?"

"Touhy. Joseph Xavier Touhy. Ring any bells?"

"Jesus Christ, you gotta be kidding me, Joey Touhy? Let me see that," Dillon said, then looked at the driver's license photo. "God, it really is him. Joey Touhy. I don't believe it."

"You know the guy?"

To Be Continued . . .

Thanks for taking the time to check out the sample of <u>Spade Work</u>, the sixth book in the Jack Dillon Dublin Tales series. Grab your copy and enjoy!

BOOKS BY MIKE FARICY
CRIME FICTION FIRSTS

A boxset of the first four books in four crime fiction series:
Russian Roulette; Dev Haskell series
Welcome; Jack Dillon Dublin Tales series
Corridor Man; Corridor Man series
Reduced Ransom! Hot Shot series

The following titles comprise the Dev Haskell series:
Russian Roulette: Case 1
Mr. Swirlee: Case 2
Bite Me: Case 3
Bombshell: Case 4
Tutti Frutti: Case 5
Last Shot: Case 6
Ting-A-Ling: Case 7
Crickett: Case 8
Bulldog: Case 9
Double Trouble: Case 10
Yellow Ribbon: Case 11
Dog Gone: Case 12
Scam Man: Case 13
Foiled: Case 14
What Happens in Vegas… Case 15
Art Hound: Case 16

The Office: Case 17
Star Struck: Case 18
International Incident: Case 19
Guest From Hell: Case 20
Art Attack: Case 21
Mystery Man: Case 22
Bow-Wow Rescue: Case 23
Cold Case: Case 24
Cash Up Front: Case 25
Dream House: Case 26
Alley Katz: Case 27
The Big Gamble: Case 28
Bad to the Bone: Case 29
Silencio!: Case 30
Surprise, Surprise: Case 31
Hit & Run: Case 32
Suspect Santa: Case 33
P.I. Apprentice: Case 34
Rebel Without a Clue: Case 35
Puppy Love: Case 36

The following titles are Dev Haskell novellas:
Dollhouse
The Dance
Pixie
Fore!
Twinkle Toes
(*a Dev Haskell short story*)

The following are Dev Haskell Boxsets:

Dev Haskell Boxset 1-3
Dev Haskell Boxset 4-6
Dev Haskell Boxset 7-9
Dev Haskell Boxset 10-12
Dev Haskell Boxset 13-15
Dev Haskell Boxset 16-18
Dev Haskell Boxset 19-21
Dev Haskell Boxset 22-24
Dev Haskell Boxset 25-27
Dev Haskell Boxset 28-30
Dev Haskell Boxset 1-7
Dev Haskell Boxset 8-14
Dev Haskell Boxset 15-19
Dev Haskell Boxset 20-24
Dev Haskell Boxset 25-29

The following titles comprise the Jack Dillon Dublin Tales series:

Welcome
Jack Dillon Dublin Tale 1
Sweet Dreams
Jack Dillon Dublin Tale 2
Mirror Mirror
Jack Dillon Dublin Tale 3
Silver Bullet
Jack Dillon Dublin Tale 4

Fair City Blues
Jack Dillon Dublin Tale 5
Spade Work
Jack Dillon Dublin Tale 6
Madeline Missing
Jack Dillon Dublin Tale 7
Mistaken Identity
Jack Dillon Dublin Tale 8
Picture Perfect
Jack Dillon Dublin Tale 9
Dublin Moon
Jack Dillon Dublin Tale 10
Mystery Woman
Jack Dillon Dublin Tale 11
Second Chance
Jack Dillon Dublin Tale 12
Payback Brother
Jack Dillon Dublin Tale 13
The Heist
Jack Dillon Dublin Tale 14
Jewels To Kill For
Jack Dillon Dublin Tale 15
Retirement Scheme
Jack Dillon Dublin Tale 16
The Collector
Jack Dillon Dublin Tale 17

Jack Dillon Dublin Tales Boxsets:
Jack Dillon Dublin Tales 1-3

Jack Dillon Dublin Tales 4-6
Jack Dillon Dublin Tales 1-5
Jack Dillon Dublin Tales 1-7
Jack Dillon Dublin Tales 6-10

The following titles comprise the Hotshot series;
Reduced Ransom! Second Edition
Finders Keepers! Second Edition
Bankers Hours Second Edition
Chow Down Second Edition
Moonlight Dance Academy Second Edition
Irish Dukes (Fight Card Series)
written under the pseudonym Jack Tunney

The following titles comprise the Corridor Man series:
Corridor Man
Corridor Man 2: Opportunity knocks
Corridor Man 3: The Dungeon
Corridor Man 4: Dead End
Corridor Man 5: Finger
Corridor Man 6: Exit Strategy
Corridor Man 7: Trunk Music
Corridor Man 8: Birthday Boy
Corridor Man 9: Boss Man
Corridor Man 10: Bye Bye Bobby

Corridor Man novellas:
Corridor Man: Valentine

Corridor Man: Auditor
Corridor Man: Howling
Corridor Man: Spa Day

The following are Corridor Man Boxsets:
Corridor Man Boxset 1-3
Corridor Man Boxset 1-5
Corridor Man Boxset 6-9

THANK YOU!

Contact the author:
- Email: mikefaricyauthor@gmail.com
- Twitter: @Mikefaricybooks
- Facebook: Mike Faricy Author
- Website: http://www.mikefaricybooks.com

Published by

MJF Publishing